SECOND CHANCE

John Wilson was born in 1953 in North London and after attending a local prep school was educated at Culford School near Bury St. Edmunds in Suffolk, where he studied English and History and was captain of cricket. Upon leaving school he joined the family business, elevating to managing director in 1988 and carries on running the organisation to this day. He has three daughters and lives with his wife in Hertfordshire.

Published Work:

Duplicity (2007)
Olympia Publishers
ISBN: 978 1905513 20 8

SECOND CHANCE

John F. Wilson

Second Chance

Olympia Publishers
London

www.olympiapublishers.com
OLYMPIA PAPERBACK EDITION

A CIP catalogue record for this title is
available from the British Library.

ISBN: 978-1-905513-93-2

This is a work of fiction.
Names, characters, places and incidents originate from the writer's
imagination. Any resemblance to actual persons, living or dead, is
purely coincidental.

First Published in 2009

Olympia Publishers part of Ashwell Publishing Ltd
60 Cannon Street
London
EC4N 6NP

Printed in Great Britain

DEDICATION

To my father Fred Wilson and in remembrance of my mother
Jean Wilson

ACKNOWLEDGEMENTS

My wife Pamela Wilson for her proof reading and punctuation

CHAPTER 1

"Where is it? For God's sake, I had it only a few moments ago. I had it in my hand and then I had this sudden urge to empty my bowels and on my return it had gone. The bloody thing had just disappeared, gone, it can't just go. It's an inanimate object, it's solid matter, unadulterated, pure modern day mechanics, a gismo. Do you know what I mean? Have you seen it?"

"No? Well have a bloody good look then."

"It must be here somewhere." I have ferreted down the sides of the chairs, having already tossed the florally upholstered cushions to the floor, and risked my delicate flesh against the spite of the tethered springs. But still the damn thing is nowhere to be found. What I will have to do is systematically search every horizontal surface, ensure my eyes pass slowly across every possible resting place, every worktop, every horizontal surface.

I stand in the middle of the room and carefully survey it, commencing in the east and rotating at a snail's pace (well perhaps a tortoise's pace) until, having passed through three hundred and sixty degrees with my eyes hawk-like in their attentiveness to spot the offending item, I return to my starting position.

Shit. outwitted by a plastic box with coloured buttons that runs on batteries.

No luck, "Shit, it doesn't add up." I retrace my steps out of my flat door, across the decoratively neglected landing to the communal bathroom, where I survey the room with an eagle eye and a mind finely tuned to discover missing items and guess what, there wedged between the cistern and the wall is my digit box.

"Digit box?" I hear you ask.

Well yes, it's metaphorical English for TV remote control device. It enables me to sit in my armchair and flick backwards and forwards between channels, avoiding advert breaks and party political broadcasts and getting out of my chair. I can summon up the teletext to list the day's programming, without having to find a newspaper. Just press a few buttons and providing I can memorise the page numbers, the screen just rolls over with an endless amount of information or tosh, depending on how you look at it. Weather forecasts, flight arrivals and departures, new or ongoing leisure events, you name it they've got it.

I can even look up the movements on the stock exchange, the ups and downs, the lows and highs, to see how my investments are performing. If I had any! I used to have some. I used to have quite a lot actually, I used to have the responsibility and authority over other people's as well, dealing for them, operating their accounts, some of which ran into millions of pounds.

My father's family originated from Cornwall, they owned tin mines in the late seventeen hundreds and when the industry floundered and the pits were closing my great grandfather decided to take what money was left and make for London in the hope of a new life. The money was still substantial and allowed him to start up in insurance, mainly high risk deals which other more established brokers wouldn't touch. Perhaps this is where I got my stockbroking brain from, you know the Midas touch which has left me where I am today, with nothing.

I would buy and sell, buy when the stocks were low and sell when they were high. A logical conclusion you think, but I can assure you logic seldom influences the international markets. Anyway that was the principal of the thing, buy the rumour, sell the fact as a very astute financier once told me. But it didn't always work, having taken tips from the newspapers, and listened to radio reports, I could assess the pros and cons and call my broker. "I would like to buy one thousand shares in" – whatever, some multi-national conglomerate, or a little-known private company. Penny shares they were a fashionable idea, any share under a pound, they are cheap to buy and therefore you can buy more of them for your money, and consequently for any one penny move in the right direction you are more quids in. And being more quids in is becoming harder to achieve these days.

But that's all in the past, before I was divorced, before I lost my home and all my financial stability, having been brutally screwed by the British legal system that automatically assumes that the female member of a partnership has naturally been wronged.

We used to live in suburbia, Weybridge in Surrey, the stockbroker belt as they call it, just outside the M25. Rachel, my wife, had been brought up in Guildford, the only daughter of a wealthy banker. They never did like me much, always thought I wasn't good enough for their daughter, I was of a similar persuasion, never being particularly charismatic or confident and my looks certainly left me wanting, but I must have held some attraction for her in the beginning.

Rachel was a beautiful girl, slim waist, pronounced hips, slender body, firm round breasts, not too big not too small, you know those perfectly shaped globes which you just can't stop gazing at and just want to cup tenderly in your hands. You know when you creep up from behind and reach round and feel the soft firm flesh it just makes you quiver, you just never want to let go. And those legs, model's legs, they just started at the ankles and just carried on going. Long dark hair almost jet black, flowed with waves and curls that laid in folds on her shoulders, just like that advert on telly years ago for some hair maintenance product where the girl shakes her head and her hair bounces and falls into a perfect style. Her smile captivated me from the first moment I clapped eyes on her. (These thoughts aren't going to do me any good, the memories are too fresh in my mind.)

She was sitting in Lyons Corner House, at Marble Arch, or that's what it used to be called then, she was seated with two other girls drinking morning coffee. I had just popped in for a coffee myself and a Danish pastry and a gander through the financial pages of *The Telegraph*. When I looked up at the opposite table. I just stared, and then I found I was trying to catch her eye in a sort of macho kind of way. Though heaven knows what I would have done if she had thrown it my way. It was one of those situations when you just think wow! This one is something different. She avoided my gaze or just didn't notice, but when they left, I followed, I didn't know why, but I just did and I had no idea what I was going to do, you know some kind of instinct that tells you to do it, because if you don't there may be consequences. But perhaps I just wanted to prolong the experience of being in her presence, kidding myself there may be something in it. The three of them were all dressed in line with the fashion of the day, you know the early nineties. They walked across Bayswater Road and into Hyde Park, with me tripping along closely behind, well not too close, but carefully trying not to make it look too obvious, with my newspaper hanging out of my pocket and my sunglasses perched neatly on my nose. It sounds a bit Gorky Park not Hyde Park doesn't it?

But that's enough of that for now, I'll return to it later having just moistened your appetite. You were beginning to get just a little excited wondering where this narrative was leading, three very delectable young ladies being followed through the leafy glades of London's most amorous Royal Park, by a young buck loaded and, primed with testosterone.

Having retrieved my digit box and returned to my first floor flat, closing the door with the aid of my foot to get the better of the sticking bit at the bottom. I padded across the cold lino and into the sitting room and took up my post in front of the TV. No need to get up again now I've got my digit box and a can of bitter at my elbow, I prefer wine but I have to be particularly careful with the pennies.

I switched on the telly and ran through the options, two Australian soaps, I could try and watch both at once by flicking between the two, it can be quite fun and does help to pass the hours. The storylines are so thin, it shouldn't overtax my concentration, but first I'll just check out the other choices, a daytime quiz show and, well surprise-surprise a cookery programme. Have you noticed how daytime television consists of game shows and soaps punctuated with cookery programmes? They even link the two occasionally by producing a competitive cookery show. Chefs seem to be the new sports stars, I don't get it, chuck a few things in a pan and stir them around, add some spices or herbs, bit of soy sauce and you turn into a folk hero. Having given it plenty of consideration, today I think I'll go with the soaps, there may be some added ingredient to stimulate my mind.

I settled down, cracked the can of bitter and took a large slug, it was warm having been left in the path of the summer sunshine. I gave the task in hand my undivided attention and if I got fed up with the script there would undoubtedly be some boobs to look at. That's another thing, why are most people in these soaps unnaturally attractive? They rarely have the communal garden moose look, girls are just not like that, most are not model material, but if you watch these programmes all the crumpet is unbelievable.

After about twenty minutes my viewing was violently interrupted by a sharp knocking on my front door, amplified by the lack of furniture and the lino-clad floor. The second phase of knocks was accompanied by a loud high-pitched shriek.

"Vincent? Are you in?"

"Shit," I said to myself. It's Hilary, I recognised her low-pitched tone, she lives on the floor above, the second floor, on her own, officially, although she has been seen escorting the odd man up the stairs. I often peep through my spyhole when I hear the main door close and I have seen a number of unidentified males being escorted past my door. We all have spyholes fitted and apart from their intended use they are certainly suitable for a bit of nosing.

Hilary, she's quite plain and a bit dumpy, in fact thinking about it, she's very dumpy and her face mirrors her figure in so much that it's round too. A less chivalrous person would most probably describe her as a bit of a porker, but not I, I have my reputation to consider and my standing in the community. Her hair is shoulder length, nondescript brown and she has a large mole on her forehead that always has at least two hairs sprouting from it, occasionally there are more. She has an irritating habit of pulling on them when she talks, which automatically draws your attention to the spot. All this being said, I've often wondered what it would be like to roger Hilary, but always dismissed the idea for another time. Perhaps I'm just not prepared to admit that I'm a bit of a coward when it comes to women, the idea is always good but when it comes to making an approach I seem to crawl back into my shell. Or perhaps it is the anticipation and the wonder which are far more exciting than the action itself. I know what you are thinking now. Is that what happened with Rachel in Hyde Park? Well you are just going to have to wait and see.

"Vincent." The high-pitched tone was repeated and I assumed my presence was requested, so with a slovenly spring in my step I ambled to the door. A quick peek into the spyhole confirmed my suspicions and magnified Hilary's chubby face into a rather loathsome expression of impatience.

I opened the door. "Hilary, how nice to see you, would you like to come in?"

She blinked.

I felt a stirring in my groin. "We could crack a can together." Statement or question I am not sure, it probably depends if one's delivery rises at the end of the sentence.

She blinked again, perhaps she had something in her eye, I thought.

"No," she said. "I've just come down to invite you to a party."

"Where?" I asked, somewhat surprised, for Hilary had never given the impression that she was ever likely to include me in her social circle.

"Upstairs, in my flat. Where did you think?"

"Well I really didn't know." I stuttered out this reposte more in surprise, than fear, as you may have thought.

"There will be quite a lot of people, so you'd better come, or go out, because of the noise and banging."

"Banging?" I queried.

She looked confused and pulled the hairs on her mole. "Banging on the floor, people dancing, that sort of thing."

"Oh I see, yes I suppose you have a point. When is it?"

"Saturday, three days' time, about eight, you could bring a bottle or something, there will be lots of people my age."

I looked a little hurt, but before I could speak, she said, "I know you are a little older but you may fit in and I will be sorting the food, you know finger buffet, bits and pieces, nibble on the hoof." She once again plucked at the protruding hairs on her forehead, I feared she may pull them free.

"Are you sure you wouldn't like to come in?" I persisted.

"No." She answered, a little too quickly I thought.

"Right, okay." I said.

"Thanks I'll see what I can do." She had edged away from the door and headed for the stairs.

I let her go. I returned to my seat and settled down in front of the TV. I just realised I haven't told you my name, you now know it's Vincent from the last few paragraphs, but not my surname. Sleeve. Vincent Orlando Sleeve. A bit 007 don't you think?

The Orlando came from my mother's side, I understand she had a soft spot for an American waster whilst she was a young wench on holiday in Florida. When she fell pregnant in the late fifties she still hadn't forgotten this fellow and once I was born she decided to preserve the memory for all time, well at least until I pop off I suppose, therefore I can't imagine the memory is likely to linger for long.

I understand my father never knew or suspected and now he never will as he left us nearly four years ago, for what hopefully may prove to be a better place. It was quite sad really he wasn't actually that old at sixty-eight but he picked up a serious bout of flu, which turned into pneumonia and he didn't appear to have the desire or determination to fight it, and within two months he was dead. It seemed a great pity, I felt bad as I had deteriorated to this low life way of living, especially as I was doing so well and my family expected the best of me.

I would like to have asked Hilary a bit more, such as what sort of party was it? What sort of people were going? Would I know any of them? What should I wear? Is it a celebration, birthday or something? I suppose she'll have asked Simon, because of the noise and banging, although in his case it wouldn't be the floor, not the ceiling. I am a bit out of touch with parties and socialising these days and I must admit the prospect of turning up and being confronted with a lot of strange faces is a little worrying.

Simon Cheek lives in the top floor flat, he's in advertising or something, he's a few years younger than me. He goes through live-in girlfriends quicker than I go through a box of Coco-Pops. Where most people ask a girl out for dinner or a drink at the pub, or to the cinema or theatre, Simon asks them if they would like to move in. And a few weeks later, presumably, he asks them if they would mind moving out, because they never seem to stay for very long. I've never been quite sure if that's before or after he's asked the next one to move in, but the turn around always appears fairly rapid.

I've had a few lively evenings with Simon at the 'Mother Shipton', a local hostelry at the end of the road, it's on the corner of Prince of Wales Road and Malden Road. I think it's been on occasions when he had run out of female company and he resorted to Mr ready-wit and conversational skills, but it's always been a good laugh.

I think he makes quite a lot of money, which makes me wonder why he is living in this dump. But I expect he spends most of it, he has an almost new bright red Porsche, that he leaves parked in the street outside, a trifle risky I would have thought. He probably spends a lot of money on his girlfriends too, he may even use his wealth to entice them into his one bed-roomed flat and subsequently his bed. As I said before Simon Cheek is a fast worker and from what I've seen of his conquests he's fairly particular as well. Unlike me he's tall, and his dark colouring and angular features hint of a Mediterranean origin. He's slender, but not bony. When Simon wears jeans, they meander to the contours of his shape.

When I wear jeans, they tend to flop and sag making my legs look shorter still.

You probably detect a hint of jealousy in this description. Well you would be right, but just a hint. Honestly. Well no one is completely happy with themselves, if they were there would be no need for beauticians. You see I'm only 5'4" and just a little plump, I think it's to do with being big boned, but unfortunately it exacerbates my squatness. I lost most of my hair before I was twenty-five, I used to have long flowing locks succulent blond, but that was in the seventies, the end of the flower power era. Love, peace and San Francisco.

By the end of the seventies I was a flat head, barring the monkish trim circling the back, but I don't mind, there is nothing I can do about it anyway.

I tried wearing wigs, but they were uncomfortable and they made me feel very self conscious. I've still got some in the wardrobe along with my entire belongings, I think I may as well get rid of them. I used to have such lovely clothes, so did Rachel. When we were dressed up together she certainly looked the business, and I just went along for the ride, a poor companion beside her. She must have seen something in me at that time. But now my sole possessions are stored in one rickety wardrobe in my bedroom.

* * * *

I open my eyes, the sound of grating gear cogs and groaning diesel engines shout through the gaps of the ill-fitting sashes of my bedroom window. The local authority's refuse collectors are carrying out their weekly destruction of the neighbourhood. They perform their tasks with scant regard for the slumbers of residents and little respect for their property either. Before their visit there is a neat symmetry to the groups of black bags stacked beside the kerb, but when they're gone, the pavements are littered with rotting remains as they sling the bags into the back of the macerator as it chugs along with little concern for the debris that falls out. Presumably they work on the principal, that if they're up and working at six o'clock in the morning, then everybody else should be as well. Well, unfortunately, that is typical of the attitude we have to put up with these days.

But enough of that, my head hurts this morning, I've just been woken by the bloody dustmen. My stomach feels as if it's been wrenched asunder by a Samurai swordsman. Something must have been off last night, I picked up a takeaway from the Indian a couple of streets away in Prince of Wales Road, a vindaloo, I hadn't tried it that hot before, it was so warm I had to wash it down with a couple of bottles of cheap Bulgarian white. The inside of my mouth was burning up and the long swigs of chilled wine brought a short-term relief. I am not sure if it was the curry or the wine that was off, but something has certainly upset my delicate stomach.

I decant myself from the bed, landing on the floor in a throbbing, sickly heap, virtually lifeless. My intentions are honourable, they are to get to the bathroom, but my muscles lie dormant, they have little movement and less inclination. I lie still, eyes closed, my back on the floor and my legs still resting on the bed, incapable of getting up. The surge in my bladder informs my, somewhat, muddled brain that a certain urgency is imperative, and my present position is likely to cause me to drown in my own urine if I don't get a move on.

Some minutes later in the kitchen I feel a little better, I lob an Alka-Seltzer into a glass and flood it with water, the resulting bubbles jingle against the side of the glass like the crashing of bells in a bell tower. I squint at the thought of swallowing this vital mixture, God, what on earth will it do to my insides? Quickly all in one gulp, while the fizz is still there, the sharpness scratches my dry throat and hurries down the tubes to my stomach, where it mingles with last night's sustenance. I hurriedly return to the bathroom and clean my teeth, scrubbing hard to dislodge the furry build-up and in an effort to dissolve the sharp and bitter taste of the liver salts. A long glance in the mirror confirms that I look just as bad as I feel, bloodshot eyes, distant and hollow. I snarl at the reflection and fall through the door to head back to my room. When!

"Hi! Vincent old chum." Simon Cheek punches me in the solar plexus in an over exuberant form of embrace.

I doubled forward in pain and queasiness tottering on the brink of retching. You know, that moment when you realise you're going to throw up, but, even though you know you'll feel better if you do, you still try to stave it off in the hope it may go away.

"I'm just off to… I'm meeting this absolutely fabulous piece of totty f…" He trailed off.

"For what?" I gurgled still clutching my midriff.

"Lunch, you know the sort of thing, round about the middle of the da… A trendy West End restaurant, oysters, lobster etc washed down with a couple of bottles of the old champers. And then who…"

"Who what?" I asked a little confused.

"Well you know, back to the old flat and make a play for…"

"Play for what?" I felt I was spending my whole time asking questions, but with Simon it was never easy to understand what he was talking about.

He looked at me quizzically. "Home base, you know Vince," and he gesticulated by rhythmically gyrating his hips.

"Won't Sarah mind?" I asked.

"Sarah?" He screwed up his face in a mystified expression.

"Yes Sarah. She lives with you."

The light dawned. "Oh that Sarah, kicked her into touch, couple of days ago, took her eye off the –"

"Ball?" I offered.

He was jockeying backwards and forwards now imitating the machoness of a rugby player. "Yep, that's the chap, ball. She had been round too long. We must have been toge... for," he considered, "six..."

"Six what?" I asked.

"Weeks of course." He looked at me as if I was mad.

"It can't have been that long, it's not even a month." I offered with no particular interest whether it was six weeks, six months or six years, but I was concerned about my stomach and the damage Simon's loosely slung fist may have done.

"Four weeks that's it. Too long, she was getting too comfortable, lowered her guard one day and out she went." He was still hopping from side to side which was adding to my already unstable sense of balance.

I didn't mention that Simon is particularly economic with his vocabulary, he either leaves words out, cuts them short or doesn't finish his sentences. This often leaves one guessing or volunteering to fill in the gaps, it can be a rather nerve wracking experience, keeping up with the conversation.

I edged back to my flat and leant against the door frame still feeling exceedingly groggy, but thankful for the support. Simon still hung around, quite obviously he wasn't late for work yet.

"Hey Vince, you going to this party Saturday night?"

"You mean Hilary's?"

"Yep, there'll be loads of extra curricular crumpet up for grabs, you know the sort of thing. Free and easy, anything goes no holds... and all that sort of bizzo."

"Right," I replied still clinging to the door frame and hoping Simon would grow tired of my lucid wit and tireless conversation and leave me to return to my bedroom and die quietly.

"Depending on my success rate this after... Vince old boy," slapping me again, this time on the shoulder. "If I'm not home too late we could have a couple of jars down the old rubber-dub-d... what do you say?"

I willingly agreed in the hope that an answer in the affirmative would send him on his way. And it did, with a spring in his step and an air of confidence in his posture he skipped down the remaining flight of stairs and banged the front door behind him. I doubted he would fail in his afternoon quest and therefore I would not be required this evening, which the way I felt at this moment was alright with me.

I delicately returned to my dishevelled bed and collapsed onto the crumpled brown sheets. I thought they never used to be brown, I felt quite sure they were once a quite pleasant shade of cream. But that was some time ago, I really must find the time to wash them, but not today.

Today I was going to make a special effort to go out in search of employment. Offer society the benefit of my wealth of knowledge and experience.What knowledge and experience, you're thinking. Well I used to have a job when I was married to Rachel.

You see I told you I would come back to it. I was a city slicker, I worked for a medium-sized stockbroker surrounded by the newly arrived computer screens, soon after the city revolution engineered by the big bang of October 1986 when the city became computerised. Suddenly the trading in the pit became obsolete and the romanticism of the traditional form of trading would be lost for ever. I really enjoyed it, the pressure was intense, especially when the markets began to slide, with a phone to each ear and my eyes glued to the screens as they changed colours with the price moves. I would shout instructions at the handset barely waiting for the confirmations before moving onto the next one. It was exciting, exhilarating even when the markets were going against me the adrenalin was pumping as I tried desperately to limit the damage and close down positions without a moment's delay, losing as little as possible. In some respects this was more rewarding than making big profits.

CHAPTER 2

The room was open plan, gloss painted walls and a grubby lino covering the floor. The atmosphere was sticky, it was a hot summer's day, the air was still and the smell of sweat hung like a limpet suspended and unmoving. A mixture of presentation stands were littered randomly around the room, advertising all different types of occupations, from refuse collectors to middle management positions and a lot of positions stacking shelves at the local supermarkets. They had just built a new Sainsbury's down in Camden Town, just up Camden Road a few hundred yards north of the underground station, and they were obviously trying hard to fill it with a collection of local misfits, I hesitated and then decided this was not for me, I must be better than that I thought.

I picked up a couple of cards, one for a clerk's position at a solicitor's practice in Russell Square and the other I felt may be a little more suitable, a delivery driver for a courier company, not one of the major ones though. The money didn't sound that good for either of them, but who knows I have probably got to take a job before much longer.

I can't keep living like this for ever, I need to return to society and stop sponging and taking advantage of the situation. This wasn't my way. I hadn't been brought up to take from the state, my parents had always worked and expected me to do the same. I felt I was letting them down, but what could I do? Circumstances had overtaken me and I was left to face the consequences.

I stood in the queue that snaked away from a desk occupied by a roughly shaven man in his mid-twenties. He was dressed in a bright red, open-necked shirt and was hunched over some paperwork, most likely a form. His pen was poised anticipating an answer from the loutish looking bruiser seated opposite him. After some consideration I decided this may take some time, as the loutish figure did not give the impression that answering simple questions was his forte. He shuffled from side to side in his chair and then leant back gazing into thin air presumably hoping some divine intervention may provide him with the answers.

I bided my time, I had plenty of it, by studying the other applicants in the queue, trying to determine their different attributes. Everyone must be good at something, even the bruiser at the front, when not beating up old ladies or stealing cars there must be something he is good at. Painting perhaps, not interior decorating, but artistic, copying beautiful scenes of English landscape, I was letting my imagination run away with me, but perhaps he could be good at interior decorating, emulsioning rooms, a bit of glossing up the woodwork or perhaps even design as well.

I glanced back at the cards I held in my hand and realised I was only fooling myself if I thought anything could come of it. My emotions are still too fragile to seriously consider taking on any serious responsibility. I tilted my head round the body in front of me to get a better look at the lady next in line. Mid-thirties, neatly dressed, some sort of business woman, I shouldn't wonder, maybe a manger at M&S or perhaps one of the other major shopping chains. Oh how the great have fallen to such lowly depths, I surmised.

I then thought of myself and felt a little more depressed, once successful, now, down and out. Perhaps all the other people in the queue were considering me in the same way and wondering what I was doing here. Whether I was some sort of sponger or a legitimate beneficiary.

Behind me another woman, scruffily dressed in a long flowing caftan, unkempt hair unwashed and hanging lankly. A joss stick burner, I thought, probably applying for a job as a social worker.

My eye strayed further back in the queue and came to rest on a casually dressed man about my age, I thought I recognised and then I took a second take. Harold I think.

"Harold." I breathed loudly, Christ I used to know Harold Blenkinsop, shit, where the hell did he come from? Christ I don't want him to see me here, but why not? I ask myself, I've seen him here, so what's the difference? He must be here for the same reason as I am, but it's the stigma of standing in the dole queue with all and sundry that is so demeaning, the notoriety of signing on once a week. But Harold, I thought he was well established in Fleet Street, he was working for a decent publication when I last had any dealings with him, I can't believe he is out of work and having to queue up with the likes of me at the job centre.

I pushed my knees forward a little so the joss stick burner was obscuring the direct line of vision between Harold and myself and considered the situation. The fact that I am in the dole queue means I am out of work. He is also in the dole queue, therefore he is out of work, so therefore the level of embarrassment should be wiped out, two negatives make a positive. I decided it was still best to keep my head down though and keep out of sight at least until I have had my interview and I can get outside and take stock of the situation.

I met Harold soon after I started work in the city, following my rather notorious university experiences, which I shall also speak of later. He was working for a freebie type local paper, investigating stories of local interest, such as 'Old lady's pet poodle savaged by German Shepherd' or 'Toddler dyes hair green to imitate ET'. Invigorating stuff, just the way to seduce the readers away from *The News Of The World*. Surreptitiously I glanced to the side of the joss stick burner and took a rein check on Harold, he was still there looking around, carefully studying his fellow unemployed.

I wondered how he had lost his job or perhaps he had just thrown the towel in.

I considered waiting for him outside after I'd had my interview, if we've both fallen on hard times we may be of some help to each other, who knows, it could be of mutual benefit.

* * * *

"This fucking beer's warm, Vince. You should know better than to take me to a bar that sells warm beer." Harold scowled into his jug and took a large swallow.

You were right, I did make a point of bumping into Harold.

Having had my brief interview with the young man behind the desk, which was fairly fruitless as there were no suitable positions, I enquired about the solicitor's clerk position. In reality it sounded far

29

more like they were looking for a tea boy. As for the courier it turned out they were looking for a cyclist to beat the London traffic in all types of weather and at all times of day, and I'm afraid I rejected that very quickly.

A little deflated I hung around outside, trying to look as inconspicuous as possible until Harold came out. I don't know why I wanted to see him, I never really liked him, perhaps, it was just curiosity. When he appeared I confronted him with a "What ho old chap, fancy seeing you here!" He responded with, "Vincent Sleeve, you bloody wanker, fancy bumping into you after all these years."

Introductory pleasantries over with, we ambled off to a bar in Kentish Town Road called the Red Snapper, snapper being the only reference to fish as their menu was decidedly burger and chips orientated.

"My Chardonnay's fine," I said. "Quite cool". However, I thought, after last night I'm not sure it's doing me very much good. The queasiness in my stomach had been stirred up again by the acidic nature of the wine. That's one thing about Chardonnays the darker yellow the colour, the more acidic it becomes and this can really get the indigestion working.

I looked at Harold and said, "How long have you been out of work then?"

"Out of work!" he scowled again, I didn't remember Harold as a scowler, just shows how the strain of life takes its toll.

"I'm sorry Harold, I assumed as you were in the queue in the job centre you were looking for a job."

He scowled again. "I work for the *Daily Star* now and I'm researching an article on unemployment. You know the sort of thing, an in-depth report on what makes the average out of work layabout tick? Is the highlight of his or her day an excursion down to the job centre? Or is there more to life? Can they make ends meet on the social? Or do they collect the dole in the morning and do a part-time job for cash in the afternoon? Or do they just beat up old ladies, mug people and demand money with menaces?"

He took another gulp of his suspiciously warm beer, shook his head as if trying to get rid of the taste, scowled again and replaced the glass beside the beer mat. He picked up the beer mat and placing it on the edge of the table, flicked it from underneath and as it rotated caught it between thumb and forefinger. An old trick we used to do when we were at university, we would build up a pile, perhaps ten or twelve high, to see how many we could flick and control, it was therapeutic.

He continued, "So, I thought I would start at the Labour Exchange and when I got there I found out they had changed it and it was now called the Job Centre. I looked around and tried to observe the sort of misfits that hang about in these sorts of places. And I wasn't disappointed, there certainly were some unconventional candidates hanging around. I made sure I kept my hands in my pockets and didn't want to be pick-pocketed on my first day on the streets."

I sat and listened feeling just a little uncomfortable as undoubtedly, before very long Harold would realise his research would come very close to me.

"But what about you Vince?"

Uh oh, here it comes.

"What are you doing round here? Not quite the area to be trading oil or pigs or whatever you lot do in the city I wouldn't have thought, or perhaps you have changed your position and are heading for higher things?" He shifted in his seat and focused on me with a knowing look of suspicion.

"Um. No." I stuttered, wondering if it was just best to come out with the truth or should I just muddle through with a few exaggerated stories of big developments in the world of high risk finance, big money positions, hedge funds, late nights in front of screens studying and tracking graphs, trying to pinpoint where to buy or where to sell. But no he would probably find out anyway and I have become too tired to lie, I have lost my heart for conflict. In fact I am being swallowed up by my lack-lustre existence, I am no longer razor-sharp, prepared to challenge and win, confident of my own abilities.

I looked Harold in the eye and continued. "Unfortunately I'm on the dole, out of work, stuffed by society, the sort of person you are planning to ridicule. In fact, probably your perfect subject, idle good-for-nothing layabout. So if you look at me carefully you may just see what makes me tick."

31

I winced, aware that I had raised my voice somewhat, confessing my leper-like predicament and I had also pre-empted Harold's accusations, fed him the ammunition to insult and ridicule me.

Harold hesitated for just a moment, obviously caught on the hop, he hadn't expected good old Vince to be caught up in such a situation. "Well, never mind, Vince old boy, it happens to the best of us."

This was revoltingly condescending and made me feel even worse, remembering my rather sick stomach and my recent realisation that my confidence had taken a bit of a battering, I was no longer a force to be reckoned with. And apart from that it didn't happen to the best of us, it had happened to me. "Yes, well it hasn't happened to you, has it?" I retorted a little put out.

"Well, no, but," he tailed off.

We sat in an awkward silence for some time, he swilling his lukewarm beer and me sipping my adequately chilled wine. Harold bought another round, feeling that I was probably not financially able to pay my way. I allowed him to do this out of sheer cussedness, I like to see people squirm and apart from that I couldn't really afford to pay.

After a suitable period had passed, Harold plucked up however much courage was needed and said, "We could put this situation to both our advantages."

I looked blankly.

He went on. "I'm doing a piece on society's spongers and the way I see it you're one of them."

I looked blankly again and as realisation dawned, felt a little hurt.

"If we put both our heads together, perhaps at your place, wherever that is," he looked worried. "Then I needn't go out on the streets and mix with all those no hopers."

"No just this no-hoper," I butted in a little aggrieved at the lack of compassion shown by my old friend.

"I didn't mean it like that old thing. I was thinking more along the lines of a bit of part-time work for you. I would be able to pay you, it may not be very much, but probably more than you are getting now. It could be a step on the ladder into freelance journalism. You're an educated fellow, English A level and all that and a few others I shouldn't wonder. You could draft out your experiences on the dole, the people you mix with, the poverty, the destitution, the depression, making ends meet on the breadline, turning to drink as your only friend and lover."

I butted in again. "Hey steady on a bit I have not turned to drink. I may have been a bit delicate this morning, but nothing more than that." My conscience pricked me at this point as I remembered the sickly heap that littered my floor this very morning when I fell out of bed.

"Sorry," he said apologetically. "But you know what I mean."

"No I am not sure I do."

He leant forward his hands open preparing to speak. "You know build it up a bit, everyone knows the papers seldom tell the truth, so why start now."

"But you're a journalist," I butted in again, "and you admit the papers rarely tell the truth, well that's a fine confession, I must say."

"Look Vince just listen and stop interrupting. What about sex?"

I looked blank again, surprised the way the subject had so dramatically changed. "I'm sorry Harold what the hell has that got to do with it?"

"Look, Vince you bloody wanker, sit back and listen, I mean girls that sort of thing. That must be different in the type of circles you move in, no high-class expensive hookers in your lifestyle. I shouldn't think you could pay for it anyway, could you? Except we all pay for it in our own way, even if it's just by giving them permission to nag us." He looked at me in a pitying sort of way, I was beginning to feel inferior, a leech on society. "What do you say? Shall we give it a go?" He beamed this sick smile in my direction, whilst taking another large swig from his glass, the beer dribbled down his chin and he mopped it up with his sleeve.

I briefly considered the offer, glad that he hadn't waited for an answer to his first question about girls as this was one area of my social life that had been severely lacking recently, so I thought I've nothing to lose. I didn't have a job and after this morning's interview at the job centre it was looking pretty unlikely that I would be joining the ranks of the employed in the near future, so why not? It may even help to get my mind working again and get me out of this stagnant existence. However, on the other hand, I didn't want to feel used, or to think someone was just offering me charity. Of course this was fairly unlikely in this case as Harold had quite obviously spotted a way of making his investigations a good deal easier for himself.

"Okay." I said having made the point of looking as though I had given the proposition considerable thought.

"Do I take that as a yes then?"

I fumbled with my glass, eyes down, giving an impression of deep concentration. "Yes I suppose you should." I answered holding out my glass for a refill, I might as well take advantage of the situation while it's there.

"Great." He leapt to his feet rummaging in his pocket for a notepad and pencil. "Phone number." He demanded.

Shit, I thought, "I don't have a phone."

"What? How the other half live."

"Look," I said waving my empty glass again, "What about another glass of wine first and then we can talk about it?"

He took my glass and picking up his pint mug, headed for the bar without another word and I sat back considering the situation. I was feeling okay again and looking forward to another glass of Chardonnay and I thought this idea of Harold's was certainly interesting, deep down I knew I had to find something to occupy my days or I would probably drink myself to self destruction on cheap plonk funded by my dole cheque.

Harold returned and placed a glass of wine in front of me and stood whilst taking a large glug of his pint of bitter. "Well, where were we?" he asked.

"You were asking me for a phone number."

"Oh yes."

"Hilary has a phone," I offered.

"Hilary? Who the fuck's Hilary"

"Yes Hilary, she lives upstairs in the flat above, there is a phone on the landing outside her flat and we call it Hilary's phone."

"Does she have a job, or is she one of your lot?"

Once again I felt hurt at this derisory remark, but realised that if this was going to work I was going to have to accept my position as a lower form of life and that Harold was an unfeeling bastard. "Yes, she works part-time in a Pizza place in Camden High Street." I sifted through my pockets, looking for the number, which I was sure was scribbled on the corner of an old bus ticket. I pulled out a number of old bus tickets, which I kept in the hope that I could pluck up enough courage to reuse them if the opportunity arose. But there was no scribbled number in evidence on any of the tickets. "I don't seem to have the number with me."

"Don't you have a mobile? No I suppose not, thinking about it they are quite modern aren't they?"

"No I don't." I responded.

"Why don't you sit down Harold? You're making me nervous standing there."

"Because I don't want to, stop harassing me Vince."

Harold sat down and gulped more of his beer and then without warning he was up on his feet again and banged his half empty jug on the table. "Now don't worry about that phone number Vince, old chum, we'll go straight round to your place now, I'm looking forward to seeing the type of squalor you live in, and we can get the phone number from this Hilary girl then." He now edged towards the door even though I hadn't finished my wine and then I started to panic realising the state I had left the flat in that morning. I didn't want anyone sniffing around using me as a guinea pig for the world to ridicule, especially now Harold had already admitted that most of what was written in the press was fabrication anyway. I could see the headlines now. 'Typical down and out's room'. And probably accompanied with a picture.

"Harold. Hold on." I followed him out into the street, he stood there fidgeting. "Which way old boy, bus, tube or cab?"

"Walk."

"What?" He looked stunned. "Oh well it's all part of the experience I suppose, must try and get into the feel of the part, like all good thespians. Live the character."

CHAPTER 3

I'm not so good again today. Had a shed-full last night. I must try and give up this lousy cheap wine. Once I'd got rid of Harold I popped out to the offy and grabbed a litre of that cheap Bulgarian white. Bunged a blue movie in the video, 'Raunchy Rita' or something, and proceeded to get plastered. It seemed a pretty good idea at the time, but this morning my throat feels like a vulture's crutch and my head's vibrating like a blacksmith's anvil.

I can't remember what happened after that, when I went to bed, if I went to bed. But somehow that's where I seem to be now, albeit on the bed still in my day clothes, not in the bed as is the normal custom. I gave Harold Hilary's phone number, we call it Hilary's phone because it's on the landing outside Hilary's flat, but I think I mentioned that yesterday, see it all goes to show my mind is muddled. I tried to encourage Harold to leave then, but he was anxious to see the inside of my hovel (his words not mine). So over a couple of warm cans of lager we whiled away an hour or so. Me surveying him, he surveying the decor and sparseness of my furnishings and his critical eye turned to a mixture of further insults as the lager kicked in.

On leaving he arranged to call me after the weekend to arrange to join me in my life as a down and out (once again his words not mine). He was going to move his bits and pieces in and sleep on the sofa and hopefully get into the life-style which I had been experiencing for the past few months. Once he had eventually gone I got stuck into the cheap Bulgarian white, and low and behold that is the reason for the way I feel now.

It's Hilary's party tonight, I suddenly thought, hope I feel better by then, although at the moment that hardly seems likely. My mind moved to the prospects of totty, untapped totty, free and easy totty and unattached and then I thought of Hilary, her plump figure and her mole with the hairs sticking out. I don't know if I'm suffering from some unusual sexual proclivity, but Hilary does seem to stir my innermost urges, unless it's just so long since I experienced a warm feminine embrace. The thought of this forced me into life and I rolled off the bed and staggered to the bathroom to survey the damage to my appearance. God. Not good, rheumy blood-shot eyes stared back at me from the blotchily silvered mirror and my naturally pale skin had taken on a mottled hue. I splashed cold water onto my face and let it circulate into my eyes, washing the rims. Having overcome the initial shock I found the tingle was refreshing and strangely warming. I then washed thoroughly and brushed my teeth in an effort to clean away the sour fluffy taste of last night and carried out the necessary ablutions.

Back in my room I caught up with the time. Ten thirty. Searching my pockets I came up with a crumpled fiver, a ten and some loose change. Two pound fifty on a greasy breakfast should do the trick and then, perhaps, a couple of quid on some deodorant and cheap après rasage. It must be worth it to try and make some sort of impression this evening, it seems a long time since I've been out partying. Anyway who knows this may be a turning point in my life, meeting Harold again, being invited to a party it may just give me a purpose and perhaps I will be able to repair the damage of the past few months.

After my breakfast I toddled off to the Post Office to collect my giro, this is the sixty odd quid a week our kind government gives me for being out of work so I can pay my living expenses. My one bed flat costs me one hundred and twenty pounds a month and the rest goes on my food, drink and electric light. I love that expression, it reminds me of the past when an ageing aunt would save her coins for the meter, she would keep them in a Toby jug on the mantelpiece and say, 'That's for my electric light dear'.

Breakfast had certainly helped and as I walked into the local supermarket I had a newfound spring in my step. So much so that my sunny good morning to a young mother with a pushchair was rewarded with a smiling acknowledgement. I perused the shelves labelled toiletries, matching and trying to convert the contents in grams to the price in pounds and pence. An almost impossible task, one most enthusiastic shoppers obviously learn to master, but in my financial predicament essential. Once I had finally selected the best value-for-money commodities, I was brutally dug in the back with a sharp implement.

"Sleeve. You old bum, how are yer?"

I turned round eager to bash my assailant firmly on top of the nose, or under the nose if he was much taller than me, when I came face to face with Hung. A name from my past, school days, times to remember, drunken interludes, orgy-filled evenings, punctuated by a little study.

"God. You look pretty shitty Vince, not the man I spent hours pulling the birds with, way back when. What you been up to?"

I smiled, somewhat deflated having thought I felt and looked pretty good after my substantial breakfast. "Hung," I acknowledged. "Yeah, you know how it is, bit low at present, trod a slippery slope and just carried on down, but who knows, should be coming back up soon." On what grounds this was based I was unsure, unless it was the prospects of helping Harold with his research, but it sounded good. He was bobbing about in front of me obviously keen to expound on his fortunes.

Hung? Why Hung you think? I know this has crossed your mind by now. The less moralistic ones among you are thinking, 'Hung like a donkey'. Others, more discernible, probably assume a connection with hung-over. Well you would all be wrong, Hung was called Hung, because his father was hung, or hanged, for a murder he reportedly, did not commit. One of the last to undergo such a final type of punishment and one that was also very influential in the abolition of such a practice. I won't say barbaric, because I'm not sure it is, an eye for an eye etc, it may well sort out our rather lawless society of today. In other words if some mindless thug beats up on some old lady, or young lady, for that matter, the most suitable punishment is to beat up on him. Not just once, but twice or thrice, until the bastard learns his lesson. But I don't imagine we are likely to return to capital or corporal punishment, especially with the lily-livered government we have at present.

Hung's real name is Mitchell Wire. A lanky emaciated looking chap, with a pale complexion, a squashed nose, large bulbous goggle eyes, that roll around his face, a little like the look of King James the sixth of Scotland and first of England as portrayed in the paintings of the time. If you were hung for beauty, Mitchell Wire would more than likely die innocent, however, from now on I am going to refer to him as Mitchell, especially as I have explained the reason for his rather obscure nickname. But as he pointed out earlier he could certainly pull the birds, perhaps they were just inquisitive, I often wondered.

When Mitchell's father was disposed of, Mitchell was only three years old so he has no recollection of the event and as there was no emotional attachment he always wore this part of his background as a sort of badge. Something peculiar to him alone, not the sort of thing everybody could boast about.

"Okay guy, let's go have some beer." He hustled me towards the checkout. "Get this junk paid for and get out of this dump and get some beer down us."

An interesting use of the word get, hardly expounds on the colourful and fruitful depth of our language or complimentary to our education system. I allowed him to persuade me and we settled down in the Hogs Head a short walk down the High Street.

After a couple of beers paid for by Mitchell, who had swallowed my hard luck story hook, line and sinker, I was feeling considerably better and even felt a rosy glow come to my cheeks and began to look forward to the evening's festivities with less apprehension.

We whiled away the next hour reminiscing about old school pals and whether the boarding school system had benefited us as individuals, especially the sixth form period, which is all we could remember with any accuracy, even though this was also somewhat cloudy. The final prognosis was probably not, seeing I was now on the dole and Mitchell was driving a forty ton artic up and down the motorways of England and Scotland delivering furniture, and as he was now telling me hitch-hikers were certainly his bag.

"Vince, you should see the crumpet positioned on the slip roads to the motorways just waiting to be picked up. Some hold up bits of cardboard with a destination scrawled on it in large felt tip, you know, like Oxford or Barnsley, though who the hell would want to go to Barnsley I couldn't possibly imagine."

"Michael Parkinson," I offered.

"What?" he looked confused.

"Michael Parkinson," I said again, "would probably want to go to Barnsley as that is where he comes from."

"Oh right," he grunted and took a large gulp from his glass before continuing. "Anyway, you don't really want to pick those ones up."

I looked puzzled, "Which ones?"

"The ones that hold up the bits of cardboard, they know where they want to go, they're positive thinking with one objective in mind, to get there. The ones you want are the scruffier looking sorts," he glanced at me quizzically, but I didn't comment. I'm becoming quite used to ridicule and being the butt of everyone's humour and disdain.

Mitchell continued. "As I said the ones you want to pick up are the type that don't care where they end up, or where they sleep, or with whom for that matter. The ones which are game on for a good time, players. You know the sort of thing Vince old boy." With this he slapped me on the back, just after I had placed my glass back on the table and fortunately swallowed my mouthful of dry white.

I nodded, not knowing the sort of thing at all and hid my confusion behind a smile. Although I am sure I must have known the sort of thing in the past, back in the days before I met Rachel.

"Those big cabs have everything you know, a nice sized bunk, curtains which you can draw all the way round the windows and there's plenty of room to get shacked up with a bird for the night. Most of them consider it's just payment for the lift, you know a ride for a ride. Just the ticket," he mused and started quite obviously reminiscing and considering some of his escapades and conquests.

"You should try it Vince, seeing you've got nothing else to do."

"Don't you need some sort of licence?" I asked.

He looked puzzled. "What to pick up birds on the road?"

"No." I said. "To drive trucks up and down the country?"

"Well, yes, an HGV, a few lessons, take the test and away you go, the open roads, the sunshine, the girls."

"Wasn't that a song, Frank Ifield, or Sinatra?"

Mitchell looked blank.

* * * *

After I'd left Mitchell Wire and the Hogs Head I headed back towards my flat, it was now after lunchtime and with my small bag of shopping I lurched through the back streets. I considered Mitchell's suggestion, that I become a long distance lorry driver, but in reality I didn't consider it at all. I knew that the training course was far too expensive for my meagre budget and the downside of living with diesel fumes and traffic jams well out weighed the upside of girls, who would most likely take one look at me and opt to wait for the next truck.

Back at the flat I climbed the stairs and shoved the key into my front door lock, before noticing a scrap of paper sellotaped to the door. It read:

'Give me a knock when you get (that word get again) in – Hilary'.

So I pulled the key out of the lock and trudged up the two flights of stairs to the second floor and tapped on the brown stained door. There were scuffling sounds from within and then the door was opened.

"Hi Vince."

"Hilary."

She looked confused as if she was expecting me to open the conversation.

"You left a note on my door, for me to give you a knock." My groin moved as I thought of giving Hilary a knock.

"Oh yes of course I did. It was while you were out my phone rang, you know the one on the landing over there."

"The one we all share?" I suggested.

"Yes, well it rang and it was this dishy sounding chap asking for you, well as you weren't here I chatted to him for a while. He said his name was Harold, we got talking and well I happened to mention my party and he said he was a good friend of yours and you would be spending a lot of time together over the next few weeks so I invited him."

I groaned inwardly. "And he said he would come?" I asked with only a little concern in my voice.

"He wants to talk to you, I've got..." (got again, see I missed the last one it's so frustrating the way people speak with such scant regard for our beautiful language) "...the numbers here somewhere," she disappeared behind the door and returned clutching a post-it note which she stuck to the palm of my hand.

"Thank you," I said. "I'll give him a call." I dug my hand into my trouser pocket and came out with a two pence and a five pence. I thought, under the circumstances that if Hilary had hot intentions on Harold, I could risk sponging a ten pence from her. "Ah Hilary," I started, "I don't suppose you could see your way clear to letting me have a ten pence to make the call, I appear to be a bit short at present?"

She blinked and simultaneously pulled the hairs on her mole and then grunted, which I took to be a yes, as she had disappeared leaving the door ajar. It seems strange that she hadn't asked me in, I'd asked her in a few days ago, even though she didn't accept, but she has asked me to her party, so why wouldn't she ask me in? Presumably she doesn't expect me to spend the evening on the landing with a glass of wine and a plate of sausage rolls and drumsticks.

She returned, smiled and handed me a warm ten pence piece. "There you are," she said. "I'll see you later," and before closing the door I am sure I detected a wink of her eye aimed in my direction.

I smiled my thanks.

I considered the situation before dropping the coin into the machine. Did I really want Harold joining the party trail? No. But I suppose the answer should be yes as I suppose if we are going to research the homeless problems and write this piece together, we may as well start now. The coin dropped with a tinkle, I dialled the number and waited.

"Hello."

"Harold, it's me, Vincent... The party, yes Hilary said... I'm not sure that she would... Oh she did, did she? well I'll just have to have a little word about that... Well you come to my flat first... Yes I suppose you may as well bring your things... And no I won't let them get muddled up with my shit... Okay... about seven."

He put the phone down and I replaced the receiver at my end, I hesitated a few moments thinking. Oh well here we go.

* * * *

Back in my room I decided to take forty winks before making myself look presentable for the evening's events and of course before that, receiving my erstwhile companion. Where to put the bugger? I thought, it would have to be the old sofa with the exposed springs, oh well if he wants to experience the lifestyle of the unemployed and down and outs who am I to worry about his comforts.

I drew the curtains lay down on my bed and closed my eyes. While I take my afternoon sleep and recharge my batteries I am going to take this opportunity to tell you a little more about my past. Having left school with six O levels and two A's, English and History, I scraped into Exeter University with a B and a C where I studied History, more by means of an idea than a real interest, although I did like the romanticism of the Middle Ages and Tudor times. One thing about History is if you look back everything always seems far more rosy than it does today, even though when you analyse it closely those times were filled with violence, degradation, poverty and total injustice, but we still smile and say what a great history we have.

Back to my college days I really enjoyed the slow easy-going atmosphere of self-motivated study and the social life was exemplary. Non-stop parties, it was the end of the hippy period, flower power, Woodstock, early seventies. Do you remember Ten Years After? They were a sixties blues band, but they pitched up at Woodstock, Alvin Lee twanging those high-pitched screaming strings at an incredible speed. I know many people would bask in the non-stop parties, booze and dope, although I always avoided the drug scene, I think I was genuinely scared of it. I used to smoke cigarettes, but didn't everyone?

I'll always remember the first time I tried a cigarette, (we called them dimps for some inexplicable reason) it was in a wooded area known as the bothy at school. I was thirteen, it tasted sweet and then one of the other boys said, take it down, breathe the smoke in deep. So I did and shit my head just swam and my legs tingled and I had to sit down, right there on the dry mud. But I became used to it, I never smoked a lot though, five or ten a day.

We were caught once, four of us up before the headmaster, six with the cane and confined to the school buildings for four weeks, it was known as perimetered. In other words we were not allowed out of the area housing the school buildings unless escorted by a master for four weeks. This was certainly designed to cramp one's style and it did, when you are living in four hundred acres of parkland it is particularly restricting to be confined to such a small area.

Anyhow I waffle, back to university. The parties were crazy events in those days, smoke-filled halls, dancing and moving to Gary Glitter, Madness and all those seventies bands. The girls, mini-skirts were at their highest point in every sense of the word and many of the girls couldn't wait to get them off. However, these joys never seemed to come my way regardless of other people's memories, but I did have a few flirtatious moments, but that was about as far as it went, I was never sure if it was because some of the girls felt sorry for me. Which was one reason why I was so surprised when Rachel actually fell for me and perhaps also that is a reason why it didn't last.

My studies went fairly well, I didn't overwork, but did enough to gain moderate qualifications that enabled me to move into the world of full-time employment. I joined a large American bank in their investment department and having done my time in the pit moved up the ladder fairly quickly to become a senior broker.

I opened my eyes, I trust you are a little more acquainted with my background now and probably even more confused as to my present lifestyle, but all will be revealed in the fullness of time.

I glance at the clock beside my bed, four thirty, best rise and make the place seem like home, you know generally kick things about a bit so Harold won't be too disappointed when he takes up occupancy with a down and out, as he is sure to put it.

Perhaps I should explain the layout of my flat before going any further. As I mentioned earlier the bathroom is shared with the ground floor flat, which fortunately, is at present empty. I have my own kitchen which has a sink unit, a base unit and a couple of wall units, which are fairly sparsely filled. Other than that there is the lounge with my sofa, an easy chair, a coffee table and a TV table which supports the TV, beneath which lies the video player on the floor. There is a small fold-away style table with two dining room chairs pushed into the corner to preserve floor space and to be honest I take most of my meals on my lap except when I have guests, which hasn't occurred so far. The bedroom boasts a large single bed or a

44

small double, depending how you look at it, one bedside table and my rickety wardrobe as mentioned previously. There are old well-worn carpet squares in the bedroom and lounge, tastefully finished off with a lino border. The small entrance hall and kitchen are entirely lino, particularly cold on the feet in winter when I have to trek out for an early morning pee.

Now back to the plot.

I pulled open the creaky wardrobe door and skimmed through the clothes hanging on the rail. I have quite a lot of clothes you may be surprised to hear. Some were completely inappropriate, some were old and out of date, you know the old flared trousers, imitating Marc Bolan poncing around like a ponce. I found one shirt that was clean and probably had been bought within the last three years, light blue with a randomly placed star design. Trousers, a couple of pairs, a light grey would possibly be more pleasing to the eye, I don't want to be too conspicuous. I take it from the cupboard and inspect the creases most of which are in the wrong place and run diagonally rather than up and down in the conventional way. I glance around my room looking for an iron that I know is not there, perhaps something else, something hard to press out the wrong creases and press in the right ones. Something I could heat up on the stove and then press down on the material, nothing. Perhaps I could borrow one from Hilary? But I expect she'll be too busy with preparing for this evening.

Then I remember there are two women living in the basement flat, I have only caught site of them from a distance. When I say two I am sure there are two there, but I think I have only ever seen one, I suspect they could be lesbians. But who knows anyway this could be a good excuse to do a bit of investigation.

So I pad downstairs and out into the street. Access to the basement flat is gained via an iron staircase from pavement level and has a separate entrance door, the number being suffixed with an 'A' where the remaining flats are numbered one to five, mine being number two. I clank down the iron treads and press the bell, I detect a slight movement in the curtains, the door opens about a foot and a thin pretty, in a girly sort of way, young woman peers through the gap. Her eyes are unseeing eyes, distant and vacant and with a pale complexion her dimpled cheeks are enhanced. Her jeans fit tightly to her curves and a round-necked top pronounce the small curves on her flat chest.

I paused before speaking. "Hello," I stuttered. "I live upstairs, on the first floor and I was wondering if I could borrow an iron. To iron my trousers, you know a steaming iron?" I thought the explanation and my gesticulations would help to convince her that I was not requesting a lump of solid steel in order to beat her over the head with, rape her, pillage the flat and make off with all her worldly goods.

"I'll just see," beckoning me with an incline of her head she disappears, I hesitate before following, taking a step inside into the hallway, it smelled musty and damp. The figure turned the corner at the end of the narrow corridor and into the rear room. I closed the door quietly and followed her along the passage hovering on the threshold of a room, probably the lounge. In an armchair wrapped in a blanket, lolled a strikingly beautiful woman, well at least the face was, which was all that was visible to me.

As I said before, I had only seen one of them and it wasn't this one, it must have been the figureless one who answered the door. She must be in her late twenties or at the most thirty-one. The lines were beginning to form to the sides of her eyes although the skin was still clear and clean. The curtains were closed and the room was warm and stuffy, the electric fire in the grate gave off a dry heat, considering we were in the height of summer and the temperature today must have reached twenty centigrade, I was surprised.

"This is Jane," the first person said clearly realising that I had crept in behind her.

"Hi," I nodded.

Jane smiled and looked even more beautiful.

"And you are?" The dimpled one again.

"Vincent, Vince," I said. "I live upstairs on the first floor," I was addressing Jane, I decided she was the decision maker, "I was just wondering if I could borrow an iron, don't worry about the board, I'll use the floor."

She nodded. "Tina fetch the iron please it will be alright." She had a surprisingly deep voice, speaking slowly she formed her words perfectly. Obviously well educated I thought. Her hair was dark brown and hung to her shoulders, the ends curled up in an old-fashioned style from the sixties. I had visions of Christine Keeler in all those black and white shots three decades ago. Her hands were interlocked resting on her lap, I noticed the neatly manicured nails and the little freckles on the backs. Her eyes though looked hurt and concerned as if something deep down was troubling her.

"Thank you, it's this party you see, tonight," I stuttered. "At Hilary's. I don't suppose you know Hilary?"

Jane shook her head.

"Hilary lives upstairs on the second floor."

"We don't go to parties," Tina had returned, she held the iron and was aiming it in my direction.

"Oh right, nor do I really, it's just that Hilary invited me because of the noise and banging." They looked confused. "Me being underneath," I added.

"Oh I see," Jane smiled, the corners of her mouth lifted slightly.

"You could come if you liked," I said, "I'm sure Hilary wouldn't mind, especially as you are also underneath and on account of all the noise and banging." I added.

"No." Tina answered, although I hadn't been addressing her, "I'm afraid Jane is not very well today."

"Oh, I'm sorry, anything I can do to help?"

"No thank you," Jane smiled again. What a smile I thought. "Although it is nice of you to offer, but I expect I will feel better tomorrow."

I took the iron from Tina and said, "Well I'd best be off then I'll bring this back later and thanks."

"Don't worry, tomorrow will do."

"Oh right then," I hesitated in the doorway trying to think of something to add. "I hope you feel better and you're not disturbed too much during the evening, with the noise. I'll pop in tomorrow then."

With this I took my leave and having looked at my watch, bounded up the external staircase two at a time. Ten past six, time had taken a turn for the worse, Harold would be here soon and things had to be done. I shoved my key in the Yale of the front door and received a sharp slap on the back.

"Vince old chap, are you up for it?"

I turned and stammered, "Up for what?" It was Simon Cheek just arrived back from wherever he had been.

"You know Vince, girls and all that sort of... The evening ahead." He was bouncing about on the balls of his feet as if this was the first time he was ever likely to see a girl. Simon, whom as I explained earlier was never short of female company was acting like a teenager on his first date, the testosterone was clearly trying to get out.

"Are you taking anyone with you?" I asked.

"Not likely, I'm on the look out, something new. Bit of skirt to play with, a few vodkas and when the time is right pop her back to the old homestead, or in this case just pop her up two flights of..."

"Stairs?" I offered.

He winked. "Yeah, right. You know what I mean Vince?"

I nodded and felt sick at the thought of going to a party to avoid the noise and banging only to be subjected to Simon banging overhead.

"What about...?" he nodded in my direction.

"Oh me," I said.

"Are you taking a bird or are you just going to play the...?"

"Field?" I suggested.

"Yeah right, Vince, you go for it. don't spare the..."

"No I won't."

"Well, must get..." he said and pushed past me, disappearing up the stairs.

"Ready," I threw after him.

I then followed and went back to my room via the shared bathroom, where I set the taps running to prepare a bath. I always feel a little bashed up and weary after a conversation with Simon. I don't know if it is perhaps because I have to participate from both sides. I thought it a good idea to sort out the titivating before Harold invaded my space and most likely my life. I was definitely having second thoughts about this one, being the butt of a journalistic exercise to enlighten the local well-to-dos how lucky they are to live in their three-bedroomed semis, was not my idea of the doorway to wealth and prosperity. But who knows? What else can I do at the moment?

And this is the first time for some months that I have actually started to mix with other people and have an incentive in life.

In the bathroom I wedged a chair in front of the door to reinforce the flimsy and loosely fitted shoot bolt and in the bath I thought whilst the hot, Ascot heated, water washed around me. I pondered my undoing and considered whether it was likely that I would be able to escape from this poverty trap. Unfortunately it was my own fault, as I mentioned earlier I'd had money and a good position and should have settled down into a standard middle-class system with two point four children. But before any thoughts of children I ruined everything, spoiled my whole future and left my wealth behind as my only epitaph to the class that betrayed me.

I never actually finished telling you how I met Rachel. I followed the three girls, you know the ones who were in the Lyons Corner House, across Hyde Park, Park Lane was to our left as we headed towards Hyde Park Corner, and then one of the other girls said her goodbyes and took a path left out of the park. The other two kept walking deep in conversation and from time to time I could hear the sound of natural laughter. I carried on following with no idea what good it could possibly do me. You know one of those times when you are just looking for a little twist of fate which would give you the opportunity to step up to the lectern and take your chance and perhaps it could change your life.

I kept my distance, about a cricket pitch behind her and the other girl, who turned out to be called Sue. When to my dismay Rachel (except I didn't know her name was Rachel then) tripped on a distorted section of tarmac and unable to put out her hands in time crashed face first into the ground. I instinctively ran forward, there was blood pouring from her nose and face, I took control as her companion appeared too shocked to be of any help. I shouted to the nearest passer-by to call an ambulance and with Sue's help, we carried Rachel onto the soft grass and sat her up against the base of a tree, I didn't want her choking on the blood from her nose or mouth. I had done a rather extensive first aid course when I was in the scouts at boarding school and was not afraid to play my part.

Checking Rachel over I was sure she had broken her arm, but her nose was okay, just a bloody mess. When she landed on her face she was thrown sideways trapping her right arm beneath her. It was bent at a peculiar angle just above the wrist. I took off my shirt and made up a makeshift sling, carefully threading her arm through the opening and securing the arms of the shirt around her neck.

I asked Sue to fetch some water from the nearest refreshment kiosk and leave me whatever she had in the way of handkerchiefs or tissues. I proceeded to try and stem the flow of blood from Rachel's nose and face by delicately padding the areas with the tissues. The blood was running into her long jet black hair and drying, matting the strands together in a sticky glue. Rachel was moaning with pain and shaking with shock and I knew I had to stay with her until the ambulance arrived and keep her warm, I pulled her close to me and let her head rest on my shoulder, the feeling of her close was nice.

Wallowing in the now tepid water of my bath my thoughts were suddenly interrupted by a crash on the staircase followed by a persistent knocking on my flat door and the words. "Hey Vince, open the bloody door."

I scrambled to my feet, careful not to slip and reaching over grabbed the towel from the floor and tried to mop up the globules of water.

The knocking and shouting persisted.

"Harold," I called. "I'm in here, in the bath, I shan't be a moment."

"Hell Vince, make it sharpish, I'm dying for a pee."

I dried myself down and knotted the towel around my middle before releasing the chair and undoing the bolt to the door. I left the bath water to run out on its own accord and no doubt form a line of dried scum horizontally around the plastic, something I always regretted the next time I used it. It all goes to show how one's standards can fall when one only has oneself to worry about.

Harold barged past me, the second person to do so in less than an hour, and positioned himself over the toilet, one hand releasing his zip and the other supporting his weight against the wall. "Oh. That's better," he moaned as relief flooded his nerve ends and he fired a stream of toxic urine at the porcelain.

Back in my bedroom I slipped on some old clothes, checked my complexion in the oval mirror on the bedroom wall, grinned and thought. Yeah and thought again, yeah right.

A classy lightweight suitcase landed at my feet, followed by. "Hey Vince, I'm sure glad that's over, I never thought it was going to stop."

I replied with a grunt.

"Where do I kip down then?"

I pointed at the sofa. "You should be very comfortable there, I'm sure I can find a few travelling rugs and a sleeping bag."

"What no spare room, no spare bed?"

"It's a one bedroomed flat, not a luxury penthouse." I replied.

"Struth, the way you bloody down and outs live Vince, I can't believe it." With this he threw himself down on the sofa.

"Well you better bloody believe it because as I understand it you are supposed to be researching this way of life for your local rag, so don't think you are going to be getting an easy ride from me."

CHAPTER 4

The music was loud, seventies dance sounds bashing out the cords, bouncing off the walls, voices shouting to be heard. Couples pressed hard against each other rocking in the middle of the floor, others cramped round the walls locked together in smooching clinches of eroticism. There must have been more than forty people crammed into the lounge and bedroom, she had opened up the bedroom to create more space. The bed was up-ended and stacked in the corner and the meagre furniture pushed to one side. Hilary had laid out finger buffet type bits to snack on in the kitchen and there were plenty of half open bottles and cans so everyone could help themselves.

Simon Cheek was grappling in the corner with a girl that must have been ten years his junior and he quite clearly had every intention of removing her from her very short hot pants and to be fair by her reactions I suspect he was going to succeed.

I noticed Hilary was being wooed by Harold, which is exactly what I expected to happen, so I suppose I wasn't disappointed. Hilary looked nice and wholesome, not too tarty and available and I had hoped she would keep her distance when it came to Harold.

I recognised quite a few other people, two or three girls who work in the pizza restaurant with Hilary and others that live in flats a few doors away. I just jogged along with the music, trying to look cool and unassuming. It wasn't really possible to start up any meaningful conversations with anyone on account of the volume of the sound system. I stuck to the light white wines to try and avoid a dodgy head in the morning knowing the volume of consumption was likely to be excessive and I picked at the food.

But somehow I wasn't bothered either, my mind kept going back to Jane sitting in her basement flat, I kept asking myself questions. Who was she? Why was she living in this basement flat with this rather unusual girl Tina? What sort of illness did she have? Was it a serious problem or was she just a bit under the weather? And most of all why did I keep thinking about her?

My arm was jogged by a pretty blonde as she danced and jived and some wine tumbled down my newly pressed shirt.

"Sorry," she yelled. I mopped up and raised my glass in acknowledgement.

"Hey come on Vince, there's plenty of crumpet for ev..." said Simon Cheek on his way to the lavatory.

"I'm fine." I replied, he hadn't waited for my answer.

Hilary arrived at my side. "How are you doing Vince? You don't seem to be joining in much." She had taken my spare hand and was squeezing it, I thought, affectionately.

"No Hilary, I'm fine. It's a great party, good food, fine wine, what more could I want?"

"You should be dancing Vince."

"Yeah, well I've never been too good at the old dancing, more suited to observing with a nice glass of wine." She was still squeezing my hand.

She took the glass from my other hand and placing it on the table pulled me to the centre of the room, grabbing me round the waist we bumped into action along with the other gyrators. I tried to object but thought what the hell, I'm only young once and started to move with the beat.

I looked into Hilary's face and smiled, I could see the hairs from her mole, her eyes smiled back at me. It felt good, I squeezed her tighter, she felt good too, I hadn't held a woman in my arms for a long time now and I liked it. The music was hard and fast and provided by The Who, it was obviously a compilation selection as it moved onto Rod Stewart's *Maggie May* and I was really starting to enjoy myself. I held Hilary close, her head nestling in my shoulder, we were of similar height and her hair was brushing my face, it smelt of peroxide.

"How are you getting on with Harold?" I asked hoping she was going to say what a shit he was.

She didn't move her head and replied. "He's a bit pushy isn't he?"

"Probably," I replied. "Well he always used to be but I haven't seen him for some years now. Did he tell you how we bumped into each other and what he was doing here?"

"He said he's a journalist for one of the national papers and he is writing a piece on the local homeless people, the way they live, their problems and how society rejects their plight and he says he will be looking for ways to improve their conditions and he is hoping he will be able to make a difference."

This I felt hard to believe, I wasn't sure Harold's intentions were motivated to help the afflicted, far more likely to feather his own nest.

"He also said you are a big part of his research."

I raised my eyes, national paper indeed and then telling Hilary I am just a guinea pig for his convenience. I pulled her closer and impulsively kissed her ear she didn't seem to mind, I felt some serious stirrings in my groin. I liked the feel of Hilary she was soft and cuddly, you know how some girls are, kind of warm unlike some of the skinny ones who feel sort of hard.

She turned towards me and I found her lips, it was as if nobody else was in the room, we were all alone with the deep base and screeching voice of Barry Gibb beating out The Bee Gee's *Staying Alive*, from *Saturday Night Fever*, if I recall correctly. We kissed long and deep and then I was slapped on the back,

"Hey Vince, leave some for the rest of us."

I turned, quite pissed off to see Harold glaring at me, eyes lost in light and bitter and a werewolf expression on his face. I ignored his lack of protocol and pulling Hilary closer to me spun us away to the other side of the room, bouncing off some other couples as we went. I shouted into her ear, "Do you want to come down to my flat, we could be alone there?"

"Vince, I can't this is my party and my flat." She kissed me hard and fast as an apology and was gone, I recovered my composure and went in search of first a glass of wine and secondly Harold, with every intention of striking him a severe blow in the ear. Having found a drink I gave it some thought, Hilary yeah, nice girl and I would be more than happy for things to go further, but I need to sort myself out and Harold's idea is not that bad and perhaps we could make it work.

I took my glass and picked up the half empty one Hilary had put down before and took them out onto the landing where I could sit on the stairs, listen to the music from a more subdued distance and relax with my thoughts.

I have got to get out of this slovenly way of life, living off the state and never having any money, it was not doing my ego or education justice, I was better than this. Perhaps I could start to do some of the writing for Harold, help form the basis for his articles, as I said before, I studied English at university so I shouldn't find it beyond my abilities to carry out some research and put down a few paragraphs. I was still uncomfortable with Harold's apparent attitude to my current situation and, as I said before, I am not sure his intentions are likely to benefit the homeless and are probably purely designed for his own ends.

Whilst sitting here and soaking up the music and atmosphere from within the flat I am going to continue telling you about Rachel. Now where was I?

She was in my arms leaning against a tree in Hyde Park bleeding all over my shirt, that certainly sounds like a good starting point, the suspension must be killing you. Rachel stayed in hospital for two days. I visited her on the second afternoon armed with flowers, grapes and chocolates. She smiled a sweet response as best she could, considering the stitches to her lips and cheek. But of course she didn't know who I was, obviously she remembered that someone had helped her when she fell, but she was in a pretty bad way and concussed. So I had to explain to her what had happened, leaving out the bit about purposefully following her from the coffee shop.

I sat on a chair beside her bed and we chatted comfortably, I remember thinking this is the girl for me and I was right. Once she was out of hospital we started dating, once a week at first and then after she was fully recovered and the plaster had been removed from her arm and the scars to her face had healed, it became more frequent. We did most of the venues young people frequent, pubs, bars, restaurants and cinemas, we tried the odd nightclub, but as I think I've said before I wasn't much of a dancer. I think it is because I am not tall enough to have the confidence to throw myself around with gay abandon.

We clearly got on well our backgrounds were similar or if you're allowed to say it these days, we were of the same class. Our parents were both reasonably well off and we had had good educations, she was studying law with hopes of progressing to one of the big London practices.

Our relationship blossomed, and we moved from holding hands and experiencing delicious cuddles and kisses in the darkened moments in the cinema, to a more intimate understanding. I remember the first time we made love, it was about three months after the accident. I went round to her house about seven one evening to pick Rachel up as we intended going to a Chinese restaurant, we hadn't booked, it was just an idea for a change. We both liked Chinese cuisine, the mixture of spices and herbs and the way they cook the flavours and it was always fun playing with chop sticks.

After we had kissed hello, she told me her parents were out for the evening, a ladies night or something and they wouldn't be back until after midnight. So it just sort of happened, we went to her bedroom and three hours later came back downstairs for a coffee. It was blissful, just seemed natural, not one of those all fingers and thumbs episodes tinged with embarrassment with neither protagonist knowing quite what to try next. We just fell into a comfortable coupling, a meeting of bodies which accentuated our desires and satisfaction. We sat in her kitchen and drank coffee, chatting and trying to find out more and more about each other, it was magic, I had never felt so at one with anybody before and I just knew we had to be together, for ever.

"Move over."

"Oh. Sorry, of course." I shoved over squeezing hard against the banister, Hilary dropped in beside me sitting on the staircase.

"You were miles away."

"Yeah. I was just thinking, you know the past that sort of thing." I took a swig of my wine feeling a little uncomfortable.

Hilary moved closer, although the space was limited and put her arm through mine. "It wasn't anything to do with me not coming down to your flat earlier was it? Because I would have done if it wasn't for the fact it is my party and," she hesitated. "Well you know I should be with my guests."

Shit. I thought. "No it's nothing like that, I just found it a bit claustrophobic in there and the music is very loud, I wanted space to think. It's nice sitting out here listening to some of these old records, they bring back memories."

She nuzzled up and bit my ear. "Another time perhaps?"

I nodded pleased with the thought, realising it was probably for the best as I had most likely drunk too much wine by now and that would most likely lead to an embarrassing level of under performance.

"You're a nice girl Hilary. I appreciate you asking me this evening, even if it was only because of the noise and banging."

She laughed and disappeared back into the flat.

* * * *

I was shaken awake and as I opened my eyes the first thing I saw was that bloody idiot Harold, dressed and quite clearly ready to go. Where I knew not.

"Come on Vince you bloody wanker, get up we've got things to do." His distorted expression loomed over me.

I rolled my clenched fists round my eyes and when I looked again he was still there. "What the hell are you on about Harold?"

"We have to get (that word again, I shuddered) out on the road Vince, see what the likes of you get up to on a Sunday. See which pavement you sit on, see if it's any different to the weekday slab. Anyway where's breakfast? I've rummaged through the fridge and the cupboards and apart from half a pack of Sugar Puffs, a few teabags and a tin of economy line custard there is nothing. Don't you fellows ever buy anything of decent quality? And also the sleeping arrangements are pretty bloody awful, the springs are sticking through that sofa. I hardly slept a wink and the noise upstairs kept going until well after two. That Hilary I don't know who she was going to end up with but she seemed to be playing the field. I thought for a while it might even have been you Vince, she seemed to be getting a bit friendly," he winked a knowing smile. "She tried it with me, but I played it cool, plenty of other fish in the duck pond you know, I'm not sure she's my type, I like them a little bit slimmer and more curvy." He was swaying suggestively from one side to the other. "Look, get out Harold and just let me get up and get dressed." (There I'm doing it now using that word 'get' showing scant regard for the English language).

Once I had washed and dressed I went into the lounge where Harold was munching through a bowl of Sugar Puffs covered in cold custard. "Hey this cold custard is tasty it makes a good substitute for milk, you ought to try some Vince."

I threw the remains of his bedding on the floor and sat down. "Now what are you on about?" I asked grumpily. Just in case you were wondering my grumpiness was caused by being woken up, not by any dodgy wine like previous mornings. And also I didn't particularly like Harold's remarks about Hilary playing the field.

I had left the party about half an hour after midnight and made my way to bed quite contented, falling into a deep sleep. My dreams took the shape of Hilary with her mole, in the disguise of Jane sitting wrapped in blankets in a soulful state in her basement flat and all in all it was a fairly pleasant experience. Having had virtually no contact with the opposite sex for many months I had met two women in the same day, one of which I had chatted to off and on and ended up propositioning, and in return received a half promise for a bit of nooky in a more suitable location. The other one, having met for the first time had made a deep impression on me, which reminded me I must return the steam iron to Jane today as promised and I must choose the most appropriate time of day in case she is still not feeling well, but of course I hoped to be able to spend some time chatting.

"Look if we are going to learn about the way society's scroungers live..." Harold had finished his Sugar Puffs and polished off the whole tin of cold custard. "We will have to roam the streets and try to mingle in with them, frequent the places they go, try to blend in, you must know all the haunts Vince."

"As I am one of them, you mean?" I interrupted.

"Well, yes I suppose you are, look at the way you live." And he threw his arms around gesticulating the lack of contents in the room. "Oh yes and by the way I am probably going to charge the old expense account and check into a local hotel rather than stay in this dump." Harold said very matter-of-factly.

I acted hurt, but secretly I was relieved, I wasn't sure I could constantly put up with Harold's cheap remarks and continuous insults, it was going to be bad enough spending the day times with him, let alone the invasion of my rather limited space during the night. Anyway I always enjoy watching my dodgy movies on my own and not having to put up with all the lewd remarks one would be subjected to by someone like Harold.

"I do have a few things to do today," I said. "So my time devoted to studying the city's low lifes may well be limited." I made a point of making a point, but knowing Harold this may well have been lost, he is without a doubt a thick-skinned bastard.

"Right. Okay then, you do what you have to do, I am going to find a decent hotel, get hold of some scruffy clothes and see you back here at say four and then we can go out for a wander and take in the local reprobates, mix and chat with a few no-hopers, make a few notes and hey presto we are on the way." He looked pleased with this, so I went along with it.

Four o'clock seemed a long way off at nine thirty on a Sunday morning. We therefore went our separate ways, in other words Harold buggered off with his light-weight trendy suitcase and I stayed in putting away the debris he had left and generally trying to tidy up.

I know what you are thinking, how can it be difficult tidying up in a tiny little flat like that? Well it is, so let's just leave it like that okay! I did tidy up and then I sat down with a hot cup of lemon tea, as there wasn't any milk, there wasn't any lemon either but I have always thought that a rather superfluous additive to milk-less tea. I relaxed and considered the past few days and then I remembered the iron, I should take it back, I borrowed it yesterday from Jane in the basement to press my trousers. I finished my rather bitter cup of tea, went to the bathroom, brushed my teeth, combed my hair and checked my complexion in the mirror. Back in the bedroom I chose a clean T-shirt, picked up the iron and shot downstairs to pavement level and then down the external staircase to the basement flat.

I banged on the door and waited, the curtains were drawn in the front room, and I was trying to remember if they were open or not when I called yesterday. As I stood there expectantly, I was certain I saw them twitch, I waited and then the door opened a fraction, Tina peering through the gap, a disgruntled expression on her face. With a cheery smile I waved the iron as my reason for being there and the door opened further, she went to take it from me, but I quickly moved it away from her grasp.

"May I come in?" I asked. "To thank Jane for letting me borrow the iron." I added by way of explanation.

She looked reluctant, but opened the door further to allow me to pass. "Yes alright."

I followed her down the passage as before. She was dressed in a heavy loose fitting cardigan, tight slacks tucked into long woolly socks and no footwear, the Bohemian look I thought.

In the sitting room Jane was positioned as before, wrapped in a blanket with just her head visible, the electric fire was warmly drying the air, even though it was just as warm as yesterday and in all honesty a typical summer's day.

"Hello again," I said.

She smiled that smile again. "Did you get your ironing done?"

"Yes thanks." I handed the iron to Tina now in the hope she would disappear and put it away, and she obliged.

"Did you have a nice party?"

"Yes it was good, I hope it wasn't too loud for you."

"No, we could hear the rumble of music from time to time and a few people were a bit noisy when they left, but it was alright. It's nice to hear people enjoying themselves."

I nodded, she smiled again and I didn't know what to say next.

"Do you get out much?" I stuttered. Because perhaps we could meet for a coffee or something? Sometime?" I stuttered again, why couldn't I be more like Simon? Be upfront and say exactly what I wanted to say?

"I'm afraid not, I don't venture out much and I am confined to this room and my bedroom. Would you like some tea?"

"Yes please, if it is not too much trouble."

"Tina," she called.

Tina floated into the room. "Yes Jane."

"Could we have some tea please Tina, and perhaps some shortbread and biscuits?" Tina disappeared as quietly as she had come.

"I am sorry to hear you can't get about, is there nothing that anyone can do to help?" She motioned me to sit down in the high-backed chair beside hers.

"It is a muscular problem in my legs, I get a lot of cramps and the muscles give me a lot of trouble, they think it is most likely ME. The doctors are trying their best and I have a physiotherapist visit me twice a week to manipulate the muscles and try to make them stronger. She also gives me exercises to do everyday, but I find these so tiring and I am not sure they do any good."

She pulled the blanket aside, she wore a three-quarter length dress, she hoisted the hem up exposing the lower half of her legs, they were milk white as if they had never been exposed to the sun and quite slim with hardly any definition on the calf at all. Almost like the legs of an undernourished child from a third world country. Her upper body was slim and neat and appeared out of proportion to her lower half.

"You must do the exercises," I offered. "You need to get stronger." I felt sorry for her it seemed such a waste for someone so young and lovely to be shut away in a basement flat all day and not being able to get out.

"What do you do all day?" I asked.

"Oh. I read a lot, I, believe it or not, crochet, which is very therapeutic. I make blankets, see this one," she thumbed the multicoloured blanket once again stretched across her knees. "Tina takes them to a market stall at Camden Lock market on a Sunday morning and we make a reasonable return for our labours, admittedly it is more for the satisfaction of doing it than the money."

Tina had returned with the tea and biscuits and we sat and chatted for a further half an hour. Tina stayed in the room like a chaperone, sitting in the corner listening, but not commenting.

I found I was emotionally drawn to Jane's charms and I wanted to help her, I wanted to take her in my arms and comfort her. Before I left I asked if I could call again and we made a date for late Thursday afternoon, with a promise that Tina would prepare a high tea. (Now there's an expression from my youth, high tea! My mother used to prepare high tea at weekends, especially if we were entertaining visitors. It would consist of cold meats, salad, bread and butter with jam and cakes).

I skipped up the metal staircase to pavement level with a feeling of euphoria coupled with a touch of melancholy. The euphoria was triggered by a heart fluttering desire that I was going to see Jane again and I was sure, with a bit of luck a romantic scenario could develop. The melancholia was brought on by her illness and the realisation that unless she could make a full recovery or at least improve considerably, we would not be able to experience the joys of normal couples. See, there I said normal. What is normal? How can you define normal? Because she can't walk easily I have categorised her as not being normal, which I felt a little uncomfortable about, I didn't want to be just like everybody else and pigeon hole her.

* * * *

Harold banged on my door about a quarter past four. "Okay come on let's get going, I've got an article to write." He was dressed in jeans torn at the knees, polo shirt and baggy jumper. Even though it was a warm summer's day there was a wind in the air and of course we were going to be out into the evening. Harold had obviously done his homework with every intention of blending in with the environment, but why should I be cynical, I am already part of the environment or so he believes.

I was dressed in my customary slovenly way, jeans, T-shirt and trainers, a habit I have been embracing for the past year or so. Very unlike the image I used to portray, but that was some time ago now and let's face it my life has changed, I have no need to dress to impress people anymore.

"Where do you think we should go?" I asked.

"Hell, I don't know, Vince you're the bloody expert," he glanced round the room taking in the sparse furnishings and lack of homely things and the empty fridge and cupboards. "Look how you live, come on make a few suggestions and we will be off."

I didn't have the energy to respond to his insults and just made a mental note that I had to make an effort to change. Clean myself up and try to give a different impression to people, it's been over a year now so it is about time I sorted myself out. I thought for a moment and then suggested, "Main line stations are probably a good starting place and the arches adjacent to them, little alleyways and back streets. The Strand and Charing Cross are notorious and parts of Soho, also Tottenham Court Road and Centre Point. Seeing it's late afternoon, why don't we just try the Kings Cross area this evening and then tomorrow we can explore further afield."

"Yeah, okay, at least that is some sort of plan."

We made our way by bus, on Harold's expense account, from Kentish Town Road heading south down Royal College Street until we finally arrived in Midland Road where we alighted, eager to feast our eyes on the finer points of Kings Cross. No sooner were we out of the relative safety of a London Route-master than we were surrounded by a group of preying leaches some were sitting on the pavement and two others stood barring our way. Their request was simple firstly money and then cigarettes and or drugs.

"I thought we were dressed for the part to look like these fucking peasants," said Harold clearly unsettled by this encroachment on his privacy. He was obviously unprepared for what could occur in this homeless environment. He carried on. "Why are they soliciting us? We are supposed to look like them, in fact Vince you are one of them."

As we started to move away a bearded strong smelling youth grabbed Harold's ankle pleading for a cigarette, Harold responded in typical fashion. "Get off you fucking moron," and kicked out with his right foot catching the youth on the shoulder knocking him back across the pavement.

The two that originally threatened us had now sat down with the others and they cried out and shouted abuse at us, they were all lying about on the ground, probably doped up, but I had a severe impression that it only needed one of them to get to his feet and make an issue of it and the whole mob would be after us.

We moved away quickly a little shaken by the experience and walked under the bridges towards Goods Way where the arches would provide some suitable shelter from the rain and wind in the colder months. This evening the weather was warm and calm and these hideaways just showed the remnants of dirty sleeping bags, sheets of cardboard, boxes and blankets. The occupants were clearly not at home, probably abroad looking for supplies. Whether they get these by begging or stealing is most likely of little consequence to them.

Ahead up the hill towards Caledonian Road there are rows of parking meters propping up a group of five or six girls dressed in very short skirts and revealing tops. As cars pass they gesticulate their intentions trying to get the drivers to pull over so they can show off their wares.

One car slows to a halt some twenty yards past the girls and waits. A tall, long legged girl leaves the group and walks to the passenger side of the car. Leaning on the open window a conversation takes place for some minutes, she then shouted back to her friends and got into the car, presumably, having set up an appropriate deal. The car drove off turning left at the T-junction.

We both stood and watched from a safe distance, Harold made a few notes and I made mental ones, although we both knew these things went on it was quite different observing them in the flesh. Another car slowed and something was said through the window and then the car sped away, one of the girls shouted after it and a wave of gesticulations followed from the others.

We watched for a while longer and similar incidents occurred every three or four minutes. I couldn't take my eyes from the girls plying their trade and the aggressive and intimidating confrontations that took place in front of us.

The girls appeared to be so young, but so grown-up at the same time, streetwise, that maybe the word for it, but I felt uncomfortable the way they clearly had no self respect. They were quite prepared to demean themselves, for what? A few quid which would probably be gone by lunchtime tomorrow.

One girl in particular looked little more than fifteen, she wore a minute top, her breasts squeezed forward, looked twice as big as they really were, her skirt skin-tight was short within six inches of her crotch. But I noticed she was always one of the first to shout abuse at the punters, when they decided the proposition on offer was not for them. I thought of my set of videos, the ones in my flat where I watch the girls on the screen, it seems innocent, but somehow it is different in the flesh. Perhaps I am kidding myself, it sounds as if I am beginning to feel a certain benevolence towards these girls.

We walked back towards St Pancras Station and stood in Euston Road, just taking in the atmosphere and the environment. The large Victorian building towering behind us, its crescent façade shadowed the setting sun as it glared down from the west. The darkness of the small windows looked sinister with the large stone reveals hiding the secrets within. We stood there for some minutes quietly watching the traffic and the bustle evolving around us. The traffic was intense and nose to tail, which in London never seems to abate. Even though it was an early Sunday evening there were plenty of people about, buses continuously pulling up at the bank of bus stops at the front of Kings Cross Station.

On the opposite side of the road outside a Ladbrokes bookmakers were a gang of youths pestering passers-by for money. Their manner was threatening, but it was clear that most of their targets had very little themselves anyway. The have-nots can't feed the poor, it doesn't work that way, surely they must realise that.

One man reacted to the request for money by answering back and telling them where to go, and he received a clubbing round the head for his trouble from two of the gang, before making off as fast as he could. He was clearly shaken and the last we saw of him was ducking into the underground obviously clutching his belongings close to him.

We stood and watched events unfold, there were things happening from every angle, the hustle and bustle of London. The warm evening air was pleasant on our backs and I think we were both content to just observe and take in the atmosphere of a very cosmopolitan city at work. We moved back from the kerb and leant against a wall of St Pancras Station, the bricks radiated heat having been kiln baked by a hot summer sun for the past few months.

Harold took a small hand-held tape recorder from his pocket and moving away from me hunched over and proceeded to speak into it, he held his left hand across his face shielding the receiver from view.

I carried on my observation, looking for incidents which I could file to memory, any little things which could be of use in constructing Harold's article. When you actually stop and watch it is mind boggling how many people buzz backwards and forwards going about their business some affecting others, but most independent and singular.

Harold returned to my side. "I usually write my notes out," he said packing the machine away in his pocket, "and only use this thing when pen and notebook would be too conspicuous, which in this environment was probably a good assessment."

I smiled knowingly.

A couple of beer swigging drunks passed us cursing and swearing in broad Irish, the clothes were torn and tatty, their beards were unkempt and contained the contents of their last meal mixed with beer froth. One made a grab for a lady's bottom as she walked past, heading in the opposite direction. She gave a yelp and walked on faster and he said, "Fucking whore!" and gesticulated behind them, they both laughed. Once they had moved on their stale smell lingered in the air, it was an overpowering, dank and dark odour that went straight to the pit of your stomach and made you want to retch.

We both looked at each other and our expressions showed our feelings and then Harold said. "That's some bloody smell Vince, I'm glad you're not like that, at least I've seen you use your bathroom."

"Thanks very much," I acknowledged.

"You know Vince, what I don't understand is why all these wasters allow themselves to get into this state?"

I shrugged. "I don't really know either, but to a lesser extent you could say it has happened to me." I may have opened myself up to further insults here.

"Yeah you're right Vince, I've told you before the way you live is bloody awful, but this is actually different." He visibly shivered. "It's as if they don't actually care, there is no self respect, no," he stuttered looking for the right words.

I suggested. "Self esteem."

"Yeah you're right Vince. Thanks."

Two scantily clad teenage girls passed in front of us and stopped attracting our attention, their skirts were no more than six inches below their crotches, legs bare down to high heeled platform shoes. Flimsy tops covered the essentials and there was no sign of any bra straps.

"Do you want a good time?" One of them said.

We stood our ground.

"No thanks." I said.

"It's only a score," said the other one.

I shook my head not wanting to get into a conversation.

"Oh come on," said the first one. "You know you want to and you won't be disappointed," and made a grab for Harold's groin.

Harold let out a shriek. "Hey, bugger off you bloody old toms," he shouted.

"Sod off you pair of shits," the first one said and they moved away looking for more suitable punters waggling their bottoms as they walked, probably trying to emphasise to us what we were missing.

"Vince. This shit's bollocks," observed Harold.

I nodded in agreement, thinking, what a profound remark for a journalist.

CHAPTER 5

Once home I was soon in bed, Harold had made off for his hotel, it was only a few streets away in Chalk Farm and he was going to be more comfortable there so why should I complain? It would be better both ways, he's got his expense account and I, well I would rather be on my own, especially now I have both Hilary and Jane to think about, I don't really want Harold hanging around all the time.

When I came in I threw a teabag in a cup and sloshed some boiling water on it, added some low fat milk, a quick stir and sat on the sofa contemplating the evening's experiences. I felt somewhat shell-shocked by the events, although I knew this sort of thing happened. I knew people lived like this, seeing it in the raw, fellow human beings subjected to this sort of degradation just to survive. Selling their bodies and their minds, not minding who they beg from or steal from for that matter. It is a dog-eat-dog existence out there.

As I drifted off to sleep I kept reliving the scenes, the young prostitute so forward and gregarious, her face and figure played on my mind. She was probably underage but she would flaunt and push herself forward for recognition, with no concern for her safety or her self-esteem as long as she could turn some tricks, make some cash and in her eyes cock a snook at society.

And the group of young men sitting on the ground asking for food, cigarettes and drugs, not necessarily in that order, were they aware of the level to which they had sunk? Probably not, but is that important when you're a down and out? All that is important is your next meal, your next fag, your next fix.

And the two girls who propositioned us, would they really do it for twenty quid? And for that matter where would they do it? We were in the middle of one of the busiest areas of London. What would they have done? Would they have led us round the corner underneath the arches or to some pokey little room somewhere?

I don't have the answers but I have a lot of questions.

I had a restless night and kept waking, my mind going round and round. A muddle of the streets of Kings Cross mixed up with Jane sitting in her basement flat and occasionally Hilary nibbling my ear suggestively.

* * * *

I rose early this morning, without a headache which recently is unusual. I had an enthusiasm for our project and I couldn't face Harold banging on the door whilst I was still in bed and hurling abuse at me. Therefore I washed quickly and decided not to shave as I wanted to blend in with the down and outs and a stubbly beard looks more unkempt. I searched for food but was unlucky, I considered knocking on Hilary's door to see if I could borrow a slice of bread or a bowl of cornflakes or something, but I rejected this thought. I raided my dole money, took a fiver and headed off to the local corner shop, as I strode along the street, Hilary caught up with me.

"Vincent, nice to see you, I hope you enjoyed Saturday evening."

"Yes it was great," I said. She was dressed in her bright red pizza uniform, obviously on her way to work.

"I thought you might have knocked yesterday, you could have helped me clear up. I stayed in all day." She was smiling and the hairs on her mole were juddering in the breeze. I thought she was going to finish this sentence with 'waiting for you'. But she didn't.

"Sorry, I didn't think. I had Harold there and we went out down to Kings Cross."

"Oh yes, doing your research. Well give me a knock tonight and you can help me finish up some of the leftovers, unless you've got something better to do?"

"Right. I will." I stuttered and she was gone, I watched her walk ahead her hips swinging, not unattractive at all I thought. My groin once again gave a flutter.

I bought bread, cheese, low fat spread and half a dozen eggs, four tomatoes and two apples and having returned to my flat proceeded to prepare two slices of toast, two eggs and a grilled tomato. I was feeling better about things, there seemed to be more purpose to my life and I thought a hearty breakfast could set me up for the day ahead.

Having finished I cleared away, I intended making more of an effort to keep the place clean in future. I checked the time it was after nine thirty. I would have expected Harold to be round by now, so I sat down to wait for him which gives me the opportunity to continue telling you about my past. Oh good I hear you breathe, never one to miss a good story are you?

It was not long after that first time Rachel and I made love in her parents' house, we made the decision to go the whole hog, you know get married, make an honest woman of the girl. Rachel's parents, her mum in particular went full speed ahead into the arrangements, the church was booked, bridesmaids signed up, Rachel's younger sister Catherine and her cousin Julie. They were all whisked off to take part in choosing dress designs in a wedding shop just off Oxford Street followed by numerous fittings.

Girls don't seem to mind this sort of thing, I had to go with the other men involved to Moss Bros in the West End and be measured for top hat and tails. All of which were delivered a couple of days before the wedding day the 1st March 1982.

I was twenty-four and my intended twenty-one, she looked absolutely radiant, her slim figure just sat so perfectly in the flowing white gown. The ceremony went without any hitches although we were both very nervous saying our vows in front of more than one hundred and fifty people, some of which neither of us knew, but the parents felt it prudent they were invited. Building social bridges, you know the sort of thing, take advantage of your offspring's occasion to mix with the well-to-do and sow some decent seeds for the future.

The reception was in a large country hotel called The Grange about three miles from the church just south of Guildford. The champagne flowed and the five course wedding breakfast was more than adequate to satisfy all the guests. The speeches went well, although I was nervous, the alcohol certainly helped and I drivelled on to much applause and good natured banter.

The best man, an old friend from my university days stabbed me with the usual mocking insults and memories of the past, in an effort

70

to gain as much embarrassment as possible from the poor bridegroom.

It was a great feeling to be the centre of attraction for the whole day and Rachel was so stunning, I felt so proud and kept thinking what does she see in me? Short, bald and not particularly good looking...

A bang-bang on the flat door shook me from my thoughts, it must be Harold. I must go. I will tell you more later, don't worry you will hear it all by the end, I am sure the suspense is getting too much and you probably have the urge to flick on a few pages. But I don't recommend that because who knows what you may miss.

* * * *

"Keep up Vince you bloody wanker," shouted Harold over his shoulder, he was striding through the tunnels of Charing Cross underground station following the main line rail symbol. The dirty beige and cream tiled walls with the grey grout were so tired and depressing, the smell of urine hit our nostrils as we approached the final staircase from the booking hall. A pile of dirty bedding was heaped in the corner under the soffit of the staircase.

Harold pulled up short as I caught him up, he said, "Look at this Vince," he pointed at the bedding. "I ask you what a bloody state."

"What?" I asked.

"Look there's a boy lying in amongst all those blankets, and the bloody smell," he covered his nose with the back of his sleeve.

I looked carefully, it was hard to discern the figure spread-eagled on the ground wrapped in a mixture of materials and cardboard. "I think he's asleep," I whispered.

"This is shit Vince, what's going on? I can't be doing with all this, all these fucking waifs and strays clogging up our city." He walked away without waiting for an answer and taking his hand-held tape recorder from his pocket started muttering into it shielding himself from the other commuters.

I moved closer to the figure and tried to determine how old he was, the blankets stirred and rolled over disturbed by my presence and faced me. The eyes were still closed, the face dirty and stained,

71

hair hanging lank and matted and a pungent odour floated on the stale air so familiar to the underground. The eyes suddenly opened and stared at me, they were bright and blue and frightened, shining against the dirty features.

"It's okay," I said quietly. I knelt down on my haunches trying to coax a change of expression or even a few words. But the figure just stared, he must have been no more than twelve years old. "Are you alright?" I asked

A small hand came out from beneath the blanket palm upwards clearly asking for money. I reached instinctively into my pocket, aware that I would find very little there, but felt anything would help, I pulled some coins out, I juggled them in my hand, they amounted to seventy-four pence. I dropped them into the open palm and the fingers snapped closed and disappeared inside the dirty blankets..

"Vince, what are you doing?" came from over my shoulder.

"Quiet," I said, "you'll frighten him." I tried to smile softly at the face to gain some confidence, but the eyes stayed bright, but expressionless.

"Come on Vince let's get out of here, this place is beginning to give me the bloody creeps," Harold was hopping about behind me. "And apart from that I can't stand the fucking smell."

"For God's sake just shut up and wait a minute, can't you see this is only a child, we must help him, if you don't like it wait outside, I'll meet you at the Eleanor Cross at the front of the station."

He scurried away and I returned my attention to the boy, whose eyes had not moved from my face. "What is your name?" I asked. But still he didn't speak, just stared, his eyes were perhaps less frightened looking, but uncertain and wary.

I decided to take my leave, but with a promise to myself to return, presuming he would most likely be here tomorrow and the next day. I stood up. "I will come and see you again tomorrow, if you want anything I could bring it then." I hesitated. "Perhaps you will tell me your name then." I said waving my goodbyes as I moved away up the last flight of stairs.

Outside I found Harold sitting on a raised kerb beneath the Eleanor Cross looking confused, we didn't speak, he stood up and we walked down the Strand towards the Aldwych, we passed people rolled up in doorways wrapped in cardboard and blankets, although I thought it was too warm to be surrounded with blankets. More often than not it was the blankets and cardboard that were left vacant like unmade beds.

We passed the busy shops, cafés and banks and then we threaded our way up Wellington Street into Covent Garden. The sun was warm, a late August day with just a hint of the autumnal feeling that would soon take over our summer. We sat in the piazza and drank coffee, provided by Harold's expense account, though reluctantly, surrounded by tourists and street entertainers, musicians, trick cyclists and statuesque figures carefully positioned to reap the most effect. Motionless, clad in obscure costumes, heavily made up features mingling in amongst the crowds, taking people by surprise merely by their presence. Caps or buckets laid on the pavements in front of them inviting passers-by to give of their loose change.

Harold took out his notebook, scribbled some short sentences and then spoke into his tape machine, I took little notice as I expected to be party to the finished article. I just reflected on the day so far and the young boy lying in the recesses of Charing Cross Station.

We sat in silence for a while and then Harold said, "Well, Vince, what do you think?"

"About what?" I asked.

"You know, all those bloody peasants lying about in shop doorways, underneath the railway arches at Kings Cross, those old toms yesterday evening, these fucking beggars always trying to tap you for a few bob. At least it will give me something to write about, it shouldn't take that long to form an adverse opinion about this lot and get it down on paper. They certainly provide the ammunition."

I looked at him, he was still scribbling away. "Haven't you got any feelings?" I asked.

He looked up. "What?"

I said. "Haven't you got any feelings? Aren't you at all concerned about the plight of these people?"

He looked at me with a weird expression on his face, surprised by my outburst.

I continued. "You don't think they want to sleep in shop doorways wrapped up in cardboard, without a change of clothes,

73

without the facilities to bath, shave and generally wash. Even to be able to clean their teeth and just carry out the normal everyday activities which we take for granted."

"I take for granted," he responded. "You're one of them Vince, remember that you live in squalor, claiming your dole money."

"Hey just hold on Harold, I am not one of them, I have just had a blip in my life, it is short term and it will be sorted out." I was beginning to feel pretty pissed off with Harold and his supercilious and pompous way of looking at things.

"Yeah okay Vince, I take your point, carry on."

I did. "Those girls yesterday evening don't want to have to walk the streets or stand on street corners touting for business, to sell their bodies for a few pounds. To be abused by perverted men who give them no respect but just use them to satisfy their own sordid needs. And what about that young boy, don't you have any concern for him? Living in a heap beneath a staircase soffit at a London main line station, don't these things make any impression on you?"

Harold looked at me in a slightly sheepish way. "Yeah. Well, I don't know," he said. "It just seems to me they are all just scrounging, why don't they get a job or something?"

"They probably haven't got the wherewithal to get a job, they probably haven't been given the opportunities, they probably haven't been taught interview techniques."

"They probably haven't tried," he added.

"That isn't fair Harold, you don't know the facts and neither do I, but I just feel you should try and give them a chance. You're writing the article, you should be viewing it from an unbiased perspective, not just from your own prejudiced position." I was getting a little annoyed at his self-righteous attitude, he may well have a point with some of the people but not all by a long way, many of these people are the victims of circumstances they have no control over.

"I still don't see why we should have to keep them all."

"Look this isn't getting us anywhere, you have a piece to write and I…"

"That's right and you Vince, you have what to do? Nothing, because you're a bloody layabout as well just like this lot," he gesticulated waving his arm in a circular movement.

I knew he was right that was the problem, but seeing these people last night and today, made me want to be able to help, do something about it, but I don't suppose I was going to be able to explain this to Harold. He was biased from the beginning.

"Come on," I said. "Let's go and do some more research, Charing Cross Road and Tottenham Court Road, by Centre Point should be a suitable area."

* * * *

Once I was back in the flat it was late afternoon, I had got rid of Harold, he was going back to his hotel where he could bash up his expense account on the pretence of a three course meal, a bottle of Merlot and a few large ports. Tomorrow he intended listening to his tape and typing up his notes so far, so I would be left to my own devices, this gave me a kind of warmth, a feeling of relief. To tell you the truth I wasn't sorry, too much of Harold can be a bit wearing.

We had walked up Charing Cross Road and turned right at Centre Point into New Oxford Street where we saw a woman sitting on the pavement in a recess where the pavement dog-legs and creates a sheltered corner from the wind. She must have been all of seventy years old, she was wrapped in old torn clothes, her legs, above frayed socks were bare and covered in ulcerated sores. She was smoking the remains of a dog-end she had rescued from a passer-by as it was tossed into the gutter. The glow smouldering through the filter as she dragged hard to get the final satisfaction from it. Her face was old, lined and haggard, but her smile gave off an assurance of years of experience as if she was laughing at us, not the other way round.

I found this a little unnerving, quite clearly this old lady who owned absolutely nothing harboured a lifetime's knowledge and perhaps we were the ignorant ones. I looked at Harold, but his expression was not easy to read, I think he was trying to fight any emotions he may have felt in order to put on an air of superiority.

I suggested Harold threw a few pounds onto her blanket, from his expense account of course, initially he said bollocks and then had second thoughts and pulled out some loose change and lobbed it at her feet. The woman smiled a knowing look and picked up the coins and secreted them carefully amongst her folds of clothing, clearly a safe place as no one would wish to delve amongst those materials .

We moved on and turned left into Museum Street and walked to the T-junction where we came face to face with the huge Greco-Victorian façade, temple-like in its appearance, of the British Museum. Its imposing presence dominating the vista from all directions we carried on to Russell Square where we read a notice stating the gates would be closed an hour before sunset and their sympathies were not in favour of the homeless spending the night among the trees and bushes within the parkland. From there we went past the buildings of the University of London and into Tottenham Court Road where the many electrical stores were full of young music fans searching for the latest means of playing their current choice. Once again we were confronted with the cardboard city phenomena, the remnants of bedding left in disused doorways awaiting the return of their owner once the bustle of the city had died down and night was to fall.

We didn't talk much, I think it was an eye opener to both of us, even if I was supposed to be one of them as Harold was only too eager to remind me at every opportunity. It was sad and I felt very humble even from my relatively, at present, low standing in society but at the same time an elation that perhaps this was the challenge I needed. Could I possibly do anything about it and perhaps change things?

We walked on and Harold kept sidling off into corners to mutter into his tape machine or quickly scribble out a bit of self-taught shorthand. We continued our trek north along Tottenham Court Road until we reached the junction with Euston Road, I looked up at Euston Tower with all the radio aerials on the roof picking up the signals for Capital Radio. We crossed the road and jumped on a bus on the other side heading east and made our way back to Kentish Town.

I was glad Harold had left me for the evening we had experienced a lot today and it also gives me the opportunity to carry on with the next part of my story. I can spare some time before I pop upstairs to share some supper with Hilary, you know finishing up the leftovers. Oh yes, you thought I had forgotten that didn't you? But I have decided I have got to come out of myself and start to live again and if that is with Hilary, so be it.

Anyway I have a few minutes to spare so here goes, pin your ears back and listen there may be a written test at the end, I haven't decided yet.

We spent our honeymoon in Egypt, a little unusual you may think, Cairo, a lovely westernised hotel amidst a jungle of poverty and degradation. The hotel had a number of restaurants based on different themes and cultures, good quality service and modern, spacious bedrooms. It was perhaps a strange choice, but we were both fascinated by early history and the pull and romanticism of the only lasting Seven Wonders of the World was too much to miss.

We had a lovely room overlooking the outdoor swimming pool surrounded by palm trees and a walled garden. There were chairs and tables and a number of loungers positioned in the shadows of the trees, with a constant waiter service providing drinks and light snacks. We spent hours lying about round the pool, except when we both felt amorous and we would rush straight back to our room to satisfy our needs. Oh the bliss of being newly married that desire to experiment and to just keep on satisfying each other.

When we did leave the hotel we would take a taxi, although this could be a questionable decision, to see the major sights, the Tutankhamun exhibition and a one day cruise on the Nile, the sort of romantic experience everyone should try. Although the river water is infected with just about every disease known to man it is still a must for young lovers. But of course the pyramids, those fantastically constructed monuments to the Egyptian pharaohs, standing so proud on the edge of the desert, by the small town of Giza is the real reason for coming. Once surrounded by the pyramids, if you just pass beyond them, you can see for miles and all you can see is pure unadulterated sand stretching way out into the Sahara Desert.

We went by taxi and were decanted outside a small shop, where we were met by a young boy, taken inside and told we could either go by camel or horse. I said we would walk, but we were told it was far too far to walk and we would have to take an animal. This is, of course, where we parted with a considerable amount of money and once we had agreed to take the mounted option, Rachel on a camel and me on a horse, we were led round the corner, about fifty yards and there were the spectacular constructions no more than a quarter of a mile away. Duped or what? Clearly a short walk would have satisfied our curiosity, and we could have carried out our tourist activities without interruption, and not needed the company of two obstinate animals and a rather dodgy and I suggest, untrustworthy guide.

I felt by choosing a horse I was at least closer to the ground, but the damn thing had a mind of its own, meanwhile Rachel seemed fairly content on her camel, but this may well have had something to do with the attention she was getting from our guide. A gooey-eyed youth who was prepared to go to any lengths to make compliments to my new wife. The only time he paid any attention to me was when he wanted money for the entrance fee, Lawrence of Arabia-style headgear and a tip at the end of the very unimaginative and uncomfortable tour. We felt robbed at the end, the constant demands for money and in all honesty very little to show for it because we constantly needed to be on our guard.

It was a good holiday though, a honeymoon to remember and brings back some very strong memories of romance, love and two people who really wanted to be together. And I honestly believed that would never change and we would be together for the rest of our lives, that was the only possibility for the future.

Well that's all for now I had better have a quick wash and change my shirt for one that has had a previous airing albeit for a short time, but it is the thought that counts.

* * * *

I climbed the stairs with purpose, an almost clean shirt on my back and my second best pair of trousers and tapped vigorously on Hilary's door and waited, and waited. I tapped again a little harder, but aware that this can sometimes rile the person inside, especially if they are indisposed or something, I stepped back in case I needed to make a hasty retreat, I still felt a little wary of Hilary. The door opened partially and a face peeped through the gap. "Oh it's you!"

Thanks a lot, I thought, some kind of welcome. "Yes," I spluttered. "You said to give you a knock and help you finish up some of the leftovers, from the party."

"Did I?" She looked confused holding the door almost closed, she carried on staring at me.

"Well, if it's not convenient," I stuttered.

"No, if that is what I said, you had better come in," and with a flourish she pulled the door wide and to my astonishment she stood there in her bra and panties with a crooked grin on her face.

I stepped in and she closed the door behind me, and said, "I must go and get some clothes on," she giggled and disappeared into the bedroom. Shouting back, "Help yourself to a drink, they're in the kitchen on the worktop, I haven't put them away yet, in fact I decided not to bother and just thought I would finish them instead."

"Thanks." I wandered into the kitchen and grabbed a lukewarm can of bitter, dragged the pull ring and swallowed two or three mouthfuls before coming up for breath, I then turned a half pint mug up the right way and poured the rest into the glass. I know you thought I was a wine drinker which is true, but when I saw the can I just fancied a beer. I leant against the worktop for support while waiting for mine host to materialise, in I couldn't imagine what.

Three or four minutes later, Hilary appeared in the doorway, dressed in a short light blue skirt and a white blouse draped loosely across her breasts dropping in the centre with one of those floppy bits of material that always seem undecided as to which way they should fall. Her cleavage was low and, oh no, I thought, where is this leading. You see I haven't been involved in the emotional side of life for a while now and in three days I have met two different women both of which have made impressions on me, albeit in different ways.

Hilary an odd-looking girl with her round face and her hair filled mole and her rather tubby figure has a rather attractive cuddly feel to her, a softness that I feel very comfortable grabbing hold of. Well I did the other evening at her party anyway and then there is Jane, fantastically good looking and just downright gorgeous but clearly not in the best of health and that therefore presents a different sort of challenge.

Oh dear this makes me sound more like Simon or Harold, the sort of people I do not wish to aspire to, that well-known lad type of attitude to women, that carries little respect and just a desire to get what they can for as little as possible.

"Vince, thanks for coming," she swooped towards me and kissed me firmly on the lips and was gone as quickly as she came. Pulling containers from the fridge and plates from the cupboard she hurriedly arranged drumsticks, quiche, potato salad, salad and rice salad on the plates in uneven proportions, obviously because we were finishing off the leftovers, I surmised. It kind of gives you licence to mix foods and tastes which normally you would steer clear of.

"Here take a plate," she said handing me an overfilled mixture of leftovers, but don't get me wrong, beggars can't be choosers and it all looked pretty appetising. "Take some cutlery from the drawer and grab me some too if you don't mind," she instructed.

I led the way to the lounge, armed with cutlery for two and plate for one, Hilary followed with her plate, salad cream and cruet. We sat side by side on the sofa and ate quickly without talking, I didn't realise how hungry I was after a day of activity. It just goes to show my idle life has made me lazy, I am not used to a busy day, but have been happier lying on the sofa and watching videos and drinking cans of beer and basically feeling sorry for myself. The food was good even if it was only leftovers and once I had finished, Hilary suggested I helped myself to some more and grab a wine glass on the way back. She was drinking red wine from one of those large cardboard party containers where the wine is stored in a plastic bag inside and is dispensed by a tap. Having topped up my plate I joined her with the red wine, refilling her glass at the same time.

I finished and put my plate on the coffee table, "Hilary, that was lovely I didn't realise how hungry I was."

"You're welcome, Vince, I am glad you enjoyed it." She moved towards me and rested her head on my shoulder, it was nice I liked the smell of her hair, clean shampoo with a hint of coconut. "Now tell me how you and Harold are getting on with your research?"

"Well we went out on Sunday evening to Kings Cross, thought we would start at a main line station and perhaps look round the surrounding area. These are likely places to find homeless people, but we did have a few problems."

Hilary had moved closer and her right arm was now tightly positioned across my stomach. I detected her breathing was more settled and consistent and I wondered if I should carry on.

"We were accosted by a group of homeless people asking for money, or anything really and one got a bit too close to Harold and..." I suddenly realised Hilary had pulled down the zip to my trousers and her hand was wedged firmly around my manhood, which to be honest was doing me proud. "He kicked out," I finished the sentence, I thought it was the right thing to do under the circumstances.

I stopped talking, putting my arm round her I cuddled closer as her hand moved up and down my shaft, the pace quickened and I realised I wasn't going to be able to hold on much longer, it had been a long time.

And... No it was too late, well I haven't been used to it recently.

"Oh for God's sake Vince what are you doing, haven't you got any self-control? I was looking for a really good shagging tonight."

"Look, I'm really sorry," I stuttered. "I haven't been in this situation for some time."

She had disappeared from the room and returned with a box of tissues and some wet wipes which she threw onto my stomach and said, "Clean yourself up."

I obeyed, before saying, "Look Hilary I am sorry, the whole situation was too much for me." With a newfound bravado I continued, "I can assure you it doesn't usually happen so easily, I used to have a bit of a reputation for having considerable staying power." I don't know where I dreamt that one up from, but I had the feeling it probably hit home.

"Well you had better re-discover it pretty quickly," she responded, "because I am in a pretty horny state." She refilled our glasses from the cardboard box with the tap on and sat in the chair opposite watching me put myself back together again.

Having taken a few large mouthfuls of the wine I knelt beside her chair and tried to take her in my arms, but she pushed me away, she was cold and unresponsive, obviously not convinced by my promises of better to come, and then without warning she turned and planted her lips firmly on mine forcing her tongue between my teeth. I held her tight and her plump body responded, softening, and I thought this feels good, she hooked one leg over mine and her groin was moving against my thigh. I was beginning to feel another arousal and I just hoped it wouldn't let me down. It's not easy for a man to work up the enthusiasm so soon after.

When I awoke my first thought was where am I? I didn't recognise the room, I rolled over, the smells were not familiar to me and I bumped into a naked body, flesh on flesh. Hilary was snoring deeply, a contented sound of satisfaction, thank goodness I hadn't let myself down or so I believed as the memories of last night came flooding back to me. I glanced at the clock, ten to six and carefully removed Hilary's arm from my stomach, sliding out of bed.

I found my clothes in a heap on the floor and slipped on my trousers and shoes, tucked the remainder under my arm and made my way as silently as possible from the room and downstairs to my own bedroom. Once in my own bed I couldn't sleep, therefore I thought this would be a good opportunity to tell you a little more about why I am here, not why I am here in this bed and not tucked up in Hilary's nice warm bed with her nice warm body keeping me warm and content, but in this out of character situation a one bedroom flat in Kentish Town.

Having returned from our honeymoon, we settled down in our new home in Weybridge, Surrey. Thirty miles from London with a direct line into Waterloo and then I would take the drain into the city, the whole journey little more than forty minutes. We had bought a large semi-detached with four bedrooms and three reception rooms, the third being very small but big enough for me to have a desk for my computer and a few shelves for some books. The rear garden was a good size with a lawn, flowerbeds and at the end a few fruit trees, I used to like to think of it as an orchard, something to boast about.

Rachel's father gave us fifty thousand pounds as a wedding present to help buy the house, I had a few thousand myself so we could re-do the kitchen and bathroom and carry out a certain amount of decorating. Our mortgage wasn't too high either, easily manageable on my city salary, especially with the annual promises of substantial bonuses available.

Rachel had her own career to follow, she had been to university in Warwick studying Law and was now a junior partner with a large law firm in Holborn. She was working hard in preparation for her exams which would qualify her as a full partner and promises of a large increase in salary and benefits.

We used to travel up to Waterloo together catching the 7.56am from Weybridge and pitching up at Waterloo at 8.25am and there we would part company. Me taking the drain to Bank, where I would walk a few hundred yards to the Stock Exchange and she would jump on the Jubilee Line to Bond Street and a couple of stops on the Central Line to Holborn walking a few hundred yards to Mid City Place where her office was on the eighth floor.

We rarely met on the way home as tying up departure times was not particularly easy as neither of us had an exact finishing time, so we would normally meet back at home. The first one in would start the dinner, peeling potatoes and chopping up some vegetables, except for one evening a week when we would go out for a Chinese or an Indian, or on some occasions we would dress up and go to a local hotel restaurant where we would enjoy traditional French-style cuisine.

We were happy living like this, it was what we wanted, to be together surrounded by our own things, just the two of us, following our careers, biding our time until the little ones came along that is. But they never did, things didn't work out that way, it all went wrong before that. Oh dear I am becoming melancholy again, it is the thought of the downfall of our marriage, the disappointment and heartache.

CHAPTER 6

I clearly did go back to sleep, I hope I left you at a suitable point in the story and didn't drop off in the middle of a sentence, especially if it was a fruity bit. I must admit I don't think I am going to find it too easy writing the fruity bits, but who knows once I get into it, there I go using that word 'get', I must be careful of that. I spent a few minutes going over the events of last night, it was good.

Once we had gone to bed, Hilary and I that is, she became gentle and understanding and we blended together in a very pleasant way. I am not sure how long it has been since I have made love to a woman, but I am sure as hell glad I did last night. It is all part of my returning to a normal existence and getting out of this rut I am in.

Realising it was Tuesday and I had the day to myself I got up and washed and made a point of not putting on the TV to avoid the habit of sitting in front of it all day. Having had some cereal I dressed and went through my dole money, and put fifteen pounds in my pocket and went to the local supermarket, where I bought some fresh fruit, apples, plums and nectarines, no bananas as they don't travel well. I then bought a zone one and two travel card and headed into the West End.

Although I hadn't admitted it I knew deep down I would end up at Charing Cross and having taken the Northern Line to Kings Cross I changed to the Piccadilly and decanted myself at Leicester Square. I then walked through the square, one of the most cosmopolitan areas in London, now that it is a traffic-free zone large numbers congregate waiting for cinemas, restaurants and queuing at the main ticket office. I went to the south east corner, crossed Panton Street and walked down Whitgift Street to the rear entrance of the National Gallery, where I stopped to admire the magnificence of the structure.

The clouds had moved in and it was just starting to rain, not hard but enough to make me hurry, the rain was warm after all the hot weather we have had recently. Carrying my bag of fruit I crossed Trafalgar Square past the fountains and dived down the underground staircase towards the Bakerloo Line. The depressing passage ways with cream and beige wall tiles and cold terracotta floor tiles, dimly lit were to say the least uninviting.

I moved quickly avoiding the crowds of busy shoppers and business people going about their day's chores. The tunnels, although a part of London's appeal also give off a damp feeling of depression and Victorian degradation, I shivered. The smells of stale air mixed with urine and smoke are particularly offensive to the nose.

I made my way to the soffit beneath the staircase where Harold and I had seen the child yesterday, mixed up with blankets and cardboard. The blankets and cardboard were screwed up and piled in the acute angle of the floor and the underside of the staircase, but no sign of the boy. I decided to hang around and see if he returned, I walked back upstairs where there were a group of young men seated on the half landing swigging from cans of lager, as I walked past them I hesitated not sure whether to ask if they knew or had seen the boy.

"What you looking at mate?" asked an Irish accent.

I didn't want to provoke a confrontation, but thought I would ask. "Yesterday I saw a young boy underneath the staircase here," I pointed below where they sat, they looked unimpressed by my remark. "I just wondered if you had seen him today?"

"Naw."

"What not at all?"

"No," this from a different voice.

A third voice responded, "Yes there has been a youngster sleeping down there for the past few nights, I haven't seen him this morning though."

"Thank you," I said. "I'll hang around for a while."

"Please yer'self."

I waved my thanks again.

I decided to leave the station and walked down to the embankment, it was still drizzling but I didn't mind. I sat on the wall overlooking the Thames, and watched the murky waters flowing out to sea, the tide was on the turn and the swell lapped against the wall with a swishing sound. I ate one of the nectarines I had bought earlier and followed it up with an apple.

Whilst I was sitting there I got to thinking about Jane, after last night with Hilary I had a pang of guilt and then thinking a week ago there was no one in my life, but now there are two women and I seem to spend a lot of my time thinking about both of them. Hilary I ended up bonking last night and Jane I really wanted to see again.

I know you are thinking I haven't mentioned her since I popped in on Sunday afternoon, when I returned the iron, but I can assure you I have been thinking about her quite a lot. Perhaps I will give her a knock when I get back this evening.

In the meantime, while I sat on the river wall, I took in the wonderful atmosphere of this industrial river that could tell so much history of bygone days. Traitors being led to the Tower of London via Traitors' Gate, even Elizabeth the first Queen of England, was taken to her prison this way. As was her mother, Anne Boleyn second wife of Henry the Eighth also entered the tower the same way before she suffered her execution within those very grounds.

Further along the South Bank towards the sea, the smugglers used to dock their merchandise and store it amongst the warehouses and taverns of Bermondsey. During the Second World War the German bombers used the river as a tracking device in their efforts to identify their targets and obliterate our great city. But that's enough nostalgic history for now, if you will bear with me I will continue my story of Rachel and my early married life.

Our life together was very comfortable, we were earning a good living between us and were building our home and life together. Admittedly we spent a lot of money on trivial and material things, but if you can afford to you might as well have what you want. I joined a badminton club where I would play every Tuesday evening, I wasn't very good but it was good exercise without taking up too much time. On Fridays I usually stayed in the city for a drink with some of my work colleagues.

Meanwhile Rachel had started attending the local parish church, St cuthberts on Sunday mornings, I didn't mind, she was brought up in the Anglican faith and therefore, why shouldn't she attend church on a Sunday. No reason at all, I took the opportunity to keep the garden tidy, you know weeding, chopping down any stray growth, a bit of pruning and cutting the grass. I would take the debris to the local council dump, where they had specific containers for green waste and generally kept myself occupied.

After a couple of months she came home one Sunday with her weekly newsletter and whilst making the coffee, showed me an item advertising an Alpha course. Some sort of bible study class, I think she was telling me she wanted to join the class, but I didn't make it easy for her and made out I didn't understand what she was getting at. I felt bad about it, but I made her ask outright, and she said, would I mind if she went out for a couple of hours every Wednesday evening?

That meant I was out Tuesday and Friday and now she was going to be out Wednesdays, I can't say I was particularly happy about it, but a feeling deep inside me told me to be wary of jealousy and to act a little more benevolently. So I did and agreed, saying it would be good for her to get out in the evenings, have some outside interests especially in local activities.

This went on for some weeks, it appeared the course took the same format as the school term. Ten or twelve weeks on and then two or three off until the summer holidays, when there would be at least a six weeks' recess before starting a new year. I didn't mind, it was actually quite nice to have an evening in on my own, until it seemed Rachel was arriving home later and later, and I thought perhaps I should mention it, surreptitiously so as not to cause an argument but just to make her realise it was getting later and later.

I looked at my watch, it was past midday, I thought I ought to go back to the station to see if the boy had returned to his lair. I picked up my bag and returned to the labyrinthal underground of a mishmash of filthy corridors and passageways and made my way to the area where I saw the boy yesterday. I passed the group on the staircase still swigging from their cans, but they took no notice. When I arrived the child was sitting up in the corner chewing on a half-eaten pasty of some sort, when he saw me he cowered away in the corner. He was dressed in torn military-style trousers, a stained sweat shirt with a baseball cap pulled down low over his forehead.

I over emphasised my smile like a long lost friend trying to instill confidence and knelt on my haunches and said, "Hello, my name is Vincent, you can call me Vince." The eyes stared back at me unrecognising, but expressing a deep awareness behind the blankness. "Do you remember I came here yesterday and left you some money?" I took from my bag an apple and held it out to him, after some hesitation he reached out and took it acknowledging his thanks with a smile which came from his mouth but not from his eyes. I tried to coax him into speech, "I am here to try and help you, not to hurt you."

He smiled again this time a little more willingly and said, "Thanks." His voice was high-pitched and hesitant.

"Why do you stay here haven't you anywhere else to go?"

He shook his head.

"Don't you have any parents or family?"

This time he shrugged his shoulders in a throwaway sort of way, non-committal.

"So when you are not here where do you go?" I asked.

He shrugged again. "Round the streets looking for money and food."

I was pleased to have got him talking and didn't want to lose the moment. "Do you beg for money?"

He shook his head.

To me this meant he probably stole it and also most likely gained his food by shoplifting, such as the pasty he was eating when I arrived. I didn't want to mention this assumption at present in case this made him clam up. I showed him the remainder of the food I had in my bag and said, "Here take it, I will bring some more tomorrow." I placed the bag on the edge of his blanket and held out my hand as a gesture of friendship. After a few seconds, he took it, his fingers were dirty but soft, I was expecting a more calloused grip.

"I will see you again tomorrow," I said and pulled myself upright.

He nodded.

* * * *

I wandered back to Trafalgar Square, the drizzle was back and the air felt dank, late August seemed to be turning into autumn earlier than expected, the warmth had disappeared over the past couple of hours. The tourists were still there in large numbers with plenty of pigeons to amuse them. The backdrop of the National Gallery, its grey stone façade blurred as the rain increased, dominated the north end of the square. I stopped and looked and I realised I felt a little melancholy and in all honesty thoroughly pissed off. Why? Probably the boy in the station was playing on my mind, I felt uncomfortable leaving him there to spend a lonely night on his own amongst some well-tuned experienced down and outs as Harold would have no doubt put it.

It must be very frightening, he looks so young and why is he there anyway? Where are his parents? What would drive someone to live like that with absolutely nothing? Perhaps there was a good reason? I didn't have the answers to any of these questions, but I thought I have to find out and I have to try and do something to help.

I was also aware my own life was changing, I had spent the past year or so feeling sorry for myself and living on the dole in a reclusive manner and I now seemed to be coming out of it. In the past week I have met Jane and have slept with Hilary and renewed an acquaintance with Harold, albeit a tenuous one, and now I am feeling a tinge of responsibility for a young boy sleeping rough in the tunnels of Charing Cross Station. Well perhaps this is all for the good, mixing with people again and new interests to help me get my life back on track.

* * * *

When I arrived back at the flat I thought I would have a wash, a shave and a quick change, and then pluck up enough courage to knock on Jane's door to see if I could spend some time with her. I know you are thinking well you have knocked before, well you're right, but on the two previous occasions I had a specific reason because of borrowing the iron and then returning it, but this time I just wanted to see her. But my plans were dashed when on opening the door to the house the vision of Harold slumped on the staircase made my heart sink.

"Vince, about time I've been sitting here for ages, where the fuck have you been?"

My inclination was to tell him it was none of his business, but I realised this would most likely only cause unnecessary friction so I responded. "I've been out doing your research for you."

He stood up and said, "Let's go and have a pint, I've been bashing about on my laptop all day getting down all the notes and formulating a piece to be proud of and thought we could run through it together. You know, to make sure we have the right emphasis."

I thought bugger, but knowing Harold's persistence I thought what the hell, Jane could wait, she didn't look as if she was going anywhere and she wasn't expecting me anyway. I pulled my pocket inside out and gestured to its emptiness.

He looked at me and raised his eyes. "Christ, you layabouts are all the same. You're as bad as that lot out on the streets begging, you could always go and get a job Vince." And then he laughed. "You could always go and sell the Big Issue."

I was getting used to Harold's insulting manner, and didn't really have the energy to fight it. In some ways I knew he had a point, but I just wished he would express it a little less accusingly.

"Okay, I'll sub you again, come on let's go," he was marching towards the door.

I thought sod the wash and followed.

* * * *

In the saloon bar of the Assembly House in the main road, we sat huddled over a few sheets of typed A4 and two pints of lager and two bags of crisps, I was munching on the cheese and onion, a weakness I developed many years ago. Meanwhile, Harold had chosen salt and vinegar, which may go somewhere to explaining his rather ruddy complexion and may I suggest irritable demeanour.

"So what do you think Vince?" Harold spoke through a mouthful of lager whilst spraying crumbs of crunchy potato.

Putting my English literature hat on, I replied, "For a start I think it is quite a good take on the homeless problems in London. However, the grammar could be tidied up." I wondered if this was likely to push him too far. Professional writers in whatever capacity, never like to be criticised about their quality of English.

"Yes, I know that," he interrupted, irritably. "I must point out, it's only a draft and the minor details are picked up by the back room staff."

I considered this excuse and remarked, "I was always taught during my education to ensure one's grammar, spelling and sentence construction should be as close to perfect as possible right from the start." Admittedly this was a little tongue in cheek, but Harold's haphazard attitude did annoy me.

He grunted.

I carried on reading and to be honest, he had put together about eight sides of A4 which gave a fairly accurate and detailed account of our two trips, firstly Kings Cross and secondly to Charing Cross where I first met the young boy.

"Yeah, it's good," I said straightening the papers and refitting the paperclip to the corner, I handed them back to Harold.

"Where do we go next Vince?" I then told him that I had been back to Charing Cross today and saw the young boy and spoke to him and that it was my intention to return again tomorrow. I could see him snarling as he glugged down the dregs of his beer and looked to me to buy him another one. I was going to stick to my guns on this one as I pointed out to him before we left the flat, I did not have the money to keep going out to the pub and apart from that, he was running an expense account.

"I thought we may try a different area, perhaps Soho," suggested Harold shrugging his shoulders. "I don't know, you're the sodding expert Vince." With this he wandered off to the bar, clearly to replenish his glass and I hoped with a bit of luck perhaps mine too.

When Harold returned he plonked a glass of white wine down in front of me not too careful about how much he spilt, obviously letting me know what he thought. We sat in silence for a while, while he swallowed half his drink and I sipped mine to make it last as he clearly wasn't going to buy me another one.

"I think I will kick along with you again tomorrow, if you want to go back to Charing Cross so be it and then perhaps we will hit Soho and see if there is a different type of no-hoper there. Perhaps the hookers are a better class than those hanging around the parking meters at Kings Cross."

"Okay," I said.

* * * *

We left the pub about an hour later and Harold said he was going to make his way back to his hotel. I was pleased, as too much of Harold is definitely too much and I thought I could revert to plan A. But I needed to get a move on as the evening was slipping away. Harold went down the tube and I decided to save what little money I had and started a brisk walk homeward bound. Hey that's an old Simon and Garfunkel song, *Homeward Bound*, I wish I was homeward bound, I found myself humming away. This brought back memories of my first day at boarding school. It was playing on the radio when I was waiting for my parents to drive me to the place I would call home for the next fourteen weeks, a poignant moment in the life of a twelve-year-old and not to be underestimated in its significance.

As I walked to the main entrance door I decided I would pop up to my flat, have a quick wash and brush my teeth, hopefully to conceal the mixture of lager and white wine, put on a clean shirt and then give Jane a knock. I was really quite excited with the old butterflies swimming round my stomach like a tank of exotics and as I slipped the key into the front door lock, the door flew open nearly knocking me back down the steps.

"Vincent, where have you been all day?" Hilary stared at me accusingly, her mole twitching in sympathy with the expression on her face.

"What?" I stuttered.

"I said, where have you been? When I woke this morning I expected to find you huddled up beside me holding me close and your hands roaming over my body, but no, the bed was bare. And then I went downstairs and banged on your door and there was no answer."

I gulped.

She looked a bit miffed, I squeezed past her and closed the door behind me, but she had managed to twist round and pin me to the wall and was kissing me in a deep and meaningful way, which reminded me that I had intended brushing my teeth and confirmed that I really should. You know when you get that mixture of fur and saliva together.

"Look hold on Hilary," I panted at the first opportunity. "I had to go out early this morning and I didn't want to wake you."

"You never used to go out early, you seemed more than happy to spend most of the day in bed if I remember rightly, and what's more you taste of beer." She had stood back and was eyeing me with an expression of disbelief. "Well we can make up for it now, come on get yourself upstairs and let's get down to it." (There you are that word 'get' again, English is such a beautiful and descriptive language it is such a pity people are so unimaginative in their choice of words).

"But Hilary," I tried to protest thinking what about my plan to visit Jane. But then for the second time this evening I thought, Jane wasn't expecting me anyway and there was always tomorrow. I stopped resisting and let Hilary lead me up the four flights of stairs to her second floor flat and into her bedroom. The room was bright and airy, the walls lined and painted with a rich cream colour, fitted wardrobes and a ribbed beige carpet. I know what you are thinking, why didn't I mention the quality of the décor after last night's sortie? Well I didn't. Okay, perhaps I was preoccupied and even a little drunk. But I did wonder how Hilary could afford all this on the wages of a pizza waitress.

The bed, where I slept last night was a double with a modern styled duvet set with matching pillow cases in a sharp pink with frills. She moved across to the single window and pulled the curtains closed. It was still light outside and the late evening sun had just dropped out of sight.

Hilary turned towards me and kissed me full on the lips, once again exploring my gums whilst grinding her groin against my crotch.

Which I must be honest was not disappointed at the attention it was receiving.

"Vince!"

"Yes," I spluttered.

"I want you to give me a fucking good rogering."

"Okay," I replied thinking it the best option on offer at the moment. She pulled me down onto the bed and fumbling with my zipper pulled my trousers off in a well-practised manoeuvre and immediately extracted my penis from my pants and before I knew what was happening she had all of it in her mouth. I thought of deep throat, Linda Lovelace had nothing on this, and just as I was beginning to swoon Hilary removed my organ from her mouth and leapt off the bed, quickly pulling off her clothes before returning to the task in hand. Bloody hell I thought, if she wants rogering she had better hold fire on this little exercise or it will be far too late, I don't think I had ever experienced such a mobile and electrifying tongue before as it whipped round and round taking in all elevations of my tool.

"Hilary," I groaned trying to pull away. "You had better stop or it will be too late."

"Again?" she responded reminding me of the previous evening.

"I hope not."

Thankfully she took my advice, sat up and then flopped back on the bed making herself available for me. I didn't need another invitation and dropped down on top of her feeling the moist warmth of her engulfing my swollen goad. I thrust and kicked and she moaned and whined until I couldn't hold on any longer when her lips delivered a powerful kiss on mine and I just had to let go.

"Shit Vince, is that it?" She was trying to push me off. "Where is your staying power?" She was off the bed, "I had better get you a drink and then see if we can get a bit more action going."

I lay back satisfied and content, but just a little wary about what Hilary may be expecting of me for the rest of the night. She returned with two large glasses of a dark red coloured claret, plonked them on the bedside table, released from under her arm a dark brown medicine-style bottle and placed it between the wine glasses.

I looked quizzical.

"Amal nitrate," she said. "It is supposed to help your flaccid dick," she flicked my member with her thumb and index finger.

"Ouch." I cried.

She unscrewed the cap and said, "Here take a long deep sniff of this." She held it under my nose. "Come on draw it right down into your lungs."

I obliged and immediately a light-headed feeling came over me, I sat up, reached for my wine and took a large gulp. Hilary looked good sitting on the side of the bed her plumpish figure warm and cuddly, her breasts full and still firm, I wanted to hold them and suck them. We drank together emptying the glasses after only three or four mouthfuls, Hilary went for the bottle and filled the glasses again. She then picked up the bottle from the bedside table, took the aphrodisiac and sniffed deeply before offering it to me again.

"Go on it's supposed to improve your orgasm," she said, "and let's hope your staying power."

Shit, I thought and I took a long draw pulling it deep into my lungs, the oxygen and fumes lightened my head and I thought, why not? So come on Hilary, I thought, let's get on with it, I am up for it now, you may well have bitten off more than you can chew.

I was proud, my erection had stabilised and was standing up there for everyone to see, except this was a private viewing and I couldn't care less anymore. Hilary lay before me like a Greek goddess, her plump body inviting and sensuous and I went to her like a man possessed and taking her fast and hard, and didn't stop as she cried out with a mixture of surprise and passion, as I pumped into her amidst her screams and cries all I could see was Rachel. The love I once had for Rachel was turned into hate, as I remembered everything she took from me, I drove harder and harder into her losing all sense of reality.

Hilary's eyes bulged beneath me and as she screamed, I came again and kept pumping and pumping, emptying everything into her. Hilary clung to me refusing to let me go and I collapsed in her arms and cried and cried. The tears streamed down my face, memories of my past beating me up and coming to the fore. I couldn't control myself and fell flat on top of Hilary and cried real tears, not tears of passion, but tears of distress and heartache.

After some minutes Hilary crawled out from beneath me, saying, "Fuck me Vince that was probably the best shag I have ever had, phew that was something else." She slumped in the chair in the corner of the room swigging the remainder from her wine glass and lighting a cigarette, the colour of the wine reflected across the room. And I remember thinking about the afterglow, the glint of the wine and the smoke rising in curls mystically towards the ceiling. Hilary sat there blowing circular smoke rings into the air, she looked surprised and at the same time relaxed. Her legs were open, there was no modesty and I could see the shining moist trickle glowing between her thighs, it looked good, but it didn't help my feelings.

I lay on the bed quietly groaning and panting from the efforts and exhaustion, but I just felt shit. I wasn't sure what had come over me, but somehow I thought I had been taking Rachel and I just wanted to take all of my hate and poverty out on her. I wanted to hurt her to make her suffer, physically by sexually abusing her, by keeping on whacking myself into her until I was spent and exhausted. But it wasn't Rachel, it was Hilary I was trying to hurt, but I wasn't hurting her, I was giving her pleasure. I was confused, none of it made any sense.

As I cried myself to sleep the room became a blur, my snivelling quietened and I slept restlessly, dreaming of the past and of Rachel.

As our married life had progressed we both followed our careers, Rachel passed her law exams with top marks and was made a partner taking on more responsibilities and was really enjoying her new position. I was also doing well and pulled off some successful deals, making large commissions for the company and consequently, some very useful bonuses for myself. I sailed quite close to the wind on a couple of occasions with many millions of dollars invested in certain stocks and I just hung on and on looking for the best time to sell. I would sit at my desk, my tie undone hanging round my neck and the top two buttons of my shirt open. My eyes glued to the screen anticipating and willing the smallest changes in prices and the slightest movement of direction in the graphs. Sweat formed under my arms and ran down my body, droplets appeared on my forehead and trickled into my eyes, the saltiness stinging. I constantly tapped my feet with impatience waiting for the best moment to pick up the phone and shout my instructions. I used to try and leave it to the last possible moment in order to eke out the maximum amount of profit from every deal to benefit the client, the company and of course me.

As I said before I earned some big bonuses, we spent a lot of money on the house, building a conservatory at the back and employing a landscape gardener to do a makeover at a cost which was on the wrong side of eight thousand pounds. I also treated myself, and bought a second hand Porsche 911, it was low mileage, only eighteen months old, but it still cost me thirty thousand pounds. I just loved the feeling of opulence and the speed and sense of wealth, but yes you are right I just wanted to show off and hoped people noticed, saying to their friends and neighbours. 'Hey, look at that guy he must have a few quid'. As I roared by with a blasting accelerator and a booming stereo beating out Dire Straits *Money For Nothing*, what was worse was me shouting out the words in time with the beat.

Our sex life was great too, as it was right from that very first time in Rachel's parents' house. She was always happy to experiment and we talked about it a lot and tried out new ideas in order to discover new satisfaction. She had a liking for gentle domination and role play and would ask me to tie her to the bed, blindfold her and tease her. At first I wasn't sure, but played along with it and to be honest I found it very exciting. When she finally came her orgasms were severe and fulfilling.

* * * *

I felt arms gripping my middle and I woke with a start, it was light outside, the sun shining bright, casting shadows across the room. I struggled to remember exactly where I was, my eyes were salting and glued with grating sand. Then it came back to me the drama of last night, I rolled onto my other side and came face to face with Hilary, her eyes still closed and her breathing controlled. The hairs growing from her mole drew my eyes, I was beginning to like their individuality, the way they stuck out in different directions like tentacles, I wanted to pull them. She was still naked and her breasts were squashed together as she lay on her side, a bit like the tubular succulence of aubergines. As she breathed out her lips vibrated and I caught a whiff of putrid air, a mixture of raw onions and boiled cabbage. I shuddered and pulled away out of reach of the airflow turning my face to the side, I just felt a need to get away, to be somewhere else, in my own flat, anywhere.

Just like yesterday I thought, why do I always want to get away? I rolled back the other way and started to sit up.

A hand slid round my waist, "Oh no you don't, you did that to me yesterday, buggered off before I was awake."

"Hey, Hilary," I cried. "Let go." She pulled me back down onto the bed and was all over me, her eyes dug deep into mine confirming her insatiable desire, although I wasn't ready she quickly aroused me and was on top of me and riding violently and ruthlessly.

"Come on Vince, I want it like last night, hard and fast, you know, I have never been fucked like that before. I like the way you thrust Vince, you've got the sense of penetration and stamina a girl needs. Come on you bastard get that arse moving," she was pounding away on top of me.

But I couldn't work up the same energy and enthusiasm, I lay there and let Hilary do the work, but it was still good, not like last night when my energy was unfounded. When I came I felt mellow, I don't think she noticed my lack of commitment but she seemed satisfied. After a suitable time to savour the afterglow I made my excuses and left. I went downstairs and lay in the bath for half an hour, thinking. I knew it wouldn't be long before Harold would be round to insult me and dig me in the ribs, I also had to make a point of going back to Charing Cross. I had to find out about the young man living under the staircase in the gloom of the underground tunnels, who he was and why he was living there.

As the warm water slopped around me and my thoughts curdled with the water I began to feel depressed and ashamed, I had used Hilary for my own ends. I was like an animal fighting against extinction determined to procreate and keep the line going. And whilst I used her I thought of Rachel and all the hurt and pain I felt for her came out in every thrust. I wanted to hurt her, to hurt Rachel and reap some sort of revenge for the way she had treated me, the way she had deceived me and finally left me with nothing. But I also

98

felt the guilt, the hurt and distress I had dealt out to Rachel, the way I had violated her, degraded her.

As I wallowed in my own self-pity, there was a loud slap on the door, I had, of course, expected it but I couldn't find the motivation to get (that bloody word 'get' again, I must try to distance myself from everybody else's slovenly speech) going.

"Come on shit face let's get going, we've got fish to fry, hares to snare and rats to trap," I heard him snigger.

I cringed, Harold was obviously refreshed and full of beans this morning, it promised to be an eventful day tinged with, no doubt, some difficult moments and testing times. "I won't be long," I shouted back.

* * * *

We started off in the King's Cross area again like last Sunday evening, the early part of the day certainly seems different to the evenings, far less aggressive and intimidating. I suppose it's the same in all walks of life, most people don't really start off too well in the mornings, but as the day goes on things seem to click into place and the energy levels rise. By the end of the working day people are ready for a glass of wine or a gin and tonic and meet up with friends and business or work colleagues. It was like that for me in the city, it seems so long ago now, if we had had a good day and closed some decent deals we would hit the bars, whoever had made the most money that day would set up the tab behind the bar and settle the bill at the end. I think it evened itself out in the end, but obviously some traders were better or more successful than others, but we were making so much money in those days it really didn't matter. Anyway the point I am trying to make is why shouldn't it be the same for the homeless on the streets? Why should they feel any different when they wake up and face a new dawn? Why should they feel anymore excited about it than anybody else? But one of the problems is as the day progresses they are carried along by the atmosphere of everyone else around them. The working classes going about their jobs, the office workers in their suits and smart clothes and by lunchtime the homeless people sitting on the pavement have earned some loose change to buy a few cans of lager and therefore, the adrenalin starts pumping and the atmosphere builds up on the streets. The downside to this is so does the aggression, the begging increases and so does the potential for crime, the insults start to fly and fights break out. It's a dog-eat-dog environment out there and there doesn't appear to be any way out.

We pitched up in the same area at the back of St Pancras Station in Midland Road where Harold had his altercation a few days ago. I wasn't so keen on going back there, but Harold said, "Don't be such a bloody wimp Vince, they're only a bunch of drunken drug addicts."

I didn't really think that was the point and chose not to comment. As we walked round the corner, the same group or as far as we could tell, were slouched in a corner within one of the station arches. They were in the process of decanting themselves from their cardboard boxes and sleeping bags, clearly preparing for another day. I was secretly hoping they wouldn't recognise us and equally determined to steer Harold away from their clutches.

"That's those bastards over there Vince," he said pointing. "I think I may just go over there and teach them a lesson."

This was of course totally futile as there were at least eight of them and I was quite sure they wouldn't think twice about giving Harold a good kicking if he started provoking them. I expect you have noticed I didn't intend getting a kicking because I didn't intend following Harold into the valley of death. I was equally sure Harold's bravado was purely for show and he had no intention of starting anything.

"I wouldn't advise it," I said. "Just remember what you are here for to carry out research, you're far more likely to glean information from people if you befriend them, build up a trust and don't antagonise them. A few more days and you will have enough information to put your article together and you can return to your cosy little flat in Notting Hill, never to tread the streets of the deprived again."

"Yes, well you're probably right, but I don't like the thought of these fucking peasants getting the better of me." He persisted.

"How have they got the better of you?" I asked. "Just look at them, they haven't got anything, they are sleeping on the streets, begging for food and a few cigarettes."

"Begging for money so they can buy cans of lager and fags and top up on their drugs habit," he sneered.

"No, just hold on a minute Harold," I was losing my temper. "Not all these people have drug habits, not all of them are just begging for money to buy beer and cigarettes and I don't think you should tar them all with the same brush."

"Just look at them Vince, they're all a fucking load of spongers, lying about doing nothing all day and probably claiming the dole as well."

This line hit home. "Okay," I said, "let's move on somewhere else." I was feeling a little fed up with this slant on my character.

We crossed the road at the traffic lights and headed down Kings Cross Road towards Mount Pleasant sorting office. There were a number of abandoned shops and almost all the entrances were occupied by a lumpy shape wrapped in blankets and cardboard. The appearance was lifeless and I thought if someone died in this position how long would it take for the body to be discovered? It may take a few days, except I expect there is most likely a unity between them and serious problems would filter through the grapevine quite quickly.

Harold was taking his job more seriously again and talking into his tape recorder as we walked, occasionally stopping to assess the atmosphere which was in many ways unpleasant. There was a pungent smell in the air, a mixture of body odour, stale alcohol and cigarettes and urine, this concoction seems to be familiar wherever you walk in these areas of London.

One of the bundles shifted and rolled towards us and sat up. "Spare some loose change sir?" came from a strong Irish accent.

"Sod off," replied Harold.

I of course couldn't afford to keep shelling out money I didn't have, and Harold clearly didn't intend dipping into his expense account, although I was sure if he did he would make sure he wasn't out of pocket.

The grubby face nodded, clearly used to this response and said, "Have a nice day," and rolled back again to continue his sleep.

We walked on and I said, "I think you should throw these people a few pennies you know. It would help you to be closer to them and you could benefit from their reactions."

"Why the fuck would I want to be close to this lot?" he waved his arms in the general direction of the body strewn doorways. "I would probably catch something."

"I just think," I continued, "you may find if you gave them a few quid they may talk to you and open up a bit and you could glean some information out of them, an insight into the way they live and why they live like this."

"Why don't I just ask you Vince, why do you live like you do?"

I could see he was beginning to be frustrated and I decided not to push him any further at the moment. Harold doesn't appear to be the sort of investigative journalist who is prepared to see both sides of the coin and I was beginning to wonder what impact his article was likely to have on society, if any at all. Mixing in this environment, I was hoping that whatever we discovered could result in helping these unfortunate people, bringing their plight to people who could make a difference. But I got the impression all Harold wanted to do was get his article written and get back to his usual lifestyle.

We carried on walking up Kings Cross Road to the junction with Roseberry Avenue and Farringdon Road with Mount Pleasant Post Office on the corner. We had left the homeless area behind us so we caught a bus which threaded its way towards the river and then made a change taking us along the Embankment towards the Houses of Parliament, before jumping off and walking up Whitehall and into Trafalgar Square. Here Harold dipped his hand into his pocket and threw a few coins into a hat laying beside a tramp seated on the pavement. A dog of mongrel extraction sat peacefully beside him. The tramp nodded his appreciation and Harold glanced in my direction before saying, "I like animals okay."

See he has got a soft side I thought smiling to myself.

"Big Issue!" rang in my ears.

"Fuck off," replied Harold.

"Right you are Sir, have a nice day Sir," came the riposte.

Harold ignored this and turning to me said, "That really winds me up Vince."

"What does?" I asked.

"Those bloody wankers always thrusting that shit in your face. All over London whereever you walk there is some bloody creep, shouting, 'Big Issue'! as if you would waste a quid on that rubbish. You can buy a copy of our paper for forty pence."

"Have you ever read one?" I asked.

He looked at me quizzically.

I repeated myself. "Have you ever read one? A Big Issue? Because, if not it seems a little insular and uninformed to comment. It may be a good read, it may be particularly informative, it may just give you a perspective on what you are trying to find out about, it may help you form a basis for your article."

He looked at me again, shook his head and moved on.

As we walked along The Strand towards Charing Cross Station a commotion built up behind us and as we turned, a small figure burst between us hotly pursued by a man shouting, "You little bastard."

The boy headed onto the cobbled area within the station entrance and as he sped across the stones, tripped on a protruding slab landing headlong on the ground. The man right behind him landed on top of him and punched him fairly and squarely on the side of the head, whilst grabbing the contents of the bag which had flown from the boy's fingers. The child rolled away and lay still, blood oozing from cuts and grazes to his hands and arms and there was an angry lump building on his cheek.

The man took a kick at the figure on the ground and walked away, saying, "Thieving little bastard, let that be a lesson to you."

Shocked, I watched him walk past us and then I turned to the child on the ground but he was no longer there, apart from two or three small stains of blood, there was no sign of him.

"Come on," I said to Harold, I had this sneaking suspicion this child was the same one I spoke to yesterday in the underground.

"Where?" he asked.

"Down the underground," I said. "I think I know where to find that young man."

"Why do you want to find him?" he responded. "He's obviously a thieving little runt who got the slap he deserved."

"Well if you don't want to come, stay here and I'll go on my own," and with this I strode off and jogged down the staircase into the artificial gloom of the station passages. I made my way to the now familiar corner beneath the staircase and sure enough shrunk against the wall, nursing a bruised cheek was the young fellow. His hands bleeding where he had hit the cobbles and I could see the dirt in the wounds. I realised these needed to be cleaned and treated otherwise they could turn septic especially living in these conditions.

I knelt down not knowing what to say, there were tears in the child's eyes, he clearly didn't want to cry, but was probably in a lot of pain physically and emotionally.

"Come on young fellow, it's not that bad, let me take you somewhere to get cleaned up and we can bandage that hand." I didn't know where I was going to find a bandage at this stage, but if the worst came to the worst I had a handkerchief in my pocket.

He just looked at me, I wasn't even sure if there was any recognition, but the eyes were bright though tearful. I held out my hand in a gesture of friendship. "What's your name?" I asked.

Nothing!

I tried again, "If you don't want to tell, I am going to call you Jack, what do you think? Well, whatever you think, I want you to come with me so we can clean up your wounds, there are some toilets upstairs on the main line concourse." Still offering my hand, I hoped he would take it and after a long silence he held out his left hand, the least damaged of the two, and let his fingers brush my palm and slowly I closed my fingers around it. Standing up I drew Jack up with me, turning I saw Harold standing behind me and I think I caught a smile turn up the corners of his lips.

Jack and I walked away hand in hand and went to the toilets I knew were there beneath the batch of kiosks in the centre of the concourse. I needed 20p to get through the barrier, I managed to rustle up one, but not a second so I suggested Jack crawl underneath after I went through. He did this with amazing agility and we found a wash hand basin at one end, out of the way of the general public. I collected a handful of paper towels and ran a full basin of warm water and set about bathing Jack's hands and cleaning the wounds before moving onto the lump on his cheek which still appeared to be swelling. I suspected it looked worse than it was and would probably look even more inflamed tomorrow when it would start to blacken and then turn yellow. Jack was brave and didn't flinch as I tried to remove the pieces of dirt ingrained amongst the blood and flesh.

Having completed the clean-up operation, the damage was not nearly as bad as it initially looked and all I needed to buy were some plasters. This I did by pulling out the last of the loose change I had in my pocket, sifting through the coins I found enough to buy a small pack of plasters and stuck them over the worst of Jack's cuts. This still left me with three pounds so I took Jack to a nearby café where we sat in a corner with a pot of tea for two and shared a scone with jam and butter. He still hadn't spoken, but he seemed pleased with the tea and small amount of food. I therefore, tried again to get a reaction.

I smiled at him as he sipped his tea. "Until you tell me differently I am going to call you Jack, is that okay?"

He nodded.

"Now perhaps you can tell me a few things like, how old are you? Where are you from? Have you any family? Why are you living," I pointed across the road towards the station, "down there? How long have you been living like this? "Take your pick answer anyone you like."

I waited hoping for a response, he was obviously wary of me I don't think he was frightened, but he didn't want to give too much away. He looked at me with bright blue eyes, the tears had dried up now and there was a new mischievousness there. He went to open his mouth and closed it again before trying again. "Sixteen."

I presumed this was the answer to the first question, but I didn't believe it, his voice was high-pitched as if it hadn't broken yet. I would have had him down for being closer to twelve. I nodded acceptance and took a large gulp of my tea, putting down the cup I waited for another answer.

Jack knew what I was waiting for too, this kid wasn't stupid but he was probably just being cautious, in this grown-up world he was streetwise he knew what he had to do to survive and he probably assumed he shouldn't trust anyone.

"A couple of weeks," he said. I presumed this referred to the time he had called the underground network home.

At this point I didn't know what to do next, I couldn't see how I could leave him to spend another night sleeping rough underground. But on the other hand, why should he trust me if I was to suggest taking him back to my flat? And would he go anyway? He hardly knew me. Besides I wanted to knock Jane up this evening, oops! I don't mean knock Jane up I mean bang on the door to her basement flat in the hope of being let in, perhaps partake of a cup of coffee and have a bit of sophisticated conversation. A touch of light relief away from Harold and his rather basic and vulgar attitude to life and also a rest from London's homeless areas.

We finished our tea and I was hoping for some more information, but nothing was forthcoming. I decided I wasn't going to gain enough trust to change circumstances today, so I would have to let him go back to his hovel beneath the staircase in what must seem like the bowels of the earth. So dingy and smelly, apart from the dangers involved for a young boy alone at night in a huge city, imagine the horrors once it is dark and you are alone with the sound of the city and the drunks, I shivered.

I stood on the corner of the Strand and Trafalgar Square and watched him walk away towards the station, a small lonely figure in a brutal world. It brought a sadness to me and I felt my eyes mist over, I knew I had to try and do something to help, but what?

He had thanked me before he went with a nod of the head and a slight smile, the bruise on the side of his face had reddened, a deeper colour coming out and distorting his features, but that would heal, the damage done to his pride may take more to repair. I intended to return again tomorrow and hoped I wouldn't have to witness a similar incident to the one which occurred today.

CHAPTER 7

I arrived home about mid-afternoon and made a point of being very quiet, I didn't know if Hilary was in her flat, but I definitely didn't want her to know I was there. Working at the piazza restaurant can certainly involve some erratic hours and I can never be sure whether she is at home or not. Therefore I crept upstairs very quietly and having taken my towel from the flat, I filled the bath as quietly as I could and jumped in for a soak. Whilst I was lying there I wondered what had happened to Harold, the last I saw of him was a gesture of a smile as I led Jack away to the toilets. I expect he probably went off to find an expensive restaurant and to have a large lunch and generally mistreat his expense account.

There are things about some people that will never change, he wouldn't spare a few coppers for the needy, but he would spend a whole heap on himself. You would have thought, considering his newspaper has sent him out to research the homeless problems, they would be more than happy and expect him to drop a few pennies into hats and cups and generally help to support the industry of begging.

I put on clean underwear and another clean shirt, inspected myself in the mirror, tinkered with a couple of spots on the side of my nose and decided not to force them too much as this could be more unsightly in the long run. I combed my hair and brushed my teeth, there was something nice about making an effort with my appearance again after months of feeling sorry for myself and never bothering. I had been living an almost hermit-like existence.

I quietly closed the door to my flat and trotted down the first flight of stairs surreptitiously glancing over my shoulder in case I was being observed. I closed the front door as carefully as possible and once outside I was down the external staircase to the basement flat and within the time it takes to strike a match I was tapping on Jane's door.

I suddenly realised I hadn't prepared a reason for calling so I would just have to bluff it out and take my chances.

After a few seconds the door opened a few inches and Tina's rather grumpy looking and familiar expression peered through the gap. I wish she would at least put on an air of interest even if it was purely for effect.

"Hello, it's me," I offered.

"I can see that," she replied. "What do you want?"

That was a good question I thought and was clearly going to stretch my powers of imagination. "I just wondered if Jane was in?" I asked.

"Why?"

"Well, I wondered if she may want anything, you know shopping or…?"

"I do the shopping," came the curt response.

"Or a plug changing, a shelf putting up, a sink unblocking, any little odd jobs I'm quite handy you know." I was really struggling now, but I was equally surprised at the speed these ideas had come into my mind.

"No I don't think so."

"Well she must want something," I said having completely run out of ideas and I was getting a little desperate too.

"No, Jane has everything she needs." Tina was trying to close the door.

I hovered on the doorstep desperately searching my mind for inspiration. "Well perhaps some advice or just a little company as I don't suppose she gets much."

Tina looked a touch exasperated and clearly was not in favour of my presence.

I then heard a voice calling from deep inside the flat. "Tina, who is it?"

Tina turned and shouted back, "The bloke from upstairs."

"I'm sorry Tina, whom do you mean?"

"The bloke who borrowed the iron last week, you thought he appeared a little strange." She glanced in my direction and then continued, "We were glad when he went."

I was beginning to feel particularly deflated and uneasy when Jane replied from the depths of the flat.

"What does he want?"

"I don't know, he appears to be waffling."

"Well ask him in, he may want a cup of tea."

"He didn't ask for a cup of tea."

"Just ask him in anyway."

I was feeling somewhat conspicuous whilst this conversation was going on as if I was of little consequence to the outcome. The door opened and Tina suggested with the nod of her head that I should step inside, I did and followed her down the corridor as before, my eyes pinned to her rear. Déjà vu, I thought.

Jane was sat just as before nestled in amongst a blanket with a shawl round her shoulders, the room was stuffy and needed a change of air. She smiled when she saw me, "Hello again, would you like some tea?"

"Yes, that would be great," I replied.

"Tina," she instructed and then to me. "Sit down." Pointing at the dining room style chair beside her.

"Thanks."

"Now to what do we owe this pleasure?"

"Well," I stammered. "I was just passing and thought I would call in and see how you were."

"Passing? I thought you lived in the first floor flat."

"I do."

"Well it seems a little odd that you would just be passing." she observed.

I was afraid she would spot this immediately, I'd said it so I decided to go in with both feet. "Well. Okay I decided to come and see how you were."

Her smile increased and lit up her face, she was truly beautiful and I felt nervous in her presence, but at the same time excited. "Oh that's nice," she said. "Well now you are here and you haven't come to borrow anything I would like to know more about you, please tell me about yourself."

Tina appeared with the tea on a tray, including a separate milk jug, sugar bowl and a plate of rich tea biscuits. You know those biscuits which resemble a lump of flat clay with pin prick holes in and taste like nothing. Having poured out our requirements she left the room with a cursory glance in my direction which I think said. 'Watch it'.

Right, I thought, you asked for it therefore you are going to get it and I spent the next two hours relating my life story culminating in the experiences of that morning with Jack and Harold. She listened intently only periodically asking one word questions and I would clarify certain points and enhance some details. As I talked I was surprised at her interest because personally to me it just sounded like anybody else's story of self-destruction and misery. But Jane appeared genuinely interested, her eyes were bright and attentive and she was full of questions.

"Well, you have had an interesting life."

"Now you had better tell me about you," I said eager to prolong the interview, because that was how it seemed as if Jane was holding court and I was the subject.

"That won't take as long," she reached for my hand and squeezed it, but didn't let go. "Perhaps another time," she said. "I am actually starting to feel a little tired now, I think the past couple of hours have taken their toll on me."

"Yes of course, I should have realised."

"No, it's not your fault, it has been lovely, I don't get many visitors. If you have got the time I would like to continue our conversation tomorrow, but of course you may be busy."

"No that's fine I would love to." I answered quickly, perhaps too quickly.

"Are you sure, it was a little presumptuous of me to assume you would be free?"

"No I had nothing planned," I said getting to my feet, "about the same time?"

"Yes." She smiled brightly and my heart melted again.

I didn't want to leave, but I knew I had to. I hesitated, trying to think of something else to say. "Would you like me to bring a takeaway in or something?" Where did that come from? I quickly worked out my finances in my head, I could pick up my dole money in the morning and therefore, could afford a few pounds on some Chinese or Indian.

"Oh that would be lovely, I haven't had anything like that for..." she hesitated. "It seems like years."

"Which would you prefer, Chinese or Indian or perhaps something else?" I wondered if I had to include Tina but wasn't sure how to ask.

"Oh just surprise me, but remember I don't eat very much."

"Right. Great." I replied and with a polite shake of her hand I was gone.

I skipped up the stairs back to my flat with a new found spring in my step and a feeling of excitement at the prospect of seeing Jane again tomorrow. You know when you are courting, perhaps you don't remember those heady days of adolescence and testosterone, a cocktail not to be mixed. When you had just been out with a girl and as long as you managed to arrange the next date you could sleep well that night. It is those times when you can't pluck up the courage to make the next arrangements and you walk away kicking yourself with frustration.

I searched the cupboards for some food and once again the options were not good, I found one of those single portion cans of baked beans wedged behind an old vase, Harold must have missed this when he raided my cupboards a couple of days ago. I grilled some toast, heated up the beans and lobbed them on top, that would do for dinner. I thought, once I had consumed it I would head for an early night.

I had just finished clearing up and was making my way to bed, I know it was only just after nine but it had been an eventful few days and I was pretty tired and looking forward to a few hours of uninterrupted peace. I had brushed my teeth and soaped and washed a few of the essential areas and was in the bedroom, about to turn the light off when there was a sharp knocking on the door. Shit, I thought, who the hell could that be? I kept quiet in the hope they would go away, knowing of course, they wouldn't and then the banging was repeated with increased venom.

Who the hell could it be?

And then. "Vince, I know you're in there."

Bugger, it was Hilary, I wasn't sure if I was up to another night of Hilary's unusual form of passion and insatiable appetite.

"Vincent, open the bloody door and let me in."

Rather than disturb the whole house I thought I had better try to appease her. "Okay," I shouted. "I'm coming." I pulled the door open not too much. just enough to converse without letting Hilary infiltrate my privacy, but immediately she saw the gap she charged the door like a raging bull, it crashed back against the frame throwing me backwards onto the floor. Hilary followed placing her right foot firmly on my chest as I lay splattered on the lino, like an African hunter championing their kill.

She was dressed in a tight-fitting white blouse and a short black skirt, beneath which she had suspenders and stockings and I could clearly see no knickers. The heel of her shoe was digging into my ribs whilst the flat section nailed down my chest.

"Hello Hilary," I offered.

"Vince, are you trying to avoid me? I expected you to come back up to my flat this evening."

"I was tired Hilary, I have had a few busy days."

"So what Vince, I know how to make you relax." With this she smiled a sinister smile and as I glanced up her skirt I realised she was not joking.

I suggested that by removing her foot from my chest it could be a good start towards making me more relaxed. She did. But before I had the chance to get up she had dropped to her knees and lowered her crotch onto my chest, her legs spread either side of my body and demanded. "Come on Vince, let's do it."

And we did and to be honest I had very little to do with it, whilst pinning me to the floor Hilary reached behind her and freed me from my trousers and then sliding back we were away and to be perfectly honest it was good. And I performed manfully, determined not to let myself down I just went along with the flow as Hilary took charge before shouting, "Come on Vince, fuck me harder."

I did and I came and I think she did as well, she was rocking backwards and forwards like Calamity Jane aboard an obstinate nag.

After a short afterglow spent on the hall floor of my small flat we moved to the bedroom, where I fell asleep with very little effort and my dreams returned to Rachel and our past life together and where was I? Oh yes.

* * * *

As our married life progressed Rachel was going out more and more in the evenings and it seemed to me, coming in later and later. She said she was attending church meetings and had been coerced onto more and more committees. You know the way churches run their affairs, there is a committee for everything and then a sub-committee to discuss what the committee has decided and then all the committees have to report to the church council. This ensures nothing has been overlooked and the church council can ratify any decisions that may have been made by other minor committees and sub-committees. The chain of authority and ratification seems to be endless and clearly no individual has any power to make a decision for themselves. You may be wondering how I know all this, well Rachel told me and I, of course, believed everything that came out of her sweet mouth.

She was on the flower committee, the fourth Tuesday club guest speaker committee, which as its name suggests meets every fourth Tuesday of every month and the committee is responsible for choosing and arranging guest speakers. She used to have a loose leaf folder with plenty of paperwork in it to substantiate her position and some evenings were spent making phone calls between other members and prospective guests or writing letters.

I really didn't mind, because one of the most important things to me was to make sure Rachel was happy and content. If she was happy I was happy too and therefore, our union could grow and mature. You see I always felt Rachel was too good for me, I was inferior and I could never understand why she would want to spend her life with me, therefore I was always looking for a reason for her to go. Always expecting the inevitable rejection, the day when I would come home from work and find a 'Dear John' letter on the kitchen worktop and an empty wardrobe upstairs.

But there was one evening, it was late November and the weather was damp and drizzly with a light fog hanging in the air. I had had a hard day and when I arrived home Rachel was just going out and with a quick peck on the cheek and an instruction that my dinner was plated, covered and in the microwave, she was gone. I had just managed to ask her where she was going and the answer was the flower committee.

I showered and changed into jogging bottoms and a T-shirt and settled down with a glass of Chablis. I fired up the microwave in order to heat my dinner. I ate with the television for entertainment, which to be honest, was lacking any form of gratification. Having finished my dinner with some ice cream, cold custard and a doughnut, you may consider this a strange mixture, but public school educates one's palate in an unusual direction.

I laid out on the settee with a copy of *Sunset at Blandings* by P J Wodehouse with background music from the Moody Blues' *Threshold of a Dream*. I was content and mellow, I finished the Chablis and was totally engrossed in the book. I played the LP through at least three times, do you remember when you could go into a record shop and ask if you could listen to a record before deciding whether or not you wished to buy it? The disc was put on the turntable and you would stand in a curved booth surrounding you with acoustic-style material and the sound was amplified all around you. Funnily enough if you ducked out of this personal enclosure you wouldn't be able to identify the record you had been listening to, it turned into a muffled squeak.

I bought lots of recordings like this in the seventies, the Moody Blues, Bob Dylan and Arlo Guthrie, and The Strawbs, do you remember The Strawbs? a hippy style three-piece country band of the early seventies fronted by Dave Cousins. 'He Was The Man Who Called Himself Jesus'. Not Dave Cousins that was the name of the song and I quote:-

'He came into the shop and looked me straight between the eyes and said you know I'm Jesus and I must have looked surprised and he said please don't be hasty no one understands, but I got a way to prove it and he lifted up his hands.

'He was the man who called himself Jesus. For a minute I was speechless then I looked into his face with sufficient lines of sadness for the total human race.

'And I said you must be joking but he slowly shook his head, and said that's what they all say, I might as well be dead, he was the man who called himself Jesus'.

This chorus was repeated three or four times before going into the second verse and then towards the end there is this great line after they had had a drink together in the local pub and Jesus had left and the singer is sitting and contemplating and he sings, 'It seemed his pint of beer had turned into a pint of blood'.

Those were the days.

Those were the days.

Those were the...

I opened my eyes and was confused, I knew where I was but my dreams had been powerful and I was slow to adapt to the familiar stark environment that I now called home. And then I thought of Hilary remembering last night, I rolled over, but she was not there, I was sure she would be, but no the bed was bare. I wondered had I dreamt it, no surely not, I could still see her writhing over me as I was pinned to the floor, her hips moving with the rhythm and... Oh dear I must stop thinking like this it will only lead to trouble. With this thought I sprang into life, washed, dressed and looked for breakfast, but to no avail.

My first stop was going to have to be the Post Office to collect my dole cheque and then perhaps I would treat myself to a café breakfast.

As I walked down Kentish Town Road I got to thinking, in less than a week my life had changed beyond all recognition. Six days ago I was slumped in my flat, curtains drawn, empty beer cans littering the floor, daytime television punctuated with blue movies and a future filled with despair. But since then I have discovered a meaning to life, I have been out and about with Harold helping with his research, I have seen the degradation on the streets of London.

Perhaps I have found a young friend who requires my help, I don't know yet but I feel I must try to help this child, to ignore the problem would be morally wrong. But it is not just that, I want to help, but there are also other changes, I have been to Hilary's party, I have slept with her three days running and I have also met Jane, whom I very much want to see more of.

I popped into Marlon's, a greasy spoon type of a café in Kentish Town Road and ordered toasted muffins and poached eggs with grilled tomatoes and tea. I sat down and looked through a *Daily Mail* which was left on the table and then I realised I hadn't waited for Harold. We had arranged to meet at my flat every morning before going off to do our research. Perhaps it was for the best, a day on my own would be a welcome change and if I could make my way down to Charing Cross I could see how Jack is and perhaps try and work out what to do about him.

My food was put in front of me and it looked good, it has not been often that I have been able to spoil myself in this way recently. But I have a better feeling about life now, things seem to be turning a corner and it is all because I am developing some interests in life and not just sitting around moping in my flat and chasing the memories of Rachel and all I have lost. I ate hungrily, mopping up all the egg yoke and juices with the toast and washing it all down with the hot strong tea.

I left the café and caught a bus down to the West End, from there I walked through Soho and Leicester Square keeping my eyes open and still trying to concentrate on the research I was trying to help Harold with. But my thoughts were very much on young Jack and what I was going to find when I reached the tunnels under Charing Cross Station.

As I walked down St Martin's Lane a scuffle broke out in front of me and in no time at all it developed into a full scale punch-up between two scruffy looking young men, probably in their late twenties. Clearly arguing over the ownership of a can of beer, presumably it was the last one and neither was prepared to give up on it. Their voices shouted insults and expletives at each other and then one threw a vicious left hook leaving the other one, the one with the can of beer, dropping like a stone backwards into the gutter just at the precise moment a black taxi passed, its nearside front wheel crushing his head between tyre and road and his face, brains and blood sprayed out over the road, the pavement and passers-by. It was as if time stood still, it all seemed to happen in slow motion, but so violently and decisively. But it had also all happened so quickly that nobody had any time to react or help in any way.

I suddenly felt sick, but I couldn't take my eyes from the scene of absolute horror, it was like a magnet pulling me towards the carnage forcing me to take in every detail so it would be imprinted on my mind forever and that is when I realised I would never forget this moment.

I saw a young woman dressed smartly in a light-coloured business suit which was splattered with slime, brains and juice. But this was nothing to the chilling screams that came from her as she jumped and leapt in a blind panic in an effort to shake the detritus from her. The noise of her screams pierced the air and my head and I couldn't free myself from the noise and horror.

I ducked into a recessed doorway and vomited uncontrollably against the shop window, my luxury breakfast had gone and my stomach muscles ached, but I still kept retching. I looked back at the scene a man in jeans and a T-shirt had already rushed to the body, which I was sure was dead. What he was going to do I couldn't imagine, but people obviously deal with these extreme situations in their own way. Some cower in the corner and do nothing, like me, others rush to help, anything to keep busy. He was kneeling by the body and then there were sirens ringing in the background, an ambulance skidded to a halt followed closely by a police car.

The doors flew open and a policewoman carefully and tenderly tried to coax the man away from the body and with her arm around him she led him towards the police car. The other officers pushed through the recently gathered crowd forcing them back to make room for the paramedics who had pulled a stretcher from the back of the ambulance and were running to the now cordoned off area.

I looked round and realised the perpetrator was nowhere to be seen, clearly he had legged it when he saw the carnage he had caused, or was it a mutual fate brought on by this diminished form of society, where there are no winners?

Having discarded my entire breakfast in a doorway I felt numb and confused and didn't know what to expect next. I found myself sitting on the pavement clearly affected by the destruction of one human body in a matter of seconds, a complete accident caused by a minor fracas between two friends squabbling over a can of beer. I still couldn't take my eyes from the macabre scene in front of me, although I still felt nauseous my eyes were drawn to the physical destruction of a human being.

A second ambulance had arrived and a female paramedic was comforting the poor taxi driver who was clearly beside himself leaning against the roof of his cab with his head in his hands and sobbing uncontrollably. She led him away towards the ambulance where he would obviously require treatment for shock before being put through questioning by the police. He clearly couldn't shoulder any blame, but no doubt his conscience would live with him forever in his dreams and nightmares.

The paramedics, having examined the body and covered it, carefully lifted it onto a stretcher and manoeuvred it into the ambulance. The police officers had cordoned off the area and were busily questioning prospective witnesses trying to attain an exact sequence of events.

I sat on the pavement and cried, I just couldn't believe what I had seen, the vision of a head being squashed between the wheels of a car and the road was completely beyond my comprehension. I don't know how long I stayed there, it may have been an hour or more and when I looked up I dried my eyes and the square was back to normal apart from a small screened off area guarded by two policemen. Obviously a secluded area for further forensic investigations to be carried out as if there was any doubt what had happened.

I stood up and walked uncertainly to the nearest pub, where I drank two large glasses of wine, paid for with money from my dole cheque which I could ill afford, but I realised how desperately I needed a drink. My nerves were mashed up and completely out of control and I swallowed the first glass in two gulps, trying to understand the sense behind God's work.

* * * *

After a suitable time I felt a little mellower if not a little drunk, the warmth of the alcohol had helped to deaden my emotions although I knew they would return as the effect wore off. Have you noticed alcohol is supposed to be a depressant, although the initial feeling is far more uplifting and the depression doesn't kick in until you start to come down?

I left the pub and carried on my walk in the direction of Charing Cross Station. There was a lot of scurrying around in the street where the accident had occurred, the area was now taped off with blue and white striped strips. There were two police officers moving amongst the passers-by with notepads, stopping some of them and asking for any information, if anyone had witnessed the incident. I wondered if I should volunteer any information but decided not to, I could always call in at a police station tomorrow. I was too fragile at the moment, I knew if I was questioned I was sure to breakdown and I really didn't have the stomach for it. All I wanted to do now was to carry on with my day, I wanted to see Jack as I had promised and make sure he was alright.

Once underground I made my way around to Jack's hideaway but there was no sign of him, his so-called bedding was screwed up in the corner. I looked around and asked a crowd of reprobates on the staircase, not the same crowd as yesterday, if they had seen him, the blank expressions told me little more than that they had had a good session on the cider and just wanted to be left alone.

I didn't know what to do, my mind was too mixed up and fuzzy the after effects of seeing this guy's head squashed like a water melon had completely halted my train of thought. I decided to leave it for today and head on back to the flat, I chose to walk so I could avoid mixing with other people, I didn't relish any conversation. As I walked I remembered I had promised to take Jane in a takeaway this evening, and even after all that had happened I didn't want to let her down.

I quickened my pace and walked easily the three or so miles back to Kentish Town, I think the open air (I almost said fresh but that would not be an accurate description of London air) helped to clear my head and made me feel a little better. It took the best part of an hour, but it was therapeutic.

Back in my flat I went to the bathroom and had a quick and thorough wash and a shave before dowsing myself in cologne. I then put on some clean clothes and made my way down the staircase and out into the street hoping I wasn't going to bump into Hilary. This was getting complicated trying to avoid Hilary because I was secretly hoping I could become involved with another girl in the same house.

Back in the High Street, I thought what should I go for, Indian, Chinese, pizza or even kebab, which I rejected immediately, I always felt a bit uncomfortable with those things rotating around on a metal prong, while someone slices strips off them. You don't know how long they have been there, left for the flies to tinker with, or if they have even been cooked properly. After much consideration I decided on the Indian, a cheaper option on the whole and always a good standby, I understand they are supposed to be the country's favourite restaurants now.

I slipped into the Raj Mahal and skipped through the takeaway menu lying on a table near the counter. Pilau rice one portion, chicken massala one portion, tandoori chicken one portion, four pappadums, and a portion of onion baji, no, on second thoughts let's have two rice just in case Tina muscles in on the party, it may help to fill us up. I was careful to check the prices, I personally would prefer a prawn dish but I wasn't sure the funds would run to that. I gave my order to the smartly dressed Asian gentleman behind the counter who offered me a free drink while I waited. After the day I have had I readily accepted a cool glass of dry white wine, took a seat at a spare table and ruminated on the last few hours. I think I was still in shock, I just couldn't accept what I had seen, it was just too horrible to contemplate.

Twenty minutes later I was knocking on the basement door to Jane's flat, armed with two brown paper handled bags, smelling strongly of rich spices. The door was opened as usual by Tina nursing a curious expression of bewilderment (no change there then, I thought) as she looked at me and then at the bags at my sides.

I held them up and said, "Dinner!" At least this was a valid statement, unlike yesterday when I was struggling to justify my existence.

She nodded and opened the door for me to pass and I walked along the corridor and then said, "Shall I put these in the kitchen?"

Tina held out her hands, took the bags from me and walked through to the kitchen at the back of the flat, I carried on into the lounge where Jane was seated as usual. The table in the corner had been laid tidily for three, bugger I thought, I had hoped it would be just for two, but deep inside I knew it wouldn't be. I can imagine it won't be long before I am tired of this chaperone.

"Hello Jane," I offered and moved over to her chair and took her hand and held it to my lips brushing the surface in a show of gallantry that even surprised me. "I've brought dinner as promised, Tina's taken it into the kitchen, I suppose she is going to dish up."

"Oh Vincent, it's lovely to see you again and thank you."

She fidgeted in her chair before starting to get up and then she said. "Do you think you could help me to the table?" She was clearly struggling.

"Of course," I said and held out my hands, she took them, hers were soft and sensual to the touch as she pulled hard against me and straightened to her full height of, I estimated, about five feet four. She looked different standing, her figure was good with a slim waist and hips and a good bust. She was wearing a clean white long sleeved blouse and a dark grey knee-length skirt and I realised I hadn't seen her legs before and I thought wow.

I flattered myself wondering if she had changed for my benefit. I looked at her face, it was so warm and her eyes dark brown and inviting, I couldn't stop looking at her. I moved her slowly towards the table and helped her into her seat, I held onto her hands a little too long and then.

"Jane, are you ready for dinner?" Tina asked from the door as she carried in plated mixtures of the Indian food I had brought in and she put them on the place mats. The pappadums she placed in the centre of the table for us to help ourselves.

"Yes, thank you Tina, please join us. Vincent would you mind opening that bottle of wine, it's a Merlot. I sent Tina out for it today. I hope you like red, I'm afraid we don't have wine very often, but I thought it would be nice."

"Absolutely," I replied, whatever she wanted was perfectly alright by me. I opened the bottle it was a screw top a wonderful invention that saved me the embarrassment of hauling on a corkscrew with a stubborn bottle wedged between my legs. I poured the pure deep red liquid into the three glasses set out on the table and smelled and tasted mine, it was nice pure and clean.

We ate freely and personally and I with great enthusiasm. I hadn't realised how hungry I was, I watched Jane closely to see how much she ate, which was little, but more so because I just liked looking at her. She picked at her food but appeared to be enjoying it, I had finished mine but I had the feeling Tina was staring at me all the time or at least after every mouthful. She ate heartily and finished soon after me. After the events of the day my appetite was not what it should be and I was careful not to eat too much as my stomach was still a little weak, a nervous feeling.

We had finished all the food except an onion baji and some rice, I suggested Tina had it and she lapped it up with a sense of greed before I could change my mind. I took the liberty of filling the wine glasses and noticed that Tina gobbled hers up without any hesitation. When she had finished she was quickly on her feet and clearing away the debris, for which I was thankful as I wanted the opportunity to talk to Jane on her own. I was keen to continue our conversation of the previous day.

Jane said, "That was really lovely Vincent, it must be years since I had an Indian, you must let me know how much it was so I can pay you."

"No certainly not," I replied.

"Well, at least let me pay for mine and Tina's."

"No it is my treat and you provided the wine and have given me tea and lent me your iron a few days ago, I certainly don't want any payment."

She smiled and said, "Thank you, you are very kind Vincent."

"But if you want to repay me," I said. "You could tell me all about yourself and continue our conversation of yesterday."

"Alright," she said. "But first you must help me to the chair." She stood up slowly and I placed myself beside her so she could take my arm to support her. I led her to her armchair where she carefully sat down and crossed her legs, left over right and her skirt rode up exposing her milky white thighs her muscles though taut looked undernourished, but still erotic. I positioned a dining room chair as close to hers as I could so I was sitting right next to her, the closeness excited me.

"Would you like some coffee? I can ask Tina to make us some."

"Yes, that would be nice."

Jane reached to the table to her left and picked up an old-fashioned bell and shook it vigorously making a loud ringing sound.

There were so many things I wanted to ask her, such as who the hell is Tina? Where does she sleep? And what hold does she have over Jane? Tina reminded me of a sinister servant from times gone by, like Uriah Heap or Jeeves without the humour, but with extreme knowledge over her mistress that ties her in. It was nagging at me and I couldn't put an exact perspective on it.

Tina came into the room and glancing at me, appeared to sneer, I suspected because I was still there, but it could have been because of my close proximity to Jane. I was not going to be intimidated and was determined to stand my ground.

"Tina, could we have some coffee please?"

Tina nodded and was gone silently, like a spirit in the night, I shuddered. Once the door was closed I said, "Well are you going to carry on?"

She nodded and our eyes met before she looked away. "I was born in Woodstock in Oxfordshire, a beautiful town on the edge of the Cotswolds and part of the Blenheim estate, the home of the Churchill family. I don't know if you knew that?"

I smiled and nodded. I did know this having specialised in the Wars of the Spanish Succession for A level and I have always had a great admiration for the first Duke of Marlborough, John Churchill, Winston's illustrious ancestor.

"My father had qualified as a solicitor in business law and progressed to barrister status where he was very successful. We had a lovely house an olde-worlde style cottage, called Sycamore Cottage named after the two large trees at the bottom of the garden. But it was far more than a cottage, there were six bedrooms, three reception rooms and a large, as we called it, veranda on the back which was more like a modern-type conservatory, a timber structure with glass panels forming the roof. It was a beautiful house and to grow up in it was an experience and a privilege.

'I had an older brother Peter, five years older in fact, but I never saw much of him, he was sent away to school when he was nine years old, a regime that my father was very enthusiastic about. He was quite a strict disciplinarian and would have done the same with me except my mother was adamant she would not let him. 'You have taken my son from me. You are not doing the same with Jane'.

"So I went to the local grammar school and was what you would call an average student, I achieved five O levels and two A's and then went to a technical college to study biology. I always wanted to be a vet right from when I was very young. I had my own horse which I was lucky enough to be able to stable in a livery at the bottom of our garden, so all I had to do was climb over the fence and walk across the field to muck out the stable and tack him up for riding. I used to love riding, it was so relaxing and I was actually quite good at it, there were local gymkhanas which I would enter and I usually came home with a few rosettes."

We were interrupted by the arrival of Tina and a tray with a coffee pot, milk jug and sugar bowl and just two cups, for which I was thankful. It does appear that Tina acknowledges her position in this strange relationship and doesn't push herself too far forward. She is also quite capable of transmitting her feelings by her body language and her moods, and I had a distinct impression she didn't think much of me. I watched her and wondered where she fitted into this strange puzzle, did she owe Jane something? Was she working off some sort of debt? Or is it possible there is something more sinister.

I poured the coffee and Jane continued. "They were old-fashioned type of parents, but very good to me, I never wanted for anything and I was brought up in a loving environment, but it was almost like being an only child as Peter was away so much and being five years older as well. When he was home in the school holidays he was always out with friends racing go-karts or tinkering with them to make them go faster. Not a sport that ever interested me, I was much keener on my horse.

"It was during my first year at college that my world fell apart, there were two major events that changed my life forever." She stopped abruptly, her eyes moistened and I could see tears flooding into them, she took my hand and squeezed it tightly. "I think I would like to stop there now Vincent, if you don't mind, I am feeling a little tired now." She sniffled and tried to smile through her tears, which made her look even more beautiful than ever and I was feeling so warm towards her.

"Of course," I said still holding onto her hand realising it would be wrong of me to push her too far.

"Thank you, perhaps if you come and see me again I will continue and tell you some more if you are sure you would be interested?"

"I would be delighted to hear more," I said. Still holding her hand I stood up and plucking up the courage lent down and kissed her on the cheek, her skin was soft and warm and I hoped it would be the first of many. "I will go now and let you rest and thanks for a lovely evening, I really enjoyed it."

"So did I, and thank you ever so much for bringing in the Indian meal, it was really lovely." she replied.

"That was my pleasure," I smiled. And with that I left, climbed the stairs to my flat with a new found spring in my step, it was past nine thirty and I was feeling good.

It is funny how with Hilary everything just happened because she was so forward and I didn't try to stop her, the whole sex thing just fired up and away we went. But with Jane I feel far more bashful, I don't want to get it wrong so I feel more reticent and nervous when approaching her, but I must admit it adds to the excitement. I just love the butterfly feeling in the stomach, it's like a drug and when it subsides there is a warm feeling of relief that brings you back down to earth.

When I reached my flat, stuck to the door with a piece of chewing gum was a scrap of paper torn from a used envelope. I pulled it off and unfolded it exposing a few words which read:

'Vince, where the fuck have you been all day (no question mark I noticed, a bit disappointing for one of our national journalists) I'll be round early tomorrow morning be up'.

I tore the note into shreds and once in the flat dropped it into the rubbish bag I kept in the kitchen. Then I went to bed to think, dream and think some more in the hope that my mixed up feelings and emotions may make more sense come the new dawn. And as I fell asleep the horrific memories of the taxi squashing the young man in the gutter returned and the vision expanded and filled my mind.

CHAPTER 8

I woke at about seven feeling very melancholy, in fact that is not quite accurate I just felt really shit. I had had a restless night with my imagination running riot. My mouth felt glued together with garlic and ghee a powerful mixture concocted by the Indian chefs.

I had dreamed relentlessly with visions of Jane coupled with motor accidents and Trafalgar square and heads exploding in front of my eyes. Jane's head kept appearing in my vision line and then my mind reverted to the black cab and Jane lying in the road without her head. I woke a couple of times sweating and hot with moisture covering my body, I rolled over and went back to sleep but the same dreams retuned tormenting my mind and giving me no respite. The night dragged on and on and as I tossed and turned I never thought it was going to end, but once I was awake and daylight shone in I got up and prepared for Harold's appearance. I must admit a day like yesterday was a change from his overpowering personality, but I wouldn't want to experience anything like that again.

Just on cue there was a violent knock on the door followed up with an abusive wave of expletives mainly aimed at me. "Hey Sleeve you bloody cretin are you up yet? We need to talk."

I opened the door with a wild flourish and said, "Yes. I'm up Harold, please come in and perhaps we could share a pot of tea together and enjoy a pleasant chat rather than keep abusing each other, or more to the point you abusing me." I stepped to one side and Harold came in glancing at me with a weird expression on his face. I don't think he quite understood my attempt at sarcasm and he clearly was not aware of the pressure I had been under over the past twenty-four hours. "Sit down." I suggested and went into the kitchen to boil the kettle returning a few minutes later with two mugs of strong dark tea, laced with a touch of milk and some sugar for Harold.

"Now what do you want to talk about?" I asked.

"Well Vince, where were you yesterday? I came round before nine thirty in the morning and there was no answer and I popped back later about lunchtime and it was the same, even in the evening you were out."

I looked at him with a certain amount of disgust. "You have absolutely no idea what I went through yesterday. I left here, collected my dole cheque."

"Huh." he scoffed.

I ignored him and continued, "Bought some breakfast and then made my way into the West End where I experienced a homeless man having his head squashed between the road and the wheel of a taxi and watched the brains, blood, eyes and gore being squirted in all directions and over most of the bystanders. I then sat in silence and cried because the shock was so overwhelming that I couldn't do anything else, I had no self control, so I went and got a little drunk, only a little because that is all my dole cheque would stretch to. You don't know what that feels like because you have an expense account, you have no idea and I am getting a little fed up with your sanctimonious attitude."

Harold looked at me with unbelieving eyes, clearly he was surprised by my outburst. "What are you talking about Vince? A head being squashed, blood and gore and guts everywhere."

I now gave him the long version and related yesterday's events in more graphic detail leaving nothing out, hoping the enormity of the disaster would perhaps in some way make him a little more aware of and even understanding of the problems people face sleeping rough on the streets and trying to survive on next to nothing. When I said I left nothing out of my story, that wasn't strictly true as I didn't mention Jane because I knew full well what sort of repartee that would start.

He appeared to be moved by my account and descriptions because he was stroking his chin and looking thoughtful and then he said, "Well we best get out on the streets again and see if we can muster up some action first-hand so to speak, so I can get some more copy down on paper, because I don't want to be mixing with the likes of this lot for much longer."

Perhaps he wasn't feeling any more benevolent after all.

He carried on, "I need to get back to my office and whack out a decent story on the old computer as soon as possible."

"How long is your article supposed to be?" I asked.

"I am looking for about four thousand words, probably spread over two editions." He stood up and headed for the door. "Let's go Vince."

We didn't talk much while we took the bus and then walked into the West End. I still felt very despondent after yesterday and the moment of impact between wheel and head constantly repeated itself in my mind and I couldn't shift it. Harold was also quiet, which was unusual, perhaps he was also affected by my experience and my mood, perhaps he had actually thought about it.

We walked across Soho Square and down Greek Street where there were rubbish sacks piled high on the pavements outside the restaurants and cafés and you could smell the leftover curries and takeaways from the night before. In a small alleyway up ahead there was a group of boisterous young men shouting and passing round cans of beer and what appeared to be a bag. At first I thought it was harmless banter just high spirits but then it became obvious there was something more serious going on.

There was a girl in the middle of the group. It was hard to determine her age but I thought late teens or early twenties, she was slim and petite with long straight blonde hair. As we came closer she was shouting.

"Give me back my bag, please," she pleaded.

The boys just laughed and threw the bag from one to another. The girl flayed her arms uselessly trying to intercept its flight but to no avail and then in her efforts she tripped, falling headlong against one of the men, catching him firmly in the stomach.

"Hey you fucking bitch," he shouted and lashed out with his fists catching her, a glancing blow as she went to the ground. We could hear her cries as the group descended on top of her and half dragged and half carried her deeper into the alleyway, further away from Greek Street. Her cries and shouts for help were muffled by the bodies surrounding her.

I looked at Harold and said, "We have got to do something Harold, we've got to help."

"Don't be a bloody idiot Sleeve there's about six of them we would probably be knifed or something, the best we could hope for would be a good beating."

"But we can't just leave the poor girl, they will probably rape her." As I said these words one of the men was standing over her as the others held her arms and legs, he bent down and slit her skirt and knickers with the blade of a Swiss army knife and threw the materials to one side. We both stood there watching, but doing nothing to help, my heart was beating with revulsion and my legs felt leaden, but still I couldn't pluck up the courage to intervene. I felt sick and disgusted, but couldn't tear my eyes from the scene, I felt so pathetic and inadequate.

The sixth man held one hand over her mouth to stop her screams while he fondled down her blouse with the other. The other man still standing over her was coaxing his penis into readiness before lowering himself between her legs where he thrust forward with sheer violence and it wasn't long before he had spent his load. He stood up taking hold of one of the girls legs and allowed the next man to take his pleasure. After what seemed like an eternity, but was most likely only a few minutes all six of them had taken their turn and had left the girl curled up in the foetal position distraught and sobbing between the corner of two buildings.

I looked at Harold again, he was still staring with frightened eyes and an expression of horror on his face.

Having emptied her bag of anything worthwhile the men calmly walked out of the alley laughing and joking and no one made any attempt to stop them although a crowd of some twenty people had gathered. People don't want to get involved these days, but are quite happy to observe others suffering.

"We should have stopped it Harold," I said.

"Look just shut up Vince, you wanker."

This often seemed to be Harold's answer when he was in a spot, to call me a wanker, I shrugged it off.

"I still say we should have done something to help, perhaps if we had tried to persuade some other people to get involved we could have stopped it."

"Look Vince, you saw the fellow had a knife, he used it to cut the girl's clothes, if you had intervened he would most likely have used it on you. It's the law of the street dog-eat-dog and all that sort of thing."

"You can't be suggesting that young girl deserved to be treated like that in twenty-first century Britain?"

He just sneered.

An ambulance arrived at the end of the alleyway and two paramedics rushed to help the girl, I was pleased to see one was a woman, it would be more comforting for her. They quickly covered her up with blankets to keep her warm and protect her modesty, but when all's said and done this seemed a little late. They then carefully checked her over before helping her to their vehicle and once inside they swung away into the traffic, turning on the blue flashing lights and the sirens and disappeared east toward Shaftsbury Avenue.

The crowd soon disbursed and Harold and I walked away without speaking, we wandered in the direction of Soho Square retracing our steps. I was wondering what our society was turning into and I sure as hell couldn't guess what Harold was thinking, it seemed to me we were hardly on the same wavelength. He seemed to have so little compassion and only really thought about himself.

Harold pulled up and sat on a wall, he removed his mini recorder from his pocket and started dictating into it. I moved away letting him make his notes and form his ideas in his head. I leant against a lamp post and then found a bench, sat down and contemplated the past few days, the ladies in my life made me smile and I was surprised how my love life and possibilities had so drastically increased in such a short time. Having lived like a hermit for the past few months the opportunities were just opening up in front of me. But then on the other hand the dangerous and violent incidents that I had experienced on the streets brought a strange contrast to my mind and I found it hard to understand, to come to terms with such abuse of other human beings, it not only worried me it actually frightened me as well. It wasn't the way I had been brought up in my middle-class public school lifestyle.

I slumped away to the other side of the road where I sat on a bench in Soho Square and my mind wandered and my past came back to me, my life with Rachel and then...

It was late when I heard the key turn in the front door, I think the sound woke me, I looked at my watch it was almost eleven thirty, I sat up. Rachel stepped into the lounge. "Still up?" she asked.

I made a point of looking at my watch again exaggerating the movement to make a point. "What time do you call this?"

"It's not that late it's not even eleven thirty yet." she replied and she was gone shouting back from the kitchen, "Would you like a coffee?"

"No." I shouted back, I was uncomfortable about this and I was also drunk, I had had a couple of glasses of port after the bottle of Chablis. I couldn't understand how a flower committee meeting could take more than four hours out of someone's evening.

She came back into the room with a mug of coffee and sat down opposite me. "Why are you looking at me like that Vincent?"

"Like what?"

"Like you have some sort of problem and you don't know how to say it." She crossed her legs pushing her skirt higher up her thighs, she always had such great legs and now they looked just as good as ever, they were bare, no tights.

I somehow didn't believe she had only been at a committee meeting about flowers, but I didn't want to accuse her outright, because immediately I did that it would be out in the open and the arguments would start.

"Look it just seems to me that, you know," I could hear my words slurring as I spoke. "A committee about flowers, what the hell is all that about?" I asked realising I may have gone too far.

Rachel sat there just looking at me.

I continued. "You seem to be out more than you are in these days, every other evening you have one meeting or another," I hesitated. "Or so you say."

She looked at me with eyes I hadn't seen before, hard and distant and I couldn't recognise or read her thoughts. "What do you mean by that Vince? What are you suggesting? Are you suggesting I'm not attending these meetings and if so where do you think I am? Or are

132

you calling me a liar?" She swilled at her coffee in the sort of smug way that really wound me up.

I held on to my patience, although it was hard. "Yes." I replied.

"Yes to which question Vincent?"

"Yes to I am suggesting you are not attending all these meetings." There I have said it, I have accused her.

"You bastard. Vincent fucking Sleeve." She was on her feet now and looked pretty bloody cross.

I staggered to my feet at the same time, albeit like any drunk does when trying to stand, and without warning she clumped me firmly on the side of the cheek with a clenched fist that Frank Bruno would have been proud of. I went sprawling on all fours across the floor landing in a quivering heap and by the time I had managed to sit up and nurse my quickly swelling face, she had left the room slamming the door behind her.

Needless to say I spent the night on the sofa and surfaced with a dry mouth and a throbbing headache the next morning to find Rachel was up, dressed and had already left for work. I slumped at the kitchen table and drank a strong dark cup of coffee, held my head in my hands and cried.

* * * *

I woke the next morning tired and depressed, my dreams had developed into a cocktail of love and violence and unwashed vagrants littering the streets. I felt sick, confused and tormented by my thoughts. I had gone to bed about ten the previous evening, there was so much rushing round in my head, I didn't know what to think. The extent of my emotions thinking about Jane and Hilary and then the violence that I had witnessed in successive days being perpetrated on the streets, just caused restless nights of tossing and turning and then once asleep, my subconscious took over and mashed up all the different situations.

Once we left Soho Square Harold announced he had to return to his hotel so he could type up the day's events and get his article on track. I just nodded and walked on aimlessly for what seemed like ages. I found myself staring up at the Eleanor statue at Charing Cross, obviously drawn to see Jack and see if he was there. I wandered down the staircases into the dull passages to the angled soffit beneath.

Jack was sat in the acute angle of the structure glancing through some old newspapers, there was a whole pile beside him. I observed him from a distance for some minutes, surprised and also pleased at the intense concentration involved in his study. From what I could see he was reading some quite in-depth pieces, which suggested to me the boy wasn't stupid but didn't explain what he was doing living in this situation. When I got closer I could see some were today's and others a few days older, I wondered how he had come about so many, probably by similar means as he had secreted the bag of goodies the other day which earned him a severe clumping from the shop holder outside the front of the station.

I moved closer and carefully sat down beside him, he didn't look at me but just said, "Hi."

"Hi," I responded. "I just wondered how you were doing?"

He shrugged his shoulders still concentrating on the paper he was holding open with his arms wrapped around his knees for support. *The Sun* may not be the best read but Jack was clearly digesting its content and not just looking at pictures of boobs and tittle-tattle.

I noticed his hands were still grazed with little pinprick scabs forming, but all signs of blood had dried up. The bruise on his cheek had darkened and a yellow hue had formed around the edges and the swelling was going down. I picked up a paper from his pile, the *Observer* and flicked through the pages casually taking in the headlines.

"Are your wounds healing?" I asked.

He shrugged again.

"Look, I'll go and pick up a couple of coffees and bring them back here. Milk and sugar?" I asked.

He nodded. Clearly conversation was no better than the last time we'd had a one-sided discussion.

I returned a few minutes later with two paper cupped coffees-to-go, with lids on, with a little spout which when sucked through dribbles its contents down your chin. Jack was still in the same position and I placed a cup on the tiled floor beside him saying. "There you are, get that down you it will make you feel better."

"Thanks," he said.

"Look Jack, I want to help you I don't like to see you living here like this, it's not right, you know, you should be at home or something with your parents. You do have parents don't you?"

He sipped at his coffee through the hole and I was right it dribbled down his chin, he wiped it off with his sleeve, unaware of my amusement and ignoring my question. I let it hang in the air promising to return to it later.

"Jack. How long have you been living like this?"

He turned towards me. "My name is not Jack."

"Well what is it then? I asked.

He hesitated before speaking and then said, "Dean."

I screwed up my face hoping he wouldn't notice and thought, Dean! What kind of a name is that I thought, boys aren't called Dean, forests are called Dean.

"Good I'm glad we've got that sorted out at last, now I will no longer have to call you Jack."

"You didn't have to call me Jack before," he observed.

As you can see the conversation was really starting to flow now, back to my previous questions. "How long have you been living like this then?" I know I asked this before but I wondered if I may get an answer now.

He took another gulp of his coffee he had removed the plastic top now realising there was less chance of dribbling and more chance of consuming the liquid. "A few weeks s'ppose."

"Why, though? There must have been something to cause this situation?"

He turned to me and I could see moisture forming in his eyes, I wasn't sure how far I should push the questioning, but I wanted to keep him talking now there was some sort of breakthrough I hoped to build his confidence in me. I wanted him to know that I had his best interests at heart and wanted to help, not make his situation worse. I was sure he was a smart boy, he was alert and probably fairly streetwise, but he was also young and existing in this homeless environment was unhealthy and dangerous.

135

I thought for a while knowing what I was about to say was most likely going to cause me untold pain and heartache. "Dean, listen to me carefully, I suggest you come and live with me for a while and we can see how we get on. I live alone in a one bedroom flat in Kentish Town, a converted house split up into five separate units, mine's on the first floor. It's nothing special but it is better than this." I gesticulated with my hand taking in our surroundings and continued. "You could sleep in the lounge on the sofa and we would be company for each other. What do you think?"

I could see he was thinking deeply about this and funnily enough I didn't know how I wanted him to respond. I knew that if he said yes, I would have to curtail my pursuit of Jane, but on the other hand it would help thwart Hilary barging in and taking advantage of me without any warning and of course it would be company and hopefully help me to start to live my life again. (I know what you are thinking, why on earth would I want to stop Hilary coming in and taking advantage of me, and thinking about it I take your point).

"I want to think about it," he replied.

"Okay." I said throwing back the rest of my coffee. "Sleep on it and I'll come back again tomorrow." I got up to go. "I'll see you tomorrow then."

He nodded.

As I walked away, he called, "Hey." I turned. "What's your name?"

"Vincent." I said. "But you can call me Vince."

I smiled and carried on walking and then he said, "And thanks." I waved my hand above my head without turning back acknowledging that I had heard him.

I then knew what his answer would be so I thought I must make the most of the rest of the day and take the opportunity to see Jane again, because if Dean was going to move in and be my chum, it would make getting to know Jane a lot harder, but on the other hand I didn't want to let him tie me down too much either.

Back at the flat the first thing I did was clean myself up and then went downstairs to the basement and knocked on her door. Tina observed her usual protocol and made my entry just as difficult as on previous occasions. I had picked up a cheap bunch of tightly bloomed roses in the High Street and now clutched them closely to my chest and out of Tina's reach. When I presented them to Jane it was wonderful to see her eyes light up with genuine pleasure and at the same time my heart melted and my legs went to jelly.

They say beauty is in the eye of the beholder, well I guess they have got to be right because to me she was the most beautiful woman I had ever seen. But when you looked deeper she wasn't stunning like some of these well-known film stars or catwalk models. She didn't even have any make-up on, she wasn't dressed in glamorous or expensive clothes, but to me she was just the epitome of beauty.

This whole feeling just made my heart flutter and filled my stomach with butterflies, you know when you are so excited and yet full of nerves at the same time.

"Oh Vincent. Thank you." She squealed and taking the flowers from me shoved her nose amongst them breathing deeply, although I doubted if there was much of a scent as they still needed to open but she appeared satisfied.

She called for Tina and asked her to put them in a vase. Turning to me she said beckoning, "Vincent come here." I did and she kissed me firmly on the lips and I must admit I didn't want to pull away. Her perfume was strong but I couldn't place it, I thought it was an eighties one when they were pungent and strong, maybe Poison or First. But it was good and her lips were soft and receptive and I liked it and I wanted more. You know how it is when you kiss someone for the first time and you are not sure what to expect. You can get all tangled up with lips and teeth and when you were much younger, braces as well.

Do you remember that, when all girls around fifteen would have a mouthful of iron strapping their teeth together and if you were lucky enough to kiss them you ran the risk of getting a mouthful of metal?

"Sit down beside me," she said.

I did, moving my chair closer to hers in the hope, if the opportunity arose, I would be able to hold her hand.

"Tina will be bringing some tea in," she said.

"Thanks. That will be nice, the other evening you said you would tell me more of your life story."

"Yes I did didn't I? Where was I? Remind me."

"You left me wondering what the two major events were that caused your life to fall apart," I offered.

"Oh yes." The tea arrived and having placed it on the table Tina fortunately disappeared without any persuasion and I was hoping Jane would carry on.

She did. "Yes it was a terrible year. Peter, my older brother having left further education took up with a group of boys racing karts, which progressed to bigger and more powerful machines and he started competitive racing in Formula Ford. He was aspiring to become a Formula 1 driver, that was his ambition and my father was fully behind him, but of course mother was more sceptical or to be honest, she was just terrified of the danger and somehow she probably knew. But yes you've guessed it he got himself killed." She hesitated, tears once again formulating in the corners of her eyes. But she brushed them away and this time I felt she was prepared to confront it, but I wanted to know more. She continued.

"He was doing practice laps, testing some new set-up or something the mechanics had put on the car and he went into a corner too fast and didn't come out the other side. As he overran the edge of the track a tyre burst and sent the car catapulting into the air, when it came down it was upside down and Peter landed on his head and his neck snapped, the medics said he died instantly and wouldn't have known anything about it. But I keep thinking he would have known all about it from the moment he lost control to the moment the car landed and although it was only a few seconds it would have seemed like a lifetime to him." She slumped in her chair, not crying but just remembering, still mourning the loss of her brother which must be some ten years ago now.

I took her hand, it seemed all I could do to try and bring some comfort to her, I wanted to hold her and hug her but this would have been a move too far.

"He was only twenty-three."

I nodded not knowing what to say, it seemed so finite the end at twenty-three when he had his whole life ahead of him. I squeezed her hand tighter.

"The funeral was a large affair at the village church in Woodstock, Mother and Father had a lot of friends and I suppose the shock of someone dying so young tends to bring the crowds in." She sniffed holding a tissue to her nose and gently blew before wiping her eyes.

I just listened I didn't know what else to do, I was hoping she would carry on so I could just let her talk, I didn't know what to say.

"It is not the same when a person dies so young he was only twenty-three with so much life ahead of him. When someone has lived their life to the full and their body is worn out and their passing is, in many respects, celebrated and although not a jolly occasion is not completely unhappy. This was not the case with Peter, it affected my parents so badly, there is something wrong about a child dying before its parents, the order is all wrong."

Jane held a tissue tightly clutched between the fingers of her right hand ready to use it if she felt a sudden need. "The day of the funeral was clear and sunny, but the air was crisp, it was late February and the atmosphere in the church was so morbid, you could have cut it with a knife. The inside of the church with its stone columns and walls were cold and reverent and an unusual feeling of peace hung in the air. Mum and Dad had provided a substantial table of refreshments back at our house, but hardly any of it was touched.

"Everywhere you looked people were weeping and crying, he was buried in the churchyard a family plot which goes back some six generations. The trouble was Peter was so young, it just didn't make any sense and clearly this is what affected most people, emotions were running high. The time round the grave was the worst, the drone of the priest, I didn't hear the words, but they seemed to go on forever and then it was all over, the thud of the soil hitting the top of the coffin was so finite."

I still had hold of her left hand, I was squeezing it. It felt moist and soft and then she turned towards me throwing herself against me and cried out, "Oh Vincent."

I hugged her close, saying soothingly, "It's alright," she felt warm and smelled sweet of Cussons Imperial Leather and I think I had decided it was Poison. (Oh sorry, I can see you're confused, the perfume I was trying to identify earlier). Our lips met and she kissed me lightly and then more deeply as if she was searching for some sort of release. Some reassurance, a promise of life and not death, that we were real and could touch and feel and be close and have feelings and as she sobbed on my shoulder my heart melted.

CHAPTER 9

I left it until late morning before taking a trip down to see Dean, not Jack I had to remember that, and see if he had given my proposal any thought. What his decision was, I thought I already knew. In preparation I made an attempt to tidy up the flat and tried out a few blankets and rugs on the sofa to see if I could make it homely or at least acceptable as a bed. But when you think about it anything would be better than lying on a hard tiled floor beneath a main line railway station. I also washed-up and put away anything that was lying about thinking the place would look better and more inviting if it was tidy. Déjà vu kicked in as it was only a few days ago that I had done the same thing for Harold expecting him to be staying for a week or so, but one night was enough before he was off to a decent hotel.

Once down the staircase I went straight to Dean's hideaway, he wasn't there so I decided to wait. I hadn't stipulated an exact time so I wasn't particularly surprised, I didn't fancy sitting amongst his mixture of blankets and cardboard, I was aware I didn't want to be associated with living amongst all this debris and apart from anything else it didn't smell too sweet. I made a mental note that one of the first things to do was to hit the launderette with all this stuff and also the clothes Dean was wearing, I may even try and lob him in as well. I hovered around and then went up to the main concourse and picked up a free handout paper and found a seat whilst I skimmed through the articles. I thought if I wasted half an hour he would probably be back by then.

When I returned sure enough Dean was sitting cross-legged munching on a pasty, where he got this I couldn't imagine, but I had my suspicions.

"Hi." I said.

He looked up and nodded.

"How do you feel?" I asked.

He nodded again.

"Are you okay?"

He nodded saying, "Yeah."

"Well, what do you think? Have you had enough time to think?"

He nodded again.

Here we go again I thought, back to the one-sided conversation and apart from that there is too much nodding.

"Well, what's the answer then?" I was trying to coax a response from him but I was beginning to think we had gone backwards not forward.

He finished his pasty and flicked the excess pastry from his fingers and then rubbed his hands together and looking up said, "Okay then. We'll give it a go."

"Good." I said not sure whether it was good or not. "Let's get your things together, perhaps if you roll that blanket out you could put all the other bits inside it."

He nodded and proceeded to follow my instructions. It didn't take long as you would expect a shirt, two pairs of socks an old coat, two blankets and a well-thumbed copy of *The Rainbow* by D.H. Lawrence, was hardly worthy of a removal company. The book was the surprising item, an old publication and of course an English classic, I remember studying it for O level. I suppose the eroticism may appeal to the young pubescent male about to embark on a journey of discovery into what makes girls tick, but I won't go into that because I fear I would need to write at least another volume. However, I was pleased to see there was perhaps some sort of literary interest there amongst Dean's inner thoughts.

We headed back to my flat where I introduced Dean to luxury far beyond his recent habitation and he appeared more than happy with it. He still wasn't talking much, but I expected and hoped this would change. I assumed there would be certain things I would have to buy like a toothbrush and a few groceries so I decided to head off to the local supermarket and give him some time to settle in on his own. Take the pressure of him a little, let him find his own way round, decide where he would like to dump his worldly goods.

I was very aware that I had to be very careful with how much I spent so I carefully studied all the special offers trying to get the best deals and value for money, buy one get one free that sort of thing.

I arrived back at the flat an hour or so later and as I climbed the stairs I was greeted by a deep base vibrating through the house. What the hell is that? I thought. It was definitely The Who, *My Generation* was beating out its message, but more to the point, why? I slipped my key into the lock to be confronted by Harold dancing round the lounge like some demented hippy and Dean sat back on the sofa in fits of laughter clutching a can of lager. My first thought was that Harold had completely lost it, a mental breakdown or something brought on by the bizarre happenings of the past few days. And then I thought, oh no. You know in that last resort sort of way when you just think, why me?

"What the hell's going on here?" I shouted above the noise and grabbed the digit box and pressed the volume control taking it to a manageable level.

"Oh Vince. Come on," yelped Harold.

"Hello, Harold, I see you've obviously met Dean. I have asked him if he would rather stay here for a while rather than in the underground system."

"Yes, I got that idea," he replied. "But I personally think you must have lost your mind, but that is up to you. I am going to be out of here soon, in fact that is what I came to tell you. I think my research at the coal face, so to speak, is up and I can go back to civilisation and construct my article."

"Really are you sure you've seen enough out on the street? Experienced enough first-hand?" I asked.

"Oh yes Vince, I've seen more than enough. I've seen a gang rape, attempted murder, I've been insulted, assaulted and offended by the sheer sight and smell of the great unwashed. Oh yes Vince, I've seen enough to last me several lifetimes. So I intend to leave you and your young friend here to carry on acting out your peasant existence of begging and living off the state, whilst I go back first to my hotel room and then tomorrow blend back into civilisation."

I wasn't going to rise to the bait. I had grown used to Harold insulting and putting me down over the past few weeks.

"Anyway my expense account is not a bottomless pit and I need to get back in front of the word processor and bash out a masterpiece of journalistic prose to provide our readers with a forthright and accurate account on what their taxes are spent on."

"Well whatever you say, Harold," I said.

"But I m not without gratitude," he said. "Because tonight is on me Vince, I am going to take you out and buy you a drink, just like all the other drinks I have bought you recently. But just to prove there are no hard feelings and to thank you for your help, because I couldn't have found all these misfits and their cardboard boxes without you, tonight the drinks and whatever you want to eat are on me."

"What about Dean?" I asked. "He has only just arrived today, we can't leave him here on his own."

Harold looked at Dean with a blank expression as if he had never seen the boy before. "Well I suppose he had better come as well."

"He's too young to go in a pub," I said.

Harold thought, took a swig from a can, I could see the cogs turning. "We'll smuggle him in, what the hell, in for a penny in for a pound. They won't notice in the Shipton, they probably wouldn't care even if they did. The boy must be sixteen so we can dust him up to look a little older, you must have some clothes he could wear. Some of your seventies stuff Vince, you know when you looked a real wanker."

I must admit I was waiting to be called that again and perhaps after this evening it may be the last time. I'll probably miss it when he's gone, hey that sounds a bit Bob Dylan.

* * * *

Well that was what we did after a bit of a clean-up, well I had a clean-up, it didn't seem to be in Dean's repertoire. So I decided I would deal with that another time, I gave him his toothpaste and brush and explained about the soap, water and towel. I know I haven't been the best example of civilised middle England for the past few months, but general hygiene and cleanliness is something you never forget.

While I washed and changed, Harold and Dean carried on drinking cans of lager, although I interspersed every so often explaining that Dean was barely a teenager. But I must admit he appeared to be handling it quite well.

We went to the Mother Shipton on the corner of Prince of Wales Road and Malden Road and to be honest it got a bit messy, they carried on with the lagers and I tucked into the Chardonnay, Harold suggested I had a bottle rather than keep on asking for another glass.

He said, "For God's sake Vince you bloody wanker have a fucking bottle and stop bothering me." He obviously had an eagle eye on his expense account, but what the hell, it was his last night mixing with us down and outs so as far as I was concerned he may as well keep buying, I am sure the newspaper could afford it.

There was a recommendation for fish and chips with a beer batter chalked up on the food board, so we all had that, I suspect the other two were seduced by the beer batter. But to be fair it was good, the batter crisp and light and the cod was succulent and fresh with big fat chips and a heap of tomato sauce splashed liberally over the top. We pushed our plates away and ordered another bottle of chardonnay and some more lagers, I noticed Dean was looking a little under the weather, but I carried on thinking he would get over it, I probably didn't appreciate how young he was. But it was only a matter of some ten minutes before he burped, leant forward and spewed lager, fish, and a mashed-up concoction of potato and ketchup across the table, I watched it drip off the edge onto Harold's trousers.

I must confess this bit made me smile, however, I suspected Harold wouldn't, but to my surprise he saw the funny side of it. But he was probably too far gone himself at this stage and just thought, what the hell tomorrow it will be all over.

It was this episode that enticed us to make our way back to my flat. Harold and I wobbled along either side of Dean who needed our support as he groaned and whined about the way he felt. It seemed a much longer walk home than it had been getting there, but finally we made it and having made an attempt to clean Dean up we laid him out on the sofa and it was only a matter of minutes before he was snoring like a grumpy old man.

Harold and I retired to my bedroom where we shared a final can of lager and in a rather silly way said our goodbyes as our use for each other had run its course. He would go back and write his article which no doubt would turn up in the national press on a day when there was very little news.

* * * *

The following morning I woke with a headache swearing I would never drink again, my mouth was full of fur and that dry stuff which makes you feel rank. Then I remembered Dean, I went through to the lounge and Dean was still out for the count, he must have drunk far too much and I had this pang of guilt which told me I should have been more responsible. He was clearly far too young to be sitting in pubs quaffing pints of lager all evening with a couple of irresponsible adults. I use the term loosely. But, still what's done is done, I can't change it now and in many respects it was Harold's last night and without his rather over-powering influence we won't be making a habit of such evenings.

I decided to cook a bit of breakfast hoping the smell of bacon would entice Dean to wake up. I had bought a few things like this yesterday evening as an enticement to make living with me a little more inviting. It gave my dole money for the week a bit of a belting, but I am just going to have to be even more careful than usual.

After I had had a bath I put the radio on in the kitchen, Capital Gold where they play a lot of the old ones from the sixties and seventies, and started up the frying pan, singing along to the music trying to make myself feel better. I toasted a few slices of bread and when the bacon hit the pan the aromas filled the room, a couple of tomatoes and it started to remind me of school breakfasts. When I turned round Dean was standing in the doorway.

"Hi.

How do you feel?" I asked.

He shook his head. "Not too good."

"Do you fancy some breakfast?"

He looked at the pans and I swear he turned green and ran out of the front door onto the landing and to the shared bathroom. I left him for a while and carried on cooking, I could always heat it up a bit later, he would feel better if he had some food inside him. The voice of experience, it always works but the first couple of mouthfuls can be difficult.

We sat down together about an hour later and both struggled through some breakfast, we left most of it but what we did have certainly helped to settle our stomachs. I put the remains back in the fridge in the hope it could be used in the near future for sandwiches or perhaps just warmed up. Every little would help now my dole cheque was going to have to stretch to two.

"Well Dean I think we ought to discuss some house rules if we are going to rub along together, don't you?"

He looked nervous and then said, "Yeah, okay."

"Firstly," I said. "I am going back to the job centre today, because to make ends meet I am going to have to get a job, I've been trying recently, but to be honest not with the sort of enthusiasm I should have been. I will have to take anything to bring some money in, bar work or perhaps retail, part-time office work even. Secondly, you should be at school, so I am not quite sure how we are going to deal with that at the moment?"

This made him look up from his plate. "No," he said. "I'll get a job, I'll find some work and it'll be fine."

"What do you mean? You're too young to have a job," I repeated my statement. "You should be at school." I was confused and wasn't sure where this would lead.

He looked at me picking bits of bacon fat from his teeth, "I don't want to go back to school, I've done that, I'll get a job."

I looked sceptical about this. Would I be doing something illegal housing a boy of this age and then letting him go out to work? It smacks a bit of Charles Kingsley's *Water Babies* where children were sent up chimneys at a very young age, climbing through the dark channels in order to sweep them.

"Well we'll see," I said. "Anyway, I want you to feel at home, look after the place, but do as you wish as well, we can work as a team to make the place homely and comfortable."

He nodded, I hoped he was keen to enter into the spirit of the thing.

"Well we will start now," I said clearing the plates away, whilst my head throbbed behind my eyes, but I was determined not to show it. I put on a brave face and retired to the kitchen, where I filled a bowl with hot water and proceeded to wash-up. I thought about the situation, if I looked back a couple of months I would never have bothered to wash-up until there wasn't any crockery left, in which case I would rinse a few items under the tap to see me through for a while.

Dean came to the kitchen door. "Okay, I'll do my best to help, but on this occasion, if you don't mind I would quite like to rest now."

I smiled understanding his feelings. "Of course," I said. "We will start tomorrow."

I must admit we both spent the rest of the day getting over our hangovers, the bacon and tomatoes with the toast acting as a good sponge for last night's alcohol, but we still had to make our own recovery. By late morning we had both settled down to sleep it off and I fell into a deep sleep of thoughts and reminiscences and Rachel bounced straight back into my dreams, but her face was Jane.

Since that evening when Rachel had struck me knocking me off my feet, things had not been the same between us, there was a distance. She only spoke to me when she had to and even then it was only to ask a question and tell me to do something, put the rubbish out, load the dishwasher. Isn't it about time you cut the grass? That sort of thing. She still carried on going out to all her church meetings and she also started going to a gym on Wednesday evenings, when she would change into a tracksuit, put trainers on her feet and with a sports bag over her shoulder leave the house usually before I got home, but always before seven o'clock.

On these occasions there would be a plated meal in the fridge for me with instructions on how long to heat it in the microwave. She never used to eat herself before going to the gym, said she would have something out once she had done the exercise, if she ate first it would give her indigestion. There was never an exact time she would come back, sometimes it was mid evening and others after eleven. If I was to question this she would just say she met up with some people for a drink in the leisure centre bar afterwards where she had had a salad or some pasta, the healthy type of options suitable to her activities.

The truth of it was I didn't know whether to believe her or not, I wanted to, but there was always this nagging doubt in the back of my mind. Something just wasn't right and I didn't know what it was. I decided to start following her, I even considered employing a private eye to do it, but I rejected this, it seemed too spooky. I would do it myself and for a few weeks I would follow her to her church meetings, and observe from a distance all the people going in and out and trying to assess any likely gigolos, but most were middle-aged women older than Rachel, two or three of her age and some older men, which in all honesty, didn't look very likely.

I didn't wait until the end of these meetings as there didn't seem much point and by the time she got home I was either curled up on the sofa watching TV or reading. I did a lot of reading in those days, I was trying to drink less after the previous incident as well, so I became involved in some very good novels. I used to pick them up from the local library every Saturday morning.

We had stopped making love at this stage, it didn't really seem the right thing to do after our fight or her fight, she being the one that knocked me out, but I suppose it depends how you look at it. The art of combat generally needs two protagonists, but on this occasion Rachel just clumped me and I went down like a sack of maris pipers. Since then she never approached me with any intimate suggestions and I thought, well one day we may get back to normal, but for now too much damage had been done. But I was prepared to wait, but for how long?

Then one evening I decided to stake out the gym, it had been bugging me for some weeks, I even consulted a colleague at work and he said, 'Vince you should check it out, I wouldn't put up with it'. Well when you think about it, he would say that wouldn't he? He's not taking the risk with his marriage, it's just the typical macho attitude, no one's going to take the piss out of me et cetera.

Anyway this particular Wednesday I was home early and I had had my dinner which was left out for me as usual. We had exchanged the usual pleasantries and Rachel had gone upstairs to change before going out and whilst I was drying up I thought to myself, tonight I will do some investigative work. So once she had left I gave her five minutes and jumped in the car, I had a three series BMW then, 2.3 litre engine, fast and responsive, just the sort of image for a city broker. I used to enjoy driving, the sense of power, speed and command over such an erratic and powerful piece of machinery.

The leisure centre was only about three miles away so when I arrived, Rachel was already there. I traced out her VW Golf and parked in a suitable spot so I would be able to view it without being easily observed. I was most likely only about ten minutes behind her so I gave her a few minutes to start her activities, took my brave pills and went for a nose round the centre. I told the girl on reception I may be interested in joining and would it be alright if I took a look around and checked out the facilities.

I walked past the squash courts and watched from the observation balcony, before moving on to the main hall, where the floor was marked out with a mixture of different coloured lines for five-a-side football, basketball and badminton courts. I then found the gym, I could peer through glass strips in the doors, the walls were covered with mirrors so I could get a full look at the whole of the room, albeit reflected from different angles. I scanned the room looking for Rachel and then I spotted her long shapely legs on one of those fast walking machines, the speed was turned up and she looked like a long distant walker, the way their hips bounced sideways with the strain of the walk. You know that sort of gunky movement when they gyrate their hips from side to side in the hope of extracting as much speed as possible from their legs.

I watched for a while appreciating her lovely figure and realising how lucky I was to have married her, she really was a stunning looking woman and I felt my stomach move with butterflies and excitement. Voyeurism can be a hypnotic tool.

I surveyed the rest of the room looking for any likely suitors, not sure whether I wanted to see the evidence or prove Rachel's innocence. There were three other women using running machines and bicycles.

Two men were using weight machines, one, probably early thirties was lying on his back and pushing up a heavy pile of metal slabs, his arm muscles straining, the veins sticking out taut. His face grimaced with the effort, moisture and sweat clinging to his skin.

The other man was younger, perhaps late twenties he was in the sitting position with his legs wrapped round circular pads on which he pulled backwards and forwards once again, moving a pile of weights up and down orchestrated by wires from the stack at the back of the machine.

The gym was clearly well-equipped and no doubt this would be reflected in the subscription and joining fees.

I was looking for some sort of recognition and sign between either of the two men and Rachel, but nothing was obvious, too much concentration on what they were doing I thought. Too much exertion, lungs expanded and muscles stretching and contracting with the effort. I kept watching hoping for a clue, anything that would give her away, but what did I want to know? Did I want her to be having an affair? I wasn't clear in my mind, if she was guilty I wanted to know, but really I wanted her to be innocent. I didn't want my life to change, I didn't want it to fall apart, it was too comfortable and I truly did love Rachel.

I realised I couldn't stay here for much longer without the risk of being noticed, so I thanked a different girl on reception saying I would give it some thought and be in touch. I went back to my car where I sat for a while and pondered the situation, wondering how I would get home before Rachel if she was to come out whilst I was still sitting in the car park.

CHAPTER 10

Dean and I slept most of the day and all the next night and then the following morning we both woke refreshed and in a funny sort of way, I thought, raring to go and this to my way of thinking was unusual. But of course a year or so ago I was always ready to perform. The city was a full-on environment with no room for time wasters or losers, if you couldn't keep up you were out. I was good in that sort of atmosphere and it paid off, the results were good and I made a lot of money for Rachel and I, we had a lovely house and a substantial bank account, our mortgage was low and we lived within our means, but never wanting for anything. But I digress, I must get into the habit of telling the story and not keep returning to the past where history is the author.

We were up fairly early, we ate ravenously after a day of almost total abstention and then I headed for the job centre leaving Dean to find his feet, and I hoped in an industrial sort of way. I sincerely believed he was not at all stupid and would easily make a success of himself, but I realised I had to be prepared to coax and guide at the right moments in order to funnel his talents down the right channel. When you think about it, it is quite a challenge really and perhaps this is exactly what I needed to put my life back on track.

I went to the job centre with a renewed attitude and a spring in my step, I needed a job and if it wasn't behind a plush desk with a contract promising bonuses and expense accounts, so what! A menial position with the expectation of a few quid in my pocket at the end of the week would suffice and could even be exciting.

"Mr Sleeve, are you listening to me?"

"Yes I'm sorry," I was disturbed from my daydream.

The young kid with the spotty face behind the desk was staring at me in a frustrated way, but he continued. "Yes as I was saying a local contractor is looking for labourers to move about materials, plasterboards, plywood, MDF et cetera so it is in the right areas for their carpenters to work on."

"You mean humpers?" I replied. I had heard of humpers before, building contractors employ them purely to hump boards about. But I wasn't prepared for exactly how hard it would be, I have never been the most physical of men.

"Well I suppose so, if you put it like that."

I gazed at the worm the other side of the desk and realised I was better than this. I had been living an inferior existence for some time now and I had been prepared to be bullied by bureaucratic assholes like this revolting little tick in front of me now, but no more, the game was up.

"I'll take it." I shuddered, wondering what I may be letting myself in for, but of course now I have responsibilities.

"Well we will just have to fill out these forms then," he pulled a bundle of paperwork from the desk drawer as if it was unusual that anyone ever actually accepted a position and having looked back at the line of individuals in the queue I wasn't at all surprised. I turned my mind off to the form filling, an essential to modern living which I find hard to adhere to. I answered the questions with a sense of robotic acceptance realising there was no way forward until this bizarre performance of communistic and autocratic theatre was acted out in order for me to become a humper. My boredom threshold was being tested, but I played along in preparation to start my career in the building trade.

I walked home anticipating my early start the following morning at a site just north of Kings Cross Station in York Way. It used to be an old cement works, now being developed into blocks of flats and it seems my job is most likely going to be moving heavy boards from ground level to the appropriate floors for the tradesman to fix. Oh well, I said I would have to obtain some useful employment to make ends meet, so perhaps this is it.

I was to start tomorrow, eight o'clock reporting at the site office to collect my hard hat and regulation steel-capped boots in order to keep within the bounds of the health and safety regulations, which as we all know are paramount and more important than the construction itself. It is strange how this pariah of regulation and bureaucracy has overtaken our general common sense and understanding of what is right and wrong. I blame it on the Russians, you may think that a little flippant, but just think about communism, *Animal Farm*, the way the pigs took over and all the other animals just fell in line and accepted all the changes. Occasionally they would question new rules and regulations, but this was short-lived and they soon lived under their suppressed conditions. Is this any different to our present government which clearly have dictatorial aspirations?

I contemplated the type of work I would be doing, I had never done much physical stuff before, but I considered myself to be fairly fit and anyway it may do me some good. As I walked home my thoughts turned to Jane and how I wanted to see her again and learn more about her and ultimately, I wanted to be able to help her. I wondered how I could make the time for her whilst not making Dean feel as if he was being ignored. I will have to give this some thought, because I don't want to make him feel uncomfortable and unwanted. Because I suspect that has probably happened often enough in his short life already, and may well be one of the major reasons why he has been living the way he has.

When I arrived home the flat was empty, but I was sure it was cleaner than when I left it a few hours ago. I had given Dean a key, I know it could be a bit risky, but I decided that if I didn't show trust towards him right from the start how could I expect him to trust me? I had to do everything I could to make him feel welcome and at home.

I loafed about waiting for what, I didn't really know, the sun had been beating down all day and it was hot, it was coming to the end of the summer but the air had been heating up for weeks and it now seemed to be constantly sweltering. London itself has absorbed the heat, the buildings and roads have acted as storage heaters and radiate a constant warmth.

At about four, I heard a key in the door and in came Dean carrying some loose bits and pieces which he placed in the kitchen.

"I've brought dinner in," he said proudly.

"Oh yes." I said a little surprised, walking into the kitchen.

"Sausages," he said, producing a string of eight from a bag, "and some rolls."

"Where did you get these?" I asked.

"In the High Street."

"Where in the High Street?"

"The butchers and the bakers, I thought that would be fairly obvious."

"I think you know what I mean Dean, how did you pay for them?" I was worried about this situation because I couldn't imagine how he would have enough money to buy dinner, but on the other hand I didn't want to dampen his thoughtfulness.

"I bought the rolls Vince." He hadn't used my name before.

"What about the sausages?" I asked.

"I only had one pound forty so I bought the rolls, I figured you had some butter and then I thought we would need something to go with the bread so I went to the butchers and I saw the sausages in the window just beside the door. They were all joined together and they looked good and juicy and the man had gone out to the back of the shop. I looked at the price and then at the change in my hand and decided I didn't have enough so I picked them up and threw them into the bag with the rolls and was gone." He was still looking pleased with himself.

"So this rather explains that incident last week in The Strand when that man chased you through the station and gave you a beating for his trouble. You had stolen from him as well hadn't you?"

He shoved his hands in his pockets and bowed his head looking a little sheepish.

I pushed him for an answer. "Well?"

He looked up. "Yeah, well last week I was hungry, it was hard finding food each day. Anyway it was only a pasty off a stall. He wouldn't miss it, you want to see how many he sells when all the tourists are around."

"That isn't the point Dean. You don't steal from anybody. Where did you get the money from in the first place?"

"Oh that's easy people throw coins in my direction when I'm sitting in the station. As they pass running for the trains they see me and chuck coins at my feet." He clearly thought this was okay, well perhaps it is.

I decided to change the subject I had made my point and hoped he would take it on board, "Okay Dean, now listen to me." I sat him

155

down in the lounge. "I have been to the job centre today and am going to start tomorrow morning on a building site in York Way. This will help us to be able to make ends meet, the money isn't bad and I want us to make a go of it. But not by stealing from other people."

He shifted uncomfortably in his seat and then said, "You. Working on a building site?"

"Yes why? What is so funny about that?"

"You don't look the sort."

I ignored this remark and continued. "You of course should be at school, you're an intelligent boy you will soak up the information like a sponge. But I am realistic enough to understand that it is not for me to try and enforce it, I am not your parent or legal guardian, I just want to be a friend and help you. As you know I was very concerned seeing you sleeping rough in the station and worried for you in what is a very dangerous environment. So I think it may be best if you were to go out and try and find some part-time work, I am not sure in what field. You can't sign on at the job centre because of your age and they will just say you should be at school. Perhaps the market stalls or some sort of labouring, I don't know, but if you give it some thought, because if we are going to make ends meet I can't do it just on my own." I smiled trying to reassure him, I didn't want him to think I was having a go at him after he had only been here for a day or so.

He smiled and appeared to be quite keen on the idea. "Yeah, okay, I will start looking tomorrow."

"Good," I said. "Now you've got a key, I would like to emphasise that you are here every evening unless you have told me otherwise, just so I can be aware of your movements for my own peace of mind, not because I am ordering you about. We will then try and eat together every evening and it will give us the opportunities to catch up on what we have both been doing during the day and will give us some sort of stability." I didn't want to lay down too many rules either, but I also wanted to create an understanding.

Dean was nodding so I was satisfied for now, we could work together.

"And one other thing –" and then I was interrupted by a sharp bang on the door. "Who the hell is that?" I said getting up and walking through to the front door, I put my eye to the spyhole and came face to face with Hilary's globe peering back at me. Shit I thought and opened the door not too far, but just enough for Hilary to force her foot in the gap followed by herself as she planted a fat, wet kiss firmly on my lips.

"Vincent, have you been avoiding me?"

"No," I stuttered, I don't know why I always stutter when I am confronted by Hilary in fighting mood.

"Or have you found someone else to amuse you?" She grasped my penis firmly with her right hand and rubbed it through my jeans and I felt a familiar stir as she looked invitingly into my eyes with a suggestive sneer.

"No," I stuttered again, "I... I'v... got..."

"Oh for goodness sake Vince stop burbling like a stuck pig," she let go of my penis and pushed me towards the bedroom.

"Look Hilary, I've got a frien..."

She pinned me to the wall with her lips pressed firmly against mine trying to prise my mouth open and when she found resistance once again grabbed my penis more firmly this time and instantly got what she wanted as I howled with pain.

When I came up for air I escaped along the wall just long enough to try and explain about Dean being next door in the lounge, but as I looked up Dean was not next door but standing an arm's length from me with a confused, albeit a humorous expression on his face.

"I..." I stuttered again.

"What's going on Vince?" asked Hilary.

This time I was determined not to stutter so I prepared myself, took a deep breath and said, "Hilary meet Dean. Dean, meet Hilary."

They both looked at each other uncertain what to do next.

"Well Vince who is Dean, some sort of relation or something?"

"No. I met Dean at Charing Cross Station." I replied.

"Vince, what are you trying to tell me?" Hilary looked askance, horrified and then I realised what she was thinking.

"No, Hilary not like that he was sleeping rough and I saw him a couple of times when I was out with Harold researching for his article and once I even witnessed him getting into a bit of trouble. And I thought, well it would be best if, perhaps he came back to stay here, with me. I just thought he was so vulnerable in that dangerous environment I was scared for him and wanted to do something to help."

"You are joking Vince, aren't you?" She had a confused expression on her face.

"No, Hilary, that is exactly what happened, I had been helping Harold with his research, you remember Harold he came to your party."

"Yes of course, I remember Harold he was a bloody lecher, now get on with it." She was looking sterner now.

"Well we did a lot of our research around The Strand and Charing Cross Station and that is where we came across Dean here," I gestured in Dean's direction hoping to divert Hilary's stare from pinpointing me. "He was sleeping rough in the angle of the soffit of one of the underground staircases and well to be honest it didn't seem a suitable environment for a young man to be living in, so I suggested he came back here to share my meagre existence."

Hilary carried on staring at me while she pulled at the hairs growing from her mole and then asked, "Okay Vince, where does this leave us?" she glared at me as she pinned me to the wall again.

"What?"

"You and me Vince, we have been sleeping together, we have been sharing some extremely satisfying experiences, I thought you may have noticed."

"Yes of course I did." I wasn't sure how to respond, I didn't want to encourage her too much because of Jane, but also I didn't want to discourage her either because, as she had said, it had been good. God what a mess to get into, only a few weeks ago I didn't have a social life and now I seem to have more than I can cope with. "It's just that I want to help Dean, there is no need for it to make any difference to us."

Meanwhile Dean was leaning against the door frame taking it all in.

"Well it quite clearly will," she responded. "You're hardly going to bundle me into your bedroom right now and bonk me senseless are you?"

I was lost for words as she was undoubtedly right. "Well no, I suppose not." I glanced at Dean whom I swear had a knowing smirk on his face, which I had a violent desire to wipe off.

"I rest my case," she retorted.

"But there will be other times," I stammered.

"I won't hold my breath," she shouted and slammed the door behind her.

I turned and looked at Dean and said, "We had better start cooking those sausages I suppose, come on I'll show you the way around the kitchen."

"Okay." He followed me into the kitchen and then said, "Is she your girlfriend then?"

"No," I said. "Well, yes I suppose so in a funny sort of way she has been, but perhaps it's over now."

And we both laughed together, it was good, it broke the ice and I felt a sort of camaraderie between the two of us developing. Boys together you know. Oh yes I can see what you are thinking old Vince has completely lost his marbles, he has refused the advances of a voluptuous young woman who bonks like a viper and befriended a waif and stray off the street. Well you are probably right, but I am not going to make that change my mind, anyway I think we ought to get on with our sausages and rolls and if I am lucky enough to find some tomato ketchup in one of the cupboards we will be in for a bit of a feast.

* * * *

The next morning I was on parade at eight o'clock dressed like a navvy and shaking like a leaf wondering if it was likely I would have the physical strength and the lack of brain power to spend the day humping boards of different sizes, different densities and constructed from different materials. Not just once but all day, from one level to another and then to a different level just in case there weren't enough on the first level and they wanted some more on the next level. I thought about it and came to the conclusion that the foreman or ganger as some of the lads called him, was instructing us just to satisfy his own ego.

The morning went fairly quickly as I was trying to concentrate my mind on carrying boards from one level to another, trying to focus on the job in hand, but once you've carried one sheet of shuttering plywood (whatever the hell that is) 4880 x 2440 x 18mm thick from one level to another you have kind of lost your enthusiasm. But just go a step further and repeat the process ten-fold and you lose the will to live.

However, there is the odd interlude when you are asked to transport plasterboards, these appear to be of similar dimensions, but are only 12.5mm thick, although to be honest this does not detract from their weight as they are packed in twos, thereby giving a total thickness of 25mm. And the corners of the staircase pose further problems as it is easy to scuff the corners of the boards, which in the case of the plywood is relatively unimportant, but as I was severely reminded by the ganger, in the case of the plasterboards it is pretty serious.

"Sleeve watch the fucking corners of those boards, fuck them up and you'll be looking to the bottom of your pay packet before you'll find any coppers."

As you can see I took to physical work like a duck to the abattoir, mesmerised and a trifle confused, but I was determined to persevere, I had to for the sake of Dean and my own future. I carried my thoughts with me. Rachel whom I had loved dearly and it was only jealousy and lack of control that drove me deep into destruction, and now Jane, a lady that I can't clearly describe because I still don't know her.

But I knew I wanted to be with her, discover her troubles, what has made her so sad, what has affected her life so deeply that she sits in a darkened room in a basement flat in Kentish Town, being waited on by a questionable companion. I am sure it must be something that I can help her with, help her come to terms with.

I feel uncomfortable with Tina's presence, or perhaps I don't trust her motives, but on the other hand why should Tina trust me? And she probably doesn't.

What a mixed up world we live in, the older we get the more confused it becomes, the more experiences there are behind us the harder it seems to cope with what we've got. Take young Dean as an example, even though he has had a pretty rough life to date, he still has very few worries because there are so few experiences behind him and there are so many more ahead. But as the years go by the tables turn and there are so many memories behind you and so little time ahead and you become confused and dare I say it again, a little melancholy. With this thought I smiled whilst carrying another eight by four sheet of three-quarter inch plywood up three flights of stairs.

There you are, did you see the way I dropped into the imperial language? I am sorry that was the essence of my education in the late sixties and early seventies, but it did seem to make more sense. Two hundred and forty pence to the pound, twelve pennies to a shilling, a florin or half a crown or two and six depending how you thought of it. Some people would call it half a dollar, an Americanism, a crown, five shillings being a crown. Crowns in more modern times were commemorative, in memory of Churchill or to note the Queen's birthday or jubilee, let's hope we don't get one for Tony Blair that would certainly be a move too far. Oops, I am showing my age. I had better change the subject.

Then there were inches, feet and yards, chains (the length of a cricket pitch) poles and perches, furlongs and miles et cetera. It was great, so much easier to understand than all this metric nonsense. I realise I have now completely confused the younger reader and some may even be considering my sanity.

You can see how my brain was working. I was just trying to escape from the mundaneness of carrying eight by four boards from one level to another with very little time to catch one's breath before repeating the operation. Well this is certainly a job for the guys with muscles for brains and doesn't suit the intellectuals, such as myself. Okay I would rather you didn't react like that, but I think you must agree I am more suited to the gentler activities than the physical, except where Hilary is concerned. There I've said it for you, I knew that one was coming.

By the time I arrived home that night my arms felt as if they didn't belong to me anymore and they were bulging throbbing appendages which I couldn't control. They hung beside me as I wandered drunkenly from exhaustion through the side turnings of

Kentish Town in a coma of tiredness and fatigue, wondering how on earth I was going to be ready to carry on again tomorrow, I didn't know.

* * * *

I woke this morning ready to jump out of bed and get ready for work when I suddenly realised it was Saturday and flopped back onto the pillow. I have now completed three days of humping boards and am completely knackered, but I plan to keep at it until I can find something easier and more suitable. The money is quite good and I was given an advance against my first week's labours yesterday so that will make things a little better. Dean has settled in to my cosy little flat quite well, so today I thought I would call on Jane as I haven't seen her for a few days. The thought of this quite excited me and I decided after breakfast I would make sure Dean was okay and perhaps suggest I took Jane out somewhere. So I decided to get up and get the day going (there I'm doing it now, a slovenly misuse of the word 'get').

Dean was becoming far more talkative and had been telling me about his background. He was brought up in Manchester by his Aunt Ellen, his father's sister and her husband, but they didn't really want him, his parents had both been killed in a motor accident. A juggernaut went out of control and crushed their Ford Escort on the M1 one wet foggy winter's evening seven years ago.

Six months ago Dean had had enough of living in an unloved situation with his aunt and hitched a ride out of the north-west and up to the capital where he has been fending for himself ever since. Before settling down in Charing Cross he had been sleeping around the Kings Cross area, but as he described it himself you get a better class of tramp in Westminster.

"Dean," I said. "How are you finding it here, are you settling in alright?"

"Yeah, it's okay, better than sleeping in the station." He hesitated, "I went down Camden Lock yesterday and mooched around the stalls, it's an exciting place you know."

I nodded. "Yes I suppose it is."

"I asked around if anyone wanted a hand, you know I would do anything and a few of them said I could move boxes around and unpack them. All the stallholders know each other so there are a group of about six doing fruit and veg and clothes and a second-hand record stall. They said they would club together and give me a bit of pocket money if I pulled my weight."

"Good, at least that's something," I said. "When do you start?"

"Today, being Saturday it's the busiest day of the week." With this he gulped down his tea and pushed his chair back.

"Another thing," he stopped and waited. "Clothes, I think you need to get a few more clothes you are restricted to one pair of trousers and a couple of shirts and to be honest they all need washing." I didn't want to push this too far, but it was definitely true.

He looked at me and then sniffed under his arms. "Yeah you're right, I'll have a look round the market, perhaps I could get a few bits instead of my wages to start with."

"Yes that's a good idea." I was pleased he had taken it so well. "Before you go Dean there is something else I wanted to mention."

He stopped in his tracks and stood waiting, I don't know what he was expecting this time.

"There is a lady who lives in the basement flat, her name is Jane, she is not in particularly good health and well, I will probably be popping down to see her later. Just thought I would let you know, in case you came back and wondered where I was."

"You're a bit of a dark horse aren't you? First it was that Hilary bird the other night and now there's another one downstairs, now what's her name?" He asked.

"Jane," I answered.

"That's nice, well good luck." he said and was gone.

I shrugged to myself, well that wasn't too hard, I hope he makes a go of it in Camden Lock, he seems the sort of boy that isn't scared of a bit of hard work.

CHAPTER 11

I shivered as I stood on the doorstep, the recent hot spell of weather had taken a turn for the worse and dark clouds filled the sky, the temperature had dropped considerably although the buildings and roads still gave off a stored warmth. I had already knocked twice and was starting to get the feeling that perhaps there wasn't anyone in, but this was unlikely I thought. I glanced at my watch just after midday and then the door opened a few inches, it was Tina as usual, she looked at me as if she had never seen me before, but I now realised this was her normal greeting.

If you saw too much of Tina you could get an inferiority complex as she always gave the impression you were so insignificant that she never recognised you.

"I was just wondering if Jane was in," I said.

I could almost see the feathers rise on the back of her neck before she answered. "She's in bed."

"Oh. At this hour?" I questioned a little too rudely I suspected.

"She is not feeling too well this morning."

"Oh, I'm sorry to hear that, um. Shall I come back later?"

She started to nod her head when I heard Jane's voice from the background. "Who is it?"

"It's the bloke from upstairs again," she called back.

"Vince," I said trying to project my voice into the passage and round the odd corner in the hope it would reach its destination. I would have thought Tina may have managed to remember my name, especially seeing as I had provided her with an Indian takeaway a few evenings ago, but still I don't think it's her style to appease people.

"Oh." The voice hesitated from the depths of the flat. "Show him in Tina, but give me a few minutes to freshen up."

After some ten minutes of hanging about in the lounge under the severe gaze of Tina who clearly would rather I wasn't there, I was ushered into Jane's bedroom, she was sitting up in bed leaning against a bank of pillows for support. She had clearly tended her beautiful hair and prepared for me, this made me feel good and I smiled broadly as she gestured for me to sit on the edge of her bed. Before sitting I kissed her gently on the cheek taking in the sweet scent of newly applied potions.

She held my hand in hers resting on the covers of the bed. "It's good to see you Vincent, I thought you were ignoring me, you haven't called in for a few days now?"

So I told her about Dean and that he had moved into my flat upstairs, she appeared very interested and was keen to meet him. I told her about my new job humping boards about, but made it sound less physical than it really was. She seemed concerned for my welfare probably thinking I was far too weak and puny to be carrying out such strong man work. We talked easily for some time with my hand resting comfortably in hers with her thumb constantly caressing and stroking it, before I asked her to continue the story of her life.

"Where was I?" she asked.

"The last thing you mentioned was Peter's funeral," I offered.

"Oh yes, Peter was dead." She hesitated, I was hoping returning to these memories would not bring on her tears again. But no she continued.

"I returned to my studies and threw all my enthusiasm into them, I was determined to make a success of my career if only to make up for Peter's early demise. And everything was going well, I was getting good recommendations from the tutors and my test results were good, but there was always this black spot at the back of my mind. There was something missing and of course it was my brother, we grew up together and then suddenly whilst I was still young he was violently taken away from me."

I squeezed her hand tightly and looked intently into her face and I felt so humble but with such a desire to reach out and comfort her and do anything I could to make everything right.

"Are you alright?" I asked.

She smiled. "Yes. I do like you being here Vincent you make me feel good and kind of content."

"I like being here as well. With you," I added. I liked the way she calls me Vincent, unlike most other people who just call me Vince or in Harold's case you bloody wanker Vince.

She smiled again, that beautiful smile, it made me think briefly of Hilary, a nice girl and a whirlwind when it came to sex, but Jane was so much more, perhaps I would even be prepared to become celibate if that was what she wanted, just to see that smile. Anything to be with her, enjoy her company and hopefully be able to help her.

She carried on talking. "It was during the next twelve months that I picked up a virus and within two days I was diagnosed with glandular fever, it was so debilitating, and my body couldn't cope with it. I just went from bad to worse, all the energy was knocked out of me. I spent days in bed and found I was getting more and more tired, my glands had gone down, but I wasn't recovering, if anything I was getting worse. I didn't know why, but I knew something was wrong, my muscles ached and I always felt tired, there was something not right. And the frightening thing was, I didn't know what it was. I went to the doctor, my mother insisted on it and she also came with me, but the doctor wasn't giving me any answers, and this made me worry more and more. Vincent!" she looked at me with fear in her eyes.

"This is when I felt really scared, I had got over the glandular fever, but something else was nagging at my metabolism like it was picking at a sore and wouldn't let go. I didn't know what to do and it took me over. Vince it actually took over my life."

"What do you mean? What took over your life?" I asked hoping for a more precise explanation and understanding of Jane's problems.

"What do you mean what took over my life? This fucking disease of course," she shouted.

I sat back and let go of her hand surprised by the sudden change in her personality, her expression was acid and I was scared, I hadn't seen that look in her eyes before. She looked wild, her eyes were wild and I didn't know what to make of it.

"I am so sorry Vincent," her persona had changed suddenly and she grabbed my hand again and then she flopped back onto the pillows, her breathing was hard and fast and she looked exhausted. Her eyes rolled, and her expression hardened and then they closed.

Her grip on my hand had slackened and within seconds she was asleep.

I didn't know what to do, I sat there motionless, but within seconds of Jane falling asleep the door opened and Tina came in, looked at Jane and then at me. "I think you had better leave," she said. "Jane needs her rest, she hasn't had a good day."

I was disappointed but accepted what Tina said, because in all honesty what else could I do? I wanted to ask Tina what the matter was, but thought better of it, in a strange sort of way Tina frightened me.

* * * *

The following morning there was a knock on my door and to my surprise it was Tina, she had a message for me from Jane. She firstly apologised for her rudeness the previous day and said she would love to see me again today, and perhaps I would like to pop in for lunch, they were having salad. Tina delivered this message in her usual uninspired droll and hardly waiting for my response, had turned to leave when I confirmed I would love to come and would knock about one if that was okay.

And this is why I was once again seated beside Jane in her lounge having finished our salad of cold meats, the usual greenery, tomatoes, beetroot and coleslaw and some very fresh French bread. She was obviously feeling better today and having made her apologies again for yesterday she appeared to be very chirpy.

Having covered the usual pleasantries I was itching to know more about, and of course, what was wrong with her? So I thought I would just come out and ask her. "Jane. I would really like to know, what is actually wrong with you? What illness is it you've got that makes you sit here all day wrapped up like this?"

She looked a little surprised as if I should already know, and then said, "ME, or to be more precise Chronic Fatigue Syndrome."

"Oh, I don't know much about that I'm afraid, I understand it can be very debilitating though." I didn't know what else to say.

"Yes," she said. "That is why I am like this." She gestured to her sitting position. "That is why other days I am like I was yesterday,

167

weak, lethargic with no energy and I get tired so easily. My temper can be short, like you witnessed yesterday, for which I feel I will always be apologising."

"How long has this been going on?" I wondered.

"It developed from the glandular fever, as I said yesterday, the swelling had gone down and the virus had gone but I was left tired and weak and I couldn't snap out of it. I developed muscle pains which made walking and moving about difficult and my energy levels dropped, but this could have been to do with the lack of exercise I was getting and therefore I was just losing my fitness. I had always enjoyed sports at school, hockey, netball and swimming, but now I couldn't imagine being able to run around a hockey field or even swim one length of the pool."

She had stopped talking, I presumed thinking of the past.

There was so much I wanted to ask. "Yesterday," I started. "You were clearly down, does that last for long? Do you get any warnings? And how often does that happen?"

She laughed. "Hold on Vincent, one question at a time. Yes I was low yesterday although I enjoyed your company I also knew I was tiring myself out and in a way that is why I snapped. It usually lasts up to about twenty-four hours, but if I get a good night's sleep, which I did last night I am usually back to normal in the morning, if you call this normal." She once again gesticulated towards her current position before continuing.

"The bad days can happen very often, but other times I can go weeks and even months without the experience. It's a bit like a migraine which can be frequently repeated and then many months can pass without a reoccurrence."

"When was the last bad day?"

She stopped to think. "Just over two weeks ago I think, yes it was a Thursday so about two and a half weeks ago, it followed a similar pattern really, starting about the same time of day and having gone to bed quite early, by the following morning I was alright again."

We were seated in the lounge side by side as before and I took her hand again, it was soft and warm and I liked the feeling as it nestled in mine. I ran my fingers over hers and along the nails which were neatly manicured to a feminine shape, the cuticles had also been carefully tended and felt polished.

She turned towards me and smiled, "I like being with you Vincent, I just wish I could be more active for you."

I saw my opportunity and leapt in with both feet. "Well perhaps you can, why don't you let me take you out?"

"Oh I don't know I haven't been out for –" she thought, "I don't know how long, it must be at least six months."

"It hasn't got to be far, perhaps just to the park or the cinema or even a restaurant." I was trying to think of somewhere simple and easy to get to, I realised our relationship could only move forward if we could get away from this room and of course, the threat of Tina overlooking our every move.

"Vincent it would be lovely but, I don't know if I could." She squeezed my hand tightly, excitedly.

"But I think this is what you need, you need to get out, you can't just vegetate in this environment forever. You need to get out, breathe fresh air and get some exercise." I hoped I hadn't gone too far, I could see a fear on Jane's face, but I also thought I detected a sense of excitement as well.

"Vincent I want you to listen to me," she looked deep into my eyes, I could feel genuine feelings and emotions. "I want you to keep coming and seeing me and during the next week I am going to come to terms with going out next weekend. I don't want to know where we are going, I am going to leave that entirely up to you, a surprise. I will find it easier that way, but I am going to make every effort to prepare myself and enjoy the experience."

I leant towards her and kissed her tenderly and then more deeply, as she put her arm around my neck she pulled me closer and tighter to her. My heart leapt with excitement and emotion and I realised finally that I couldn't let this woman go, I just had to do everything I could to build a relationship and to help her with her problems. Then I whispered through her hair. "Leave it to me."

* * * *

I worked through the next week humping boards from the delivery area to all floors and distributing them to different rooms as requested by the carpenters. There were four of us operating in pairs, I was working with a fellow called Brett, he was a body builder, he spent a lot of time moving weights in the gym and he used the job as an ideal way to keep up his fitness levels as well. We got on quite well although I couldn't really describe him as an intellectual, but he certainly made me laugh with some of the stories he told about his evenings out with his friends. The lifting and straining, whilst supporting the weight of some of the eighteen millimetre boards took a toll on my muscles and with Brett's joking and funny remarks on occasions I was doubled up with pain from my stomach muscles.

The plasterboards were joined together in pairs and I found them very difficult to control because they had added flexibility which the more solid boards and MDF didn't have. I would stagger up the flights of stairs looking forward to the slight reprieve on each landing and then Brett would jog back downstairs to collect the next one, where he would have to wait for me at the bottom. It was hard, but I also felt it was doing me good and I was becoming much fitter and dare I say it, stronger too.

I spent my evenings trying to keep Dean company, who I must admit I was beginning to like very much, he is an intelligent boy and all he really needs are some decent breaks. Perhaps I will be able to contribute to this in some way or another. He was always up early and had always left for the market by six thirty, which gave me another half an hour or so to tidy up the flat and if possible peel some potatoes or prepare something for the evening. He had chosen a few clothes from the stalls so at least he had enough for us to put into operation a rotation system.

He would come back tired as I did and after our meal we would watch the TV or play some of my old records, he liked The Beatles and The Kinks and I was trying to educate him in the appreciation of Bob Dylan, however this was a little more difficult.

Like me he was doing a lot of physical work during the day and was happy to lounge about in the evenings and go to bed early. We kept off the beers and wines after the episode with Harold and restricted it to a couple of glasses at weekends. This was also essential to keep the finances in order.

During the week I only saw Jane once on the Wednesday evening. I told Dean where I was going and he said go ahead with a smirk on his face and by the time I came back he was fast asleep on the sofa.

Jane and I just talked and I tried to find out more about her illness without appearing to pry or upset her. We agreed I would take her out on the Saturday, providing she was strong enough of course, and not having a bad day. I would decide where we would go and as I was being very frugal with my money I would be able to afford a black cab if necessary.

I also hadn't seen Hilary since the afternoon when she burst out of my flat slamming the door behind her, until I came back on the Wednesday evening from Jane's and I caught a glimpse of her climbing the stairs ahead of me arm in arm with… I looked carefully trying to identify the human shape, it was Simon Cheek.

Well. Well, I thought, he gets everywhere. They were both talking very loudly and swaying from side to side I suspect a little too much wine had been imbibed. Oh well, I thought to myself, perhaps it's for the best. Although the sex was good with Hilary it was purely a carnal desire, I didn't have the same deep feelings that were building and growing inside me with Jane and I expect there was no possibility of a long-term relationship with Hilary and would I want that anyway?

I kept quiet until the door of Hilary's flat closed before climbing the staircase to my own front door.

* * * *

I wanted to find a way of helping Jane, I wanted her to get well, I wanted her to start living again. I was sure her illness, although very debilitating was more in the mind than a physical phenomena, though it was undoubtedly affecting her muscles, movement and energy levels. But could this be because of lack of exercise and lack of confidence, her confidence had been severely dented following the death of her brother and then the glandular fever. Which can be a very nasty virus and then she threw everything into her studies, probably over-working and then her health, just nose-dived.

I visited the local library on my way home from work on the Friday afternoon, we always finish an hour earlier on Fridays so it gave me some time before they closed. I searched through a number of medical publications trying to learn all I could about ME, its cause, cures and its effects on the individual and those around them. I photocopied a number of pages which I could take away with me to study in more detail, I wanted to learn enough about the illness so I could understand what she was suffering and how best I could help.

I read through the sheets and it seems as if Chronic Fatigue Syndrome is most likely brought on by stress and is more likely to affect adults between the ages of twenty and forty. It seems as though the usual period for the illness to last is about four years, but of course it could be more, or it could be less. The symptoms are quite wide ranging and presumably one doesn't necessarily suffer from all of them, they are as follows: muscle pain, sleep disturbance, tiredness and difficulty in concentrating, abnormal temperature control, memory loss and emotional and mood fluctuations.

Whilst reading this I tried to relate each symptom to how I interpreted Jane's conditions, she obviously has muscle pains and difficulty walking, she is affected by tiredness and finds concentration difficult. Well it all seems to tie up but what can we do to cure it, the books say there is no specific treatment, but medication can be used to reduce allergic reactions and relieve pain. However, lifestyle changes, such as increased rest and reducing stress can help to diminish the power of the virus, also exercise, however little can be of valuable help.

If I can put more interest back into her life this could go a long way to generally making her feel better and perhaps quicken her recovery. With this in mind I felt a little better and thought if I could formulate some sort of plan to improve her lifestyle I may be able to bring her out of this debilitating state.

* * * *

I thought I had better explain to Dean about Jane or did I just want to talk about her? When a girl gets into your soul like Jane has with me, you just want to tell everyone. You just want to talk whether anyone wants to listen or not.

It was Friday evening and we had both come in from work, Dean was cleaning himself up in the bathroom, something I always had to encourage him to do before we sat down for our dinner. I was cooking a mixture of fresh vegetables which Dean had brought in from the market stalls: peppers, courgettes, mushrooms, onions and baby corn, thrown some soy sauce in with it, cubed chicken breast and some rice. I can hear what you are thinking this is a bit different from a few weeks ago when I was living off cheap wine and bread and water and with little choice in the cupboards.

"Dean," I said when he came back into the lounge, "you know I told you I was going to see Jane in the basement flat on Wednesday?"

"Yep," he called.

"She is not at all well, she has an illness called ME, it is very debilitating, meaning she hasn't got any energy, she can't move about easily, her muscles hurt et cetera. Well I am going to take her out this Saturday, she hasn't been out for a long time."

"Where are you going to go?" he asked.

"I still don't know, because of her lack of easy movement it is very limiting."

"So the zoo's out then," he observed.

I smiled. "Yeah I suppose it is."

"There's always McDonalds," he suggested.

"I am not going to take her to a burger bar."

We carried on eating in silence, I could see he was thinking and then.

"What about Covent Garden, I've been there quite often this summer. You've got all the street entertainers, the cafés and bars, it's a really full-on sort of place and if the weather's good you could just sit around and take it all in."

"Yeah, that is a good idea, providing it's not too much for her. I'll have to take a cab." I was pleased with his suggestion.

"Well that's alright you're loaded now," he laughed.

I smiled knowing full well I wasn't loaded but aware that now I was working things were not as tight as they used to be. Perhaps I would give it a go, I thought, it certainly would be a nice place to go, the weather was still promising although the summer was drawing to a close. It would probably depend on how mobile Jane was, but I would just have to wait and see.

CHAPTER 12

Saturday morning and the sky was clear, I was up early checking out the weather conditions. I had arranged to pick Jane up at ten. I opened the front door and strolled up the road a few yards, no wind and a bright morning promising to be quite hot. I trotted back upstairs and shoved a ten pence in the phone box to arrange for a taxi to pick us up at ten fifteen, then I jumped in the bath in an attempt to make myself clean and fresh for the day ahead. When I came out of the bathroom Dean was on his way out the door and I said, "Early start?"

"Yeah I'm doing a shift on the fruit and veg stall today, Alf is letting me serve the customers, weighing out the things for myself."

"Good." I said. "Enjoy yourself."

"Thanks and you," he laughed and was gone.

I looked after him pleased with the way the boy was turning out, he had a nice personality underneath the rough exterior, but I could see it was softening now he was living in a more controlled environment.

I dressed semi-casual, I wanted to look smart not scruffy and swallowed a bowl of muesli, smiling to myself. It was only a matter of a few weeks ago when the most imaginative cereal in the cupboard would have been Rice Krispies.

The newfound Vincent Sleeve was now starting to come out of his own depression which had lasted long enough, although I must confess you still haven't heard the real cause of it. Just keep your attention span intact and it won't be long before you learn the real truth as to why I am living in a one bedroom flat in Kentish Town.

But more of that later, now I know I have your full attention I must finish getting ready, put all the finishing touches in place and make sure I am downstairs at ten o'clock. Which of course I was, in fact five minutes early. I hovered on the doorstep for a little while, probably scared of Tina, but eventually I knocked and to my surprise the door was opened by Jane, smiling and dressed in a summer dress with a cardigan over the top. She smiled and beckoned me in and offered her lips to kiss which I did without hesitation.

"How are you Jane?" I asked worried that the day could be ruined before it had even started if she was having a bad one.

"I feel fine today," she said. "Quite energetic in fact." And she did a twirl to show me what she meant.

We took the taxi from outside the house and Jane was exhilarated as we sped through the London streets towards Covent Garden, I had asked the cabbie to drop us outside the Theatre Museum in Bow Street, opposite the Marquis of Anglesey and then we could walk through to the piazza. It was clear she hadn't been out for some time and she was acting like a child seeing the buildings and sights and the hustle and bustle for the first time. The sun was shining brightly now and she cuddled up to me in the back of the cab, her eyes flicking from side to side trying to take in as much as possible.

Once the taxi had dropped us off, Jane held tightly onto my arm and we walked slowly through to the piazza, stopping to look at some of the street entertainers as we passed. She particularly liked the statuesque figures dressed and painted to look like the tin man or other fabled characters. One was dressed in 1920s style upper-class clothing stood-stock still in the running position with his tie starched out behind him as if the wind was holding it up. It was so authentic this stationary figure in amongst the moving crowds was actually compulsive viewing as we stood and looked, waiting for any sign of movement.

In the background was a violinist playing some easily recognisable jazzed up pieces amidst the hubbub of voices and laughter. This is one of the wonderful things about London, the constant activity and atmosphere, the smells wafting through the air of cooking, garlic, burgers and oriental spices.

I looked at Jane and smiled, she was clearly so happy and she looked so beautiful. I wanted to store this memory, this vision in my mind for eternity. I was a little worried that she may run out of steam and we would have to curtail the day, but for the moment we would enjoy it.

She caught me looking at her and smiled.

"Are you okay?" I asked. "Enjoying yourself?"

"Oh, Vincent it's wonderful," and she laughed.

"Let's go and sit over there and have a coffee we can then just relax and soak up the atmosphere and you can rest as well."

"Oh, Vincent I'm alright, but I would like a coffee."

We sat at one of the outdoor tables overlooking the jugglers and the musicians, drinking cappuccinos and eating the little biscuits that came with it. I had thrown caution to the wind today and decided whatever she wanted she could have and I would worry about the money tomorrow. When it came to lunchtime we stayed where we were sitting at a table where we could easily observe what was going on and soak up the atmosphere. Jane ordered seared salmon with rocket salad on a bed of saffron rice and I had haddock and salmon fish cakes with a dill sauce and some spinach and chips. This was certainly an extravagant treat for me after the past few months of living like a peasant.

Jane turned to me and said, "Vincent this is absolutely lovely I can't remember when I last enjoyed myself so much and now you have almost finished your lunch I want you to continue your story and tell me why you are living like you are in a one bedroom flat. Clearly you weren't brought up like this and you have already told me about your wife and how you were suspicious of her going out in the evenings and what she may be up to, but what happened next? While you talk I can sit here and rest my eyes and the sun is so warm and with the music playing in the background it is idyllic."

I was certainly pleased that Jane was happy to rest so I agreed to proceed with my tale (see I told you it would be coming along soon).

"Okay Jane I will start from when I followed Rachel to the leisure centre one evening." I reached over and took her hand as she leaned back and closed her eyes.

"I sat in the car park of the leisure centre for some time. I had the car radio on low, just as a background noise. The car was becoming colder I switched on the ignition, the outside temperature gauge showed it was down to three degrees and falling, I suspected. I wondered how much longer to wait, when the automatic doors of the leisure centre slid open and Rachel came out closely followed by a man. I looked carefully to see if it was one of the others who I had seen in the gym, but I couldn't be sure. But I could be sure they were together, because before the doors had closed behind them he had draped his arm around her shoulder and was directing her into the car park, past her car to a large four wheel drive parked in an adjacent row. He flicked a key fob, the lights flashed and the doors unlocked and he stepped into the driver's seat while Rachel got in beside him.

"It was a while before the engine started, but the car still didn't move. I decided he had probably fired it up to activate the heating and warm the inside up. I quietly opened my car door and slipped out keeping low beneath the roof line and made my way between the parked vehicles, shielding the line of vision with the car Rachel was sitting in. You know like you see on the television shows, like *The Bill* or the older ones like *The Sweeney*. I crept closer and closer until I was just two vehicles width away, the wind was getting stronger and had a bitter bite to it. My face was cold, my eyes moist and my nose running, I pulled a tissue from my pocket and dabbed at my face. I peered through the windows of the other cars, but it was difficult to get a clear vision of the occupants and what they were doing. But whatever it was, in my eyes, it couldn't possibly be innocent, I was wound up with a severe bout of jealousy.

"The engine let out an idle drone and pumped out a stream of toxic fumes. I strained and strained my eyes to try and make out the features and movements of the occupants inside, the windows were steaming up and I couldn't tell what was happening, it was no good, I couldn't risk moving any closer, so I carefully made my way back to my own car. Whatever was going on in that car I was sure Rachel was a willing participant.

"After some twenty minutes of sitting in my car with my eyes glued to the four-by-four, I decided to leave the car park of the leisure centre and drive home. I stopped off at an off-licence on the way and bought a bottle of chilled Chablis. Once I was home and had turned on the TV. I opened it. I sat watching *News at Ten* drinking the cool dry wine and snacking on cheese and biscuits, when I had eaten enough I put my feet up and laid back on the sofa. I kept mulling over and over in my mind what I had witnessed and wondered what I would say to Rachel when she did come in. My mind was in turmoil and I knew whatever I said, the result could only cause an argument.

"When I heard the key turn in the lock I was no further forward, (I know what you are thinking, déjà vu, this is what happened last time she came in late and I was sitting on the sofa drunk). Well perhaps you are right, but this time I was not drunk, I was only halfway down my second glass and I was completely in control of myself.

"'You're late', I said looking at my watch.

"'Am I?' she hesitated and then said, 'Sorry'.

"And she was gone from the room.

"I stood up, re-filled my glass, took a large swig and followed her into the hall. I wasn't quite sure where she had gone so I listened for the noises of movement and narrowed it down to the bedroom. I made my way up the staircase and as I did so I was getting more and more angry, what I had seen tonight had clearly been going on for some time behind my back and I was going to have it out with her now, once and for all. When I entered the bedroom, her clothes were strewn across the floor and I could hear the shower running in the en suite bathroom and I suddenly thought, she would have had a shower at the gym after her workout. So the only reason to have a shower now, especially before getting too close to me, would be to wash away any smells or odours she may have picked up from having close contact with another man. Why else would she rush straight into shower before hardly saying hello or having a coffee?

"I sat on the bed and waited listening to the water splashing against the shower tray in intermittent bursts as Rachel moved around beneath the spray. After some minutes the noise stopped and I heard her slide open the door and reach for her towel, I still waited while she dried herself and then the familiar hiss of the deodorant spray. A few moments later she came back into the bedroom and I noticed a slight check in her step when she saw me sitting there, she had a towel pulled round her middle and tucked in, more like a man would, leaving her breasts exposed. This stirred me inside with desire, although I was so angry, as always the sight of Rachel made me melt and this was no exception.

"Didn't you have a shower at the gym?" I asked.

"No, why should I?"

"Because every other time after you've done your workout you do, you don't usually leave it until you come home'.

"I stood up and she backed away from me pulling the towel up over her breasts.

"'Well today I didn't," she stuttered, "I wanted to get home so I thought I would have it now."

I leant down and picked up her knickers, the ones she had left on the floor and she made a grab for them tugging them from my grasp. As she moved away from me I swung my right arm in an arc, my clenched fist catching her firmly on the side of the face, she dropped like a stone to the floor and I was on top of her immediately, my hands clenched around her throat, I was like a man possessed, it was all so instinctive, something just triggered inside me and I couldn't stop myself. I knew I was going to ruin everything, but I couldn't help myself, it was like pushing the self-destruct button.

"Who were you with tonight?" I demanded.

"She gurgled back at me. "Let go of me you bastard."

"Not until you tell me who the fuck you were with this evening?"

"No one."

"I squeezed harder. "I saw you Rachel."

"She slackened her struggle. "Have you been spying on me?"

"I squeezed harder and I could see her eyes bulge in fear, "I saw you in the car park at the gym with that man sitting in his car, the engine was running to keep you warm, which was probably necessary seeing as you had no clothes on." (Yes you're right a cheap shot).

"When she didn't answer, I then hit her again across the face, the blood rushing to the surface and a large bruise quickly forming. I pulled the towel from her, exposing her body and sunk my hands into her breasts pulling and squeezing them, trying to hurt her I wanted to remove the feeling of that man's touch, I didn't want her to be able to remember him.

"Although I am ashamed to admit it now the experience of the violence linked with sex had aroused me and I plunged my hand between her legs, parting the lips and forcing my fingers inside, I wanted to hurt her not pleasure her. I pulled my erection from my trousers with the other hand and plunged into her, Rachel was crying by now, I will always remember that sound, but at the time I couldn't stop. I just wanted more and more, I wanted revenge and I punched her in the face as I thrust deeper and deeper inside her and she just sobbed and sobbed. She had gone limp and I punched her again to wake her up, but she didn't resist anymore, her eyes were wet and distant, she lay there while I finished and ejaculated inside her and she just stared at me.

"I stood up, leaving her on the floor not moving, her eyes glazed over, not seeing. I straightened my clothes, took a kick at her and missed, stubbing my toe on the pile of the carpet, I yelped and left the house never to return."

I looked back at Jane her eyes were still closed, I wasn't sure if she was asleep or not, I had been concerned about telling her the last bit, but decided if I wanted to progress this relationship further, it would not be a good idea to start with any secrets. I had made the decision not to leave anything out and to tell the whole truth just like it was and although I wasn't proud of it, I hoped she would understand.

"Don't stop Vincent, there must be more."

"No I think that is enough for now," and I squeezed her hand.

She opened her eyes and smiled, "I would like to say it was a good story, but it isn't really is it?"

"No, I am afraid it isn't," I said. "But I didn't want to keep anything from you," I replied. "I wanted you know everything."

"Thank you, I appreciate that."

When we left the table we walked slowly past some of the small shops and stalls, stopping briefly to look more closely at some of their wares. I bought Jane a carefully fashioned bouquet of artificial flowers and handed them to her whilst bending down on one knee. Her eyes were filled with happiness and sincerity and when I stood up, I kissed her tenderly on the lips and she hugged me close. We stood like that for what seemed like ages in amongst the crowds of people, completely unaware, but completely happy.

We hailed a cab in Bedford Street and arrived home late afternoon. I left Jane on her doorstep, she insisted I should come in but I was so concerned she would be far too tired and it would be best if she had an early night. I promised to come down and see her the

181

following morning. Reluctantly she agreed, knowing it was for the best, we kissed again and I took those wonderful memories away with me.

Once upstairs in my flat, Dean had clearly been in and raided the fridge and the bread bin and gone out again, and there was no note explaining where. Which was one of the rules I laid down at the beginning. I thought it would be a good idea if we both left little notes to say where we had gone. I didn't bother and settled down to a quiet evening with a couple of glasses of Soave, the television and my memories of a truly wonderful day with Jane. I considered my expectations for the future.

CHAPTER 13

The following morning I went down to see Jane as promised, I had already checked on Dean who had come in late and was now clearly sleeping off what was the after-affects of a rather suspicious evening's entertainment. The odours were not just alcohol and I struggled to put my finger on it and decided I would broach the subject when he was awake.

Tina once again was conspicuous by her absence and Jane opened the door to me and let me in, she looked just as gorgeous as yesterday and I kissed her lightly on the corner of the mouth. You know one thing that has been puzzling me since I first met Jane and Tina, is where do they get the money from to live in a flat in this area, pay the rent, the utility bills and buy food and necessities? I don't want to just come out and ask, but I need to find out. And when does Tina go out? Because presumably she is the one that goes shopping and that sort of thing, and what's more who the hell is Tina?

"How are you feeling?" I asked. "After all your exertions yesterday."

"I feel good, I slept like a log, I went to bed soon after I got home, I just had a coffee first and then I was away."

"Where is Tina?" I asked as she led me through to the lounge.

"Tina?"

"Yes, where is she? She wasn't here yesterday when I picked you up either," I persisted.

Jane hesitated. "She's gone out shopping, would you like a coffee or tea or something stronger or lighter?" She was gabbling.

"You're gabbling," I said.

She frowned and said, "Sorry."

I suddenly realised I was sounding a little too demanding. "Yes I'm sorry too, I didn't mean to question you. I would love a cup of tea."

She went through to the kitchen and I followed, she flicked the switch down on the kettle and it started to whirl. She took two mugs from a cupboard and ladled loose tea into the tea pot, "I don't like teabags," she said and stood waiting for the kettle to boil. I stood behind her, circling her waist with my arms pulling her close to me, the warmth of her body fused with my own. She felt good and warm and comfortable and then she swivelled in my arms and putting her arms around my neck, kissed me tenderly and deeply and I knew everything I always wanted was here in my arms.

We kissed for what seemed like an eternity and then she said, "Do you really want a cup of tea?"

I shook my head.

She let go of me and taking my hand, led me through the flat to her bedroom, I swallowed nervously as I let go of her hand and watched her turn away from me as she removed her cardigan and then her blouse before turning back to face me. Her face was serious but smiling at the same time and I couldn't help but smile back, I was so excited I could hardly contain myself, but I was so aware that whatever I did I must not spoil the moment. I sat on the bed and beckoned her towards me and welcomed her into my arms pulling her against me, I buried my face in the softness of her belly and held her tightly taking in her smell and perfume. I remember trying hard to think what the scent was, Poison or First, but I still couldn't decide, and then I was taken over by the emotion of the situation.

I carefully and slowly reached up and undid her bra strap, I was scared, the last thing I wanted to do was take things too fast and frighten Jane off, but I don't think I had any need to worry, she came to me like Juliet to Romeo. I released her breasts they were small yet perfectly formed, I touched them lightly and then cupped them in my hands appreciating the softness and warmth, before caressing the nipples between my thumbs and forefingers. They became hard and erect to my touch and I looked up and Jane's face had an expression of pure pleasure and this aroused me even more. I pulled her down onto the bed and quickly pulled off my shirt and trousers, before moving on top of her and kissing her so deeply and I hoped it would never end. I found her skirt and expanded the elastic and pushed it down to the floor and then pushed my hand inside her knickers and I heard her gasp as I touched the silky moisture of her lips and then my fingers rested on her clitoris as I gently moved backwards and forwards. Jane moaned with pleasure and reached down to free my penis from my pants, I was so hard I was scared I may embarrass myself, but before that could happen she opened her legs wide and I thrust inside her and I must admit to my shame I had a brief thought of Hilary, (see I told you this is an honest tale) but in a moment it was gone and I was totally enveloped in Jane. I felt the sweat breaking out on both our bodies as the pace increased and I came and I think she came and I think we both came together and I know it was wonderful and I didn't know what to do next so I just rolled away and waited for her to comfort me.

My emotions were so severe, I was confused, I had visions of Rachel and Hilary and then Jane and I realised in that split second that Jane was the only one for me. We had coupled and everything was right and perfect and it was then that I cried, my body shook with passion and meaning, I felt Jane's arms around me comforting, but not knowing why I was crying, not realising it was from pure happiness.

We dozed for what seemed like hours and when we awoke we made love again this time we took more time over each other and our movements were slower and less urgent and our satisfaction gentler but no less conclusive. I lay in her arms and whispered, "I love you."

She was asleep but I swear she smiled and nodded at the same time, as if she really knew and then I fell asleep too and we slept together all Sunday afternoon wrapped in each others arms with not a care in the world.

When we awoke the sun was low in the sky it shone dimly through the basement window reflecting off the wall and casting shadows across the bed. I stirred first and rolled over out of Jane's arms and carefully slipped off the bed not wanting to wake her. I suspected the past two days was far more excitement than she had been used to for a long time, I thought it may be best to leave her to rest as long as possible. I pulled on my pants and headed for the kitchen, I thought I would make myself a cup of tea and perhaps prepare something for Jane when she woke. I opened the bedroom door and walked into the passage which was dark as there was no natural light, I yelped in fear and surprise as I came face to face with a figure hiding in the gloom.

"What!" I exclaimed.

"Oh it's you," said Tina scowling in total disapproval.

I decided the best form of defence was attack and said, "I was just going to make a cup of tea."

"Why would you be doing that?" she asked.

A question to which I really didn't have an answer. I couldn't say, because I had been bonking Jane all afternoon and now I felt a little thirsty and how would I explain why I was walking round in a strange flat in my underpants? I suppose it was lucky I stopped to put them on at all. I stuttered again, it seems I'm back to the lack of confidence thing again, "Um, I don't know."

"What do you mean you don't know? I find you wandering around in our flat in your underpants saying you are going to make a cup of tea and when questioned as to the sanity of this remark your only response is you don't know why you are doing it."

This was the longest speech I had heard Tina give. But I was acutely aware this wasn't going to get me off the hook now and I was going to have to put some serious thought into this. Tina was standing blocking my path with arms folded.

I know this sounds a little weak but I couldn't come up with anything any better. "I'll go and put some clothes on," and with this I headed back to Jane's bedroom.

"What are you doing Vincent?"

"Just putting some clothes on," I responded.

"Oh don't, come back to bed, I don't want to get up yet, I want you to cuddle me."

I must admit after being confronted with Tina this was a far better proposition and I almost succumbed. No, I cannot tell a lie, I chucked aside the clothes I was putting on and slipped back under the duvet and into Jane's warm embrace. It was so good and I must admit I didn't give a second thought to Tina, the poisoned dwarf.

* * * *

It was early and a typical English autumnal morning, pleasantly warm but the bite of winter was not far away. I was on the bus chugging south down Eversholt Street towards Euston Road on my way to work. I had now been humping for almost a month and I was beginning to feel I was growing muscles on my muscles, body building was not out of the question, but not really in my desired circumference. If my old colleagues in the city could see me now they would never believe it, they always thought of me as a weedy non-athletic sort of fellow, but a pretty competent trader. But now I was turning into a fit, muscular, manual worker plying my trade on a large building site and compared with the money I was earning in the city, being paid a pittance, but at least I was earning and it meant I could support myself, and Dean was also bringing in a few quid making us self-sufficient. Not like in *The Good Life*, but in our own little way we were making ends meet.

But things were starting to look up, the site foreman, a chap called Bruce, had decided I was not on a par with all the other low-witted humpers and labourers on the site and my brains could be put to better use and presumably my muscles and fitness were not up to scratch. So perhaps I wasn't doing as well as I thought I was.

Today I was to start a new position in the site office where the plans are laid out and we have telephones and facsimile machines. Bruce thinks I could be quite adept at checking material stocks, typing out orders and faxing them through to suppliers, making telephone calls and generally ensuring the tradesmen are in their designated positions and all the necessary materials are readily available to them.

I am not sure if I should feel honoured at this unexpected acceptance of recognition that perhaps I had some sort of ability and was not a complete moron. However, I was not going to become over-indulgent or parsimonious in my newfound position but just accept it for what it is, moving forward towards my rehabilitation.

I still had to wear my hard hat and boots especially when I went round the site, but at least it's a step in the right direction and to be honest I was feeling pretty pleased with myself. I may not be suited and booted like I used to be, but I will be in some sort of office position, even if it is only in a prefabricated site hut on a building site.

I sat back in my seat, the bus was only half full. In a strange sort of way I was looking forward to my new position and I felt I was returning to the office type environment I knew so well, the diffused lights flickering and pulsing their way through the day and night when I was on the New York desk. When I could sit at my work station and control things, screens lit up in front of me with graphs and movements, price indexes dictating my day, telephones ringing just waiting for an impulsive instruction. I had control over millions of US dollars every day and now I am excited about being promoted from humping eight by four boards from one floor to another to an office job in a portable hut looking at plans and typing out orders and faxing them to suppliers.

I sat in the back seat on the lower level and picked up a discarded newspaper which someone had left on the seat to my left. I flicked through the pages glancing at the headlines and reading a little further when something attracted my attention. And then I turned the page and there staring back at me was Harold's smiling face, I say smiling, probably more of a smirking supercilious expression was exuding from the page.

It read 'Harold Blenkinsop's – LONDON EXPERIENCE'.

I looked closer and then started to read:

The streets of London are paved with gold, a misnomer, I suggest. I have spent three weeks living amongst the homeless of London. An experience that has taught me a great deal about life and the way society has forsaken some of its citizens. As a middle-class man brought up in middle England, who is unaware of the social problems, poverty and degradation that we have created I have been shocked into action.

I spent these three weeks living rough with a friend I met some years ago, we slept rough mingling with people who have nothing and at times were desperate. Desperate for help, desperate for money, desperate for food, even a cigarette or a can of beer would be gladly accepted. But our undercover operation would not allow us the luxury to be so charitable and give into their needs, our experience was to live first-hand and learn from their way of life, trying to understand the problems they have to encounter on a daily basis. We only succumbed to these hardships for three weeks, they have to withstand the weather conditions, the ignominy and the degradation on view to the world day after day. There is no hiding place, this is London the greatest capital in the world, they are on view to all the tourists who visit this great city, they are our ambassadors, they are representing our country. Is this something to be proud of to treat our citizens like this?

My particular path led me to the back streets of Soho, The Strand and the arches surrounding Kings Cross Station, to the depths of the underground passages at Charing Cross. Men, women and young children wrapped in dirty soiled blankets rolled in cardboard boxes for added warmth and protection. Begging for money to buy food, or just begging for food, a few crumbs to give some sustenance to their weak and emaciated bodies. Any small token to bring a smile to their faces, a few coppers which means so little to you and me but is like a line coming up on the football pools to them.

Some are disabled or crippled and their day consists of sitting where they have slept the previous night and where they will sleep tonight and asking passers-by if they could spare a few coppers. Just a few coppers for a cup of tea or a sandwich or a meat pie anything to keep body and soul alive. I have seen an old woman slumped on the pavement in Tottenham Court Road, with swollen feet and legs covered in ulcers, her only pleasure is to beg for dog-ends so she can strip out the dregs of tobacco and roll them into a passable cigarette. She would beg a light for this privilege and then carefully smoke it ensuring she gains every bit of destructive smoke from it.

There are also those who try to make a small contribution to the society they live in by selling the Big Issue on street corners, a publication produced to inform the general public of the plight of the homeless, and for a pound this can be purchased from the sellers. This is their only job, their only means of employment to stand on the streets all day trying to coax people into parting with one pound so they may afford sustenance enough to live on.

And then there are others who are more naturally talented, trying to busk their way out of poverty. They play their versions of

189

well-known pieces, usually, Bob Dylan or Beatles covers, or other well-known artists. Performed in the labyrinths of underground tunnels with a hat or instrument case laid out in front of them to collect the change generously thrown their way as a gesture of appreciation, or is it just patronising?

I saw a child, no more than twelve, beaten by a shopkeeper outside Charing Cross Station accusing him of stealing from his shop and left to lick his wounds on the cobbles like a dog. What happened to that child? I will tell you, he was looked after by a bystander, picked up off the ground where he was laying in his own blood and taken to a local wash room and cleaned up and because there was nothing else that could be done the child was left to return to his pitiful existence, lodged in a corner beneath a staircase in the underground tunnels beneath the station complex.

I returned there a few days later, undercover, and sure enough he was still there, dirty torn clothes sitting munching on a half-eaten pasty. How he came by this food I have no idea, it could have been bought from money kind passers-by had thrown his way, he may have been given it or he may have been forced to steal it thereby creating a similar spectacle to the one I witnessed a few days earlier.

Another incident happened in Trafalgar Square. I was strolling down St Martin's Lane when a fight broke out over the ownership of a can of lager and following some pushing and shoving, punctuated with plenty of abusive language, the altercation became more serious. An accurately placed right hook landed firmly on the side of the chin of the man with the can, sent him backwards into the road where he was struck instantaneously by the wheel of a taxi which rode over his head, crushing it between itself and the road. I rushed forward, forgetting my undercover disguise and was the first to the scene in the hope I could save this poor unfortunate human being, but it was immediately clear that he was dead. In fact there was so little left of his head that he was unrecognisable.

It was after this incident that I realised how unjust life is, just because of the luck of his birth this man was left on the streets to beg for his existence and these circumstances brought him to the moment when his life was snuffed out over the ownership of a can of lager.

I reflected on this afterwards and sat on the grey worn stone steps of St Martin's in the Fields and cried. The reality of life on the streets had come home to me. It is dog-eat-dog out there, the primeval instinct for survival overcomes all sense of civilisation and for the sake of a can of lager a human being dies.

I also witnessed a gang rape in broad daylight on the streets of our fair city

A group of six men picked on a teenage girl, manhandled her into an alleyway and took turns with her. Whilst four held her down, one to each limb they followed each other until they had had their fill. I tried to help, but on my own I was useless, I was beaten back and decided I would be more useful calling for the police, I ran in search of a phone box with one of the gang hot on my heels, I managed to lose him in an alleyway before being able to make the call.

In twenty-first century Britain, should we be neglecting our citizens like this? Are we happy that people live on the streets with nothing more than what they stand up in? That they have to beg in order to have enough money to buy the bare essentials to stay alive. There are also the added dangers of the night, prowlers and drunks.

Firstly prowlers who themselves may only be looking for survival and like the wolf or the wild cat, they do not care whom they hurt in achieving their goal. If it means our twelve year old boy is thoroughly beaten for a fifty pence piece or a sausage roll that is the law of the jungle.

Secondly and probably more of a problem the drunks, who for a bit of fun will pick on some unsuspecting homeless person wrapped in his/her only possessions, and beat them to a pulp purely for the entertainment.

As a civilised westernised country we should be ashamed of such negligence to our own people and the complete lack of care that we appear to show. We seem to nonchalantly accept that it is alright to have adults and children living on the streets of our major cities. It is considered to be the norm and consequently nobody does anything to remedy it, the problem is just swept under the carpet and left to fester and rot like so many other things that our politicians ignore. My three weeks mixing and living amongst the homeless of London took place in August, when the weather was good and warm and on some occasions very hot.

Imagine what it is like in winter or summer for that matter just sleeping in shop doorways only to be woken by the retailers opening their premises the following morning and kicking you back onto the streets. But in the winter months around Christmas time, when everybody is expected to think of his brother man, severe cold sets in, perhaps snow, rain and wind, bitterly cold freezing temperatures, but still your only home is the shop doorway or some corner lodged between two buildings or underneath the arches of one of the main line stations wrapped in the same familiar blankets.

What are your thoughts? Do you think of betrayal by your fellow human beings or just an acceptance that your lot was mapped out for you when you were born?

I must express my sympathy and heartfelt concern for all those poor individuals living out there on the streets of our great city, but at least I can now say, I know what it feels like, because I've been there.

* * * *

I had got off the bus and was now walking up York Way by the time I had finished the article, I stopped and sat on a wall and thought. I was totally confused and then I was just bloody angry. I couldn't believe what I had read, Harold's total misconception of the truth, he had taken certain incidents and used them to his own advantage, suggesting he was right there in the thick of it. He claims he had been living rough in the West End of London, sleeping on the streets with homeless people, mixing with them, living their life. It just wasn't true, all he had done was wander round the streets helped by my local knowledge and then disappeared back to his three star hotel for the night. His article suggests he was first on the scene when the man was hit by the taxi, when he had only related what I had told him. He lived rough amongst those on the streets, but there was no mention of the three star hotel and expense account that was the reality.

In his article Harold gives the impression he was sympathetic to the homeless people when in reality he was intolerant and aggressive towards them. I was very unhappy about this misinterpretation of what actually happened and carried on my way to work.

I spent the morning in my new position making material lists in the porta-cabin, popping out to the site and checking with the foremen on their requirements, making phone calls to suppliers and then typing and faxing orders. I was enjoying it, there was a sense of responsibility not just a mindless conveyor belt moving eight by four boards from one stack to another, amidst a rumble of shouting and abusive conversation. However, I still couldn't get Harold's article out of my mind, the complete lies and untruths, it makes you look at the press in a completely different way. You know the way people joke about the papers. 'Well I read it in the paper so it must be true'. I think that was how the *Sunday Sport* was developed, making up the most bizarre scenarios like man from outer space fathers child with underage mother and then there was a picture of a chap with sticky out ears, a young woman in revealing costume and a baby that could feasibly be a cross between galactic races. I don't know if you knew this but the *Sunday Sport* was founded in a back street in Islington, by a few young men who thought it would be a good joke.

But I am digressing from the storyline, as you must have noticed we have moved on a month, so you are thinking what has happened with Jane? Is Tina still a pain? What about Hilary? Well I think you've probably guessed that one, Simon's charm, wit, large car and most likely large penis has seduced her to the extent that she has completely forgotten about poor old Vince.

And then there is Dean, how is he progressing?

Well I think the only way to answer these questions is to start another chapter.

CHAPTER 14

Dean had settled in very well and to be honest was making a reasonable fist of things, he was a good lad and I was very pleased the way things were going. He hadn't taken too many liberties and had more or less obeyed the house rules. He was serving on the stalls full-time now, selling fruit and veg and the store holder, a fellow called Steve, seemed more than happy to let him open up on his own in the mornings at the beginning of the week when the market was less busy, and he also rewarded Dean quite generously for his labours. He also got on well with the other stall holders whom he would fill in for occasionally and I thought, yeah I think he could make a good go of this. In a funny sort of way I had developed a kind of fatherly pride in what he was doing, it made me feel good, and at home the flat felt more like a home now, a place that was nice to come back to, because it was lived in and alive.

But Dean was a quiet lad and kept his thoughts to himself and there was obviously a lot hidden away in his mind, and I presumed a lot in his past which he hadn't told me about. I was conscious not to rush him and hoped he would tell me what he wanted to in his own time.

Of course I had been spending far more time with Jane, now things had got started, I wasn't going to let her go. Her condition has certainly been improving during the past few weeks and I do sincerely believe it is connected with our relationship, allowing her more interests in life and helping to lift her depression. She still gets tired very easily, but between us we make sure we don't plan too strenuous activities, like if we go for a walk at weekends we don't take it too far.

We had been to the cinema a couple of times, but most evenings we just stayed in talking and enjoyed being close to each other. To me she was without any doubt the most wonderful person I had ever met, but there was always one thing that bothered me and I suspected always would. Why would such a wonderful person take any interest in me? I wasn't actually a particularly good catch, I am short bald on top with my monk's ring and there is a distinct middle-aged spread protruding from my waistline, and of course I have fallen from grace, lost my wife and lost my job.

It doesn't make much sense, but I am not complaining, as long as it lasts I couldn't be happier. The only fly in the ointment is Tina, it turned out that Tina was a second cousin of Jane's who some six years ago had become pregnant by some undesirable and the family had employed a back street abortionist to practise his art. This may explain her obvious dislike of men, anyway the evil deed having been carried out, Tina was in many ways no longer accepted by her family except for Jane, who during her illness took Tina under her wing. And hence they moved in together with Tina acting as a sort of adult companion and carer.

Soon after Jane and I had first slept together, clearly under the surveillance of Tina albeit from another room, I obviously was keen to repeat the experience and thankfully Jane was of like mind. So to be honest and to limit the vulgarity to a minimum I spent every other night with Jane, at first I was very uneasy about Dean, but I decided not to beat about the bush, but just tell him the truth and he was fine about it, anyway he had probably seen plenty of worse things on the streets and me wanting to sleep with the woman I was now clearly in love with, was hardly going to shock him. I think he was pleased with the added freedom he could enjoy with having the flat to himself more for a while.

It was during one of these evenings that I continued telling Jane the results of that terrible evening when I attacked Rachel. I wanted to tell her the whole truth and keep nothing from her, but I was a little worried that she may think if I have raped once what is there to stop me raping again.

"After I left my house in Weybridge for the last time leaving Rachel lying on the floor of our bedroom, I took my car and drove out to the nearest motel, I realised I shouldn't be driving at all but I didn't know what else to do. I needed to get away and I needed to think and motels seem so impersonal, no one is likely to remember you ever being there, unlike hotels where you are likely to receive more attention. I paid cash at the desk, took a room and lay on the bed with the light off all night without sleeping and just thinking, although my thoughts from time to time were punctuated with tears. I really didn't know what to do, I couldn't go to work because I couldn't face it. I still loved Rachel but I knew what had happened was irreparable and there was no going back. I knew there was no way Rachel would consider having me back, our relationship had been steadily getting worse over the past few months and well I knew after this that was the end.

"With all these thoughts and realisations going round in my head I was heading for a nervous breakdown, over the next few weeks I took to the bottle and spent a number of nights in casualty and one in a police cell to sober up. I was still staying at the motel, because I had my credit cards and a substantial bank account, or thought I had until one day I realised my bank account had been frozen.

"Having made contact with Rachel, who clearly was not going to make conversation, I had been back to the house on a few occasions to collect some clothes, post and some essentials. They were left on the doorstep by pre-arrangement and I believe she had probably left the house before my appointed time. It was via these letters I discovered how my finances and possessions were being dealt with behind my back.

"Rachel's father was a powerful man with considerable influence, and from the moment he learned I had raped his daughter he had set the wheels in motion to strip me of everything I had and owned and to totally ruin me. And you can bet your life he managed it, I lost everything, the house, the money from my bank accounts and my credit cards were cancelled, although they were the last thing so I managed some free living on those. I think he had found it hard to actually track down how many cards I had.

"Whilst all this was going on Rachel had put divorce proceedings in place and I realised I had no means of defence and I suppose I didn't deserve any either. That was half the trouble I knew I was guilty. Whatever she had done I had no right to attack her like that and even if she forgave me she would never be able to trust me again, so I became resigned to the fact that that was the end of my marriage and I would probably never see Rachel again.

"The divorce was pushed through in about six weeks, I didn't contest anything, there was no point, I just accepted it all, and by this time I had left my position in the city, realising I was not stable enough to return and try to take the responsibility for other people's money. After two weeks of solid drinking and lying about in my motel room I took the initiative to sign on the dole and find a flat to live in, realising I could not carry on like this paying hotel bills with no income coming in. I punted round north London and finally came up with something I could afford in Kentish Town, I had decided to leave Surrey and move to north London where I had no memories in the hope I could make a new start and not bump into people who knew me. A strange idea when you think about it, but I just wanted to put the past behind me.

"And that is why I am here today."

Jane rolled along my arm and kissed me firmly on the cheek. "And I'm so glad you are," she whispered.

We had been lying on her bed for most of the evening, just talking and chatting and I had managed to tell her about the remainder of my past. I had been totally honest and I just hoped she would appreciate that, I was still nervous, terrified she would reject me. I couldn't believe I had anything to offer such a warm-hearted beautiful woman, but when they say beauty is in the eye of the beholder, it somehow helps to make everything clear and pigeon holed. I have never been a great philosopher, but I would clearly love to know the answers.

We melted into each others arms and I said, "Thank you."

"For what?"

"Everything."

She glanced up, an enquiring look on her face.

"Just for being you," I explained.

She smiled and we kissed before falling asleep.

* * * *

The following morning we woke early to a lot of banging and strange noises within the flat and I couldn't determine what they were, I also had to check my whereabouts, I wasn't clear where I was. It was Saturday so it was a little surprising, I unfolded myself from Jane and got out of bed, putting on my trousers and shirt I opened the door.

"Where are you going Vincent?" I loved the way she still called me Vincent and hadn't fallen into the slovenly abbreviation.

"Just to see what all the noise is."

"It's only Tina, she's probably making breakfast or something."

It was then that the door flew open flattening my nose first and then myself against the wall.

"Oh. It's only Tina is it?" And with this Tina was standing there glaring at Jane who was now sitting up with the duvet wrapped round her and suddenly fully awake.

"I'm sorry Tina, is something wrong?" asked Jane.

"Yes it bloody well is, I have had enough of this, ever since he," she threw a gesticulative arm in my direction without doing me the honour of turning to look at me, "started coming round every other day and now it appears he is staying nights as well. I am not prepared to put up with it any longer Jane, it is him or me, either he goes or I do."

She was clearly cross and I wasn't sure this is what I wanted to hear, I felt I could be on stony ground with this one and there was a fair chance I could lose the vote and be the one to be evicted. You know what it's like when women club together, they have this inbuilt allegiance towards their gender based on some sort of preconception that all men are bastards and only good for one thing, and when all's said and done, the truth is, they can make do without that.

"Look Tina, there is no need for this, let's calm down and talk about it." Jane was struggling out of bed, I plucked her dressing gown from the hook on the back of the door and threw it in her direction.

"No Jane I'm serious, I have packed my things and there is a taxi picking me up in," she looked at her watch, "twenty-five minutes. I am not joking it was never supposed to be like this you know that."

"Look," I said.

Tina turned on me and said, "No one asked you to comment, you're the whole fucking problem, why don't you just fuck off?"

The expression on her face could commit murder and she stared hatred into me and then it dawned on me, she was in love with Jane and I had come along and messed it all up, the possibilities of her being able to form her own relationship with Jane, it was all my doing. So Tina was a lesbian and had been living this dream, carrying out this caring position, looking after Jane in the hope that one day she would be able to live with her and as she recovered from her illness presumably planned to expand their friendship into a full-blown relationship. Perhaps this was brought on by her unfortunate experience with the pregnancy and the abortion, but that is just me surmising about something I know absolutely nothing about. But did she always have a dislike of men? And a love of women? To be honest I was surprised, but when I looked back on it everything did actually make sense.

I decided it may be best if I made myself scarce and wait in the lounge, I didn't want to desert Jane completely and run upstairs to my flat, but I just felt what needed to be said between them would best be said without the main topic of their disagreement hovering in the background trying to look invisible. I slipped through the door and made for the lounge where I sat quietly trying to hear the conversation but only picking up a few words, they were clearly both getting quite upset and in some ways I felt quite sorry for Tina, but not as sorry as I would feel for myself if Jane decided I was the one to be rejected. Looking at my watch I realised that Tina's taxi would be here within ten minutes.

As I listened more intently I heard the raised voices and Jane saying, "I am not giving up on Vincent now, when I have only just found him."

"Well in that case that is it, our relationship is over."

"What do you mean our relationship?" asked Jane.

"I love you Jane, there now I've said it."

"What? What do you mean?"

"I love you Jane don't you understand, I wanted us to be together to live together, like," Tina hesitated. "Like..."

199

Jane helped her, "You mean," her voice sounded shocked, "like lovers, don't you?"

"Yes," came the reply.

I had moved out into the hall to hear more clearly, but ready to make a quick exit if necessary.

"But Tina, I love you too, but as a friend and companion, not in the way you want I am not like that."

"Well in that case I will leave as I said, I can't stay under these circumstances, I always hoped we could make it together. But clearly now he has moved in it is not to be."

And the door was pulled open and Tina pushed past me as if I didn't exist, tears filled her eyes, she picked up her bags and struggled with the front door.

Under normal circumstances I would have offered help, but this didn't seem appropriate, so I just watched her struggle until she had manhandled the two cases and large bag through the front door and slammed it behind her.

Only then did I return to Jane's bedroom, she was sitting on the bed with her head in her hands, I didn't know what to say, so I sat down beside her and put my arm round her and she flopped her head onto my shoulder. She sobbed silently for what seemed like an eternity until finally I convinced her to lie down and close her eyes. I was concerned about her ME and whether the stress and strain of the last hour, bring on a relapse and make her worse again.

I made her a mug of hot, sweet tea and let her sleep, I sat in the next room whilst she slept, careful not to disturb her and hoping that she would be okay and not sure if I should wake her so I decided to leave her sleeping.

I went up to my flat about lunchtime, I had left Jane sleeping soundly, I thought she would probably rest for the remainder of the day and I didn't want to disturb her, although I was keen to know what she was thinking about me and whether things may have changed. You know when you really care for someone and there is a slight hitch in your relationship, you always think the worst.

I mooched around my flat, Dean was at the market so I had the place to myself, I cleaned up a bit and bunged on some old Bob Dylan tracks *Blonde on Blonde* and *Blood on the Tracks* and then followed with *Slow Train Coming*, his religious period, they suited my mood, uncertain, questioning and to be honest scared.

I was not sure what would be the outcome of today's events and I was frightened. When I feel depressed I often play Dylan and although his lyrics and voice could drive some people to drink, with me it lightens the mood and my worries and concerns can disappear. No I am only kidding, I couldn't see my immediate problems dissipating into obscurity simply by listening to Bob Dylan, but I always find his music therapeutic and wholesome. He must be America's greatest poet, but I don't suppose there is a great deal of competition.

I decided to cook something light and easy for Jane to have when she woke, I thought if I could take over Tina's domestic duties it may be a lot easier for Jane to come to terms with her sudden exit and perhaps accept me more easily.

I went back to her flat late afternoon, I had left the door on the latch so I could get back in and to my relief she was still asleep. I thought the more sleep she had the less likely she would take a turn for the worse, especially after she had been doing so well.

I went through her kitchen cupboards and freezer and came up with some smoked haddock which I poached in some milk and boiled and mashed a small amount of potato for substance. I made some homemade parsley sauce with milk, dried parsley and corn flower and some pepper, it wasn't bad actually, but not up to the standards you can get in the packet mixes. I left it to one side so I could just heat it up in the microwave, she certainly had a much better equipped kitchen than I had, but I quite enjoyed practising my culinary skills again.

Jane woke naturally at about six thirty, I was sitting at her side and I hoped greeted her with a reassuring smile telling her everything was alright. She looked at me at first confused and then realisation dawned and she smiled and held out her hand, I took it and the warmth soothed my mood.

"Would you like something to eat?" I asked. "If not I could heat it up tomorrow."

"You've made something already?" She sounded surprised.

"Yes, are you surprised? I'm quite domesticated, modern man you know," I was trying to make light of the situation, "you know with Tina leaving and what effect this could have on you."

"Oh Vincent you're so sweet, I will try some."

"Do you want to sit up and have it in bed? And then perhaps you could rest again," I was so worried she was going to relapse.

"Yes, I think that may be best."

I put a blanket round her shoulders as she sat up before going back to the kitchen and microwaving the prepared plate and dressing it with the parsley sauce. She made a vain attempt to eat it and to be honest she left very little haddock and about half of the mashed potato.

I ate mine sitting in a chair opposite her, it was quite good even if I do say so myself, the parsley sauce was a little bland but did a pretty good job of juicing it up, a little more seasoning perhaps but not bad for a makeshift effort.

"That was lovely Vincent, thank you. I think if you don't mind I am going to rest again, I hope you don't think I am being horrid to you just taking advantage of your kind nature, but I am not quite myself at present."

"No of course not," I replied, "anything to make you feel better."

"Vincent?"

"Yes."

"Just one thing, I would like you to lay with me tonight, when you come to bed I just want you to hold me close until morning and I know everything will be alright."

"Of course if that is what you want, I will just clear up and will be with you in no time."

"Thank you, Vincent."

I watched her settle down and she was asleep in no time and do you know, to this day Tina's name has never been mentioned again, it is as if she never existed.

* * * *

It was Monday morning when I woke, Jane was still breathing heavily so I decided to edge my way out of bed careful not to wake her. I had had a restless night and was glad I had not disturbed Jane. It was Harold that was bugging me, I was still fretting over his article and I had made up my mind I was going to go and have it out with him. I decided if I was to work through my lunch hour and then ask if I could leave a bit early I could get over to Wapping for about three thirty, then if I had to wait for him I would.

I made Jane a cup of tea, kissed her lightly on the lips and explained I was off to work and may be a little late home. I also told her not to worry about dinner as I would bring in a takeaway, because I may be a little late. We had talked all day Sunday about how she would manage now she was on her own. I was going to do all the shopping and make sure there was always enough bits and pieces in the freezer. Where possible I would make a sandwich in the morning and leave it wrapped in cling film for Jane's lunch and then cook the evening meal when I came in. It was important that she didn't try to do too much and undo all the progress she had made. It was a pity I was not going to cook on this first evening of our new regime, but she supported me knowing that I had to go and ferret out Harold because it was playing on my mind and I wouldn't be able to rest until I had been able to confront him. I had told her my reasons and how Harold's article had been so misguided and mainly untrue.

The office block just off Wapping High Street was not quite what I expected, not the modern opulence one has come to expect from our over-indulgent press. This was more of a brick-built, cheaply converted warehouse on three floors, with Georgian-style crittal window frames which don't provide very much natural light. The reception consisted of a dimly lit room about three metres square with a seventies style G-plan desk along one wall and a bank of two fluorescents hanging from the ceiling on chains, not what I had been used to in the city.

Behind the desk sat a middle-aged woman with a copy of *The Sun* open in front of her, a telephone switchboard system and a signing in book for visitors to one side. She had one eye on the newspaper and the other on her fingernails where she was deftly filing away in order to shape the rather long points and make them even sharper. Every so often she would dig the file underneath a nail and flick out some sort of debris.

"Good afternoon," I offered.

She looked up quizically.

"I would like to see Harold Blenkinsop please."

She gazed blankly and flicked some more detritus onto the floor.

"He does work here doesn't he?" I asked. I felt I had to keep the conversation going as there was little response from the other side of the desk.

She looked through a list of names which she pulled from beneath her newspaper and brought her finger to a halt saying, "Yes."

"May I see him then?"

"Name?" she enquired.

"Sleeve, Vincent Sleeve," I said.

"I will try his line," and with this she dialled a three digit number and waited for an answer. "I have a Vincent Sleeve in reception for you." She listened and then continued, "I don't know." She held her hand over the mouthpiece and looked at me. "Are you sober?" she asked.

"Of course I'm sober and what's that got to do with it anyway?"

She returned to the phone. "He says he is. Okay I'll tell him. He says he'll be down in a few minutes, you can sit over there," she said gesticulating in the direction of two rather well-used armchairs.

"Thank you," I said and sat down. Whilst waiting I spent the next few minutes running through in my mind exactly what I was going to say to Harold Blenkinsop, journalist extraordinaire, intolerant of the homeless and first-rate ponce.

Some minutes later the door to the left-hand side of the reception desk opened and Harold appeared scruffily dressed in an open-necked shirt, jeans and a rather limp hanging sports jacket weighed down by full pockets.

"Hey Vince you bloody wanker, to what do we owe this pleasure? Have you got some blinding story for me? Middle-aged woman mothers chimpanzee or ten year old boy seduces teacher, you know the sort of thing."

I should have expected this sort of greeting. "No nothing like that, I just wanted a chat, perhaps we could go for a drink somewhere?"

"Yeah, why not? The Prospect of Whitby is in the High Street just round the corner, it's a pretty good watering hole." He pointed over my shoulder. Turning to the receptionist he said, "Carol, if anyone wants me I'll be at the bar."

Carol nodded and we were gone.

* * * *

The Prospect of Whitby originally dates from 1543 and in the seventeenth century was a meeting place for smugglers, when it was known as 'The Devil's Tavern'. Having burnt down it was rebuilt and renamed The Prospect of Whitby after a ship that was moored locally on the River Thames. It was refurbished in the late 1970s in a common style of the day incorporating fibreglass imitation beams and artex walls and ceilings with small alcoves suitable for drinkers and lovers alike.

Harold and I sat in a bay window overlooking the Thames as it flowed out to sea, he with a pint of lager and I with a large glass of chardonnay and on this occasion my plea of poverty did not bear fruit as Harold had said, "It's about time you bought a bloody drink Vince."

I could see this was going to be a difficult conversation as Harold was obviously on the offensive, so I decided the best thing to do was to buy the first round. Although I was not flush, at least I could afford a couple of drinks now.

"How are you getting on with that bird Vince? The one with the beard."

I deliberately chose to ignore this remark, "I'm sorry?"

"You know, that bird that had the party."

"Party?" this was a poor effort at misunderstanding, but I don't think Harold was any the wiser, he is not particularly perceptive.

"You remember Vince, that bird with the hairs growing in long strands from her face, she was all over you if I recall correctly, she made a play for me first, but I put up the barriers, I had decided she wasn't for me."

"Hilary," I said, I had to put him out of his misery.

"Yeah, how's it going? Have you got to home base yet?"

I ignored this as well and said, "She's knocking about with Simon Cheek the chap who lives on the top floor."

"Really," he said looking confused, he clearly had no idea who Simon was.

"I thought he was a bit of a poof?"

I thought that was enough small talk and decided to get to the point, the reason why I was here to confront Harold about his article. "Harold it's about that article you wrote, the one we researched together."

He looked at me before taking a large gulp from his jug, his expression was not one of confusion this time, but a touch wary.

"Well," I continued. "It seems from reading it…"

"Oh you've read it have you?" He sounded surprised, which seeing it was available for national scrutiny was a bit strange.

"Yes," I replied, "but as I was saying it appears to me that all you've done is report the things that I told you and turned them round making out that you were the one who was sympathetic to homeless people. Which quite frankly was not the case at all, you were the one who abused, insulted and would have had them all dragged screaming from the streets and incarcerated in the Tower of London, if you had had your way."

"Are you questioning my professional integrity Vince?" He was glaring at me, the muscles on his neck pulsing threateningly.

I wasn't going to be beaten back at this stage, because his was little more than an unscrupulous fraud. "Well to be honest Harold I suppose I am, some of those things just weren't true. You weren't present when the taxi ran that fellow over. You didn't sleep rough on the streets in a disguise, as you claim in print, you wandered round the streets in the day abusing anyone who asked if you could spare some loose change and at night you went back to sleep in a three star hotel. You didn't try and rescue that poor girl being raped, you didn't go and phone the police, you weren't chased by one of the gang, in fact when I said we must help her you didn't want to get involved.

When it was suggested you purchase the *Big Issue* you roundly told the seller where to go. In fact Harold, the truth is it's all a string of lies, the only truth is that these things actually happened, but not to you, you weren't the hero, you weren't even there." I wondered if I had gone too far.

"Vince you're a bloody wanker."

"No, Harold I'm not a bloody wanker. All I wanted was to see the truth in print in the hope perhaps that it could do some good. There was no sincerity in your experiences, you went into it with no sense of care or understanding for the unfortunate people sleeping out there on the streets. You just don't bloody care."

"Look Vince, what the fuck does it matter who made the phone call? Who cares who was there when some bloody layabout was squashed in the gutter? And so what if I didn't actually sleep in a cardboard box in a shop doorway? The principles are there, I wrote what we saw, or you saw and I took down the information and formulated an article which was informative and that's what sells papers. And that is all my bosses and more importantly the share holders are interested in." He finished this sentence and then finished his lager, stood up and waved the glass in my direction as he walked towards the bar, I took this to mean he was going to buy me another one so I nodded my response.

I didn't know what to make of it now, I suppose he had a point, did we ever believe the press was an honest medium? Probably not, but does that make it right? No it doesn't. Shouldn't the most important thing be the people on the street without a home, money or anyone to care for them? This got me thinking as Harold returned with the drinks.

"Thanks," I said taking a mouthful, the cool dry liquid easily ran down, making me feel better.

"Cheers," said Harold raising his jug. "No hard feelings?"

I smiled. "No I suppose not, but I just got really pissed off with the different perspective in which the article was presented, I thought we went through quite a lot in those few days, we saw some pretty ugly sights. In fact I saw the ugliest sight of all and I can assure you the death of that young man haunts me without warning. It comes at me during the day, when I just have a full-blown colour vision of that moment of impact, but the worst nightmares are during the small hours, I get scared and it makes you think how cheap life really is that it can be snuffed out so easily. And when you see it in print it seems to almost glamorise what is actually a horrific situation."

"That's the industry Vince, the papers are designed to inform the public, they don't always do it in the way the punters may like. And you also have to remember the public don't always like to hear the truth, they need protecting from their own feelings and emotions, they like to think everything is cosy and it's only hearsay that people are really living out there on the streets. Vince they don't believe it because they don't want to, that's why Shelter and similar charities were started. Now you could question that as well, but if I was you I wouldn't bother, life's too short."

I looked him in the eye and could see there was little compassion and Harold didn't really care what happened to other people. He was just reporting and building up a story to satisfy his own ego and enhance his career. This made me think there must be more that can be done for these poor unfortunate people.

I stood up and drained my glass and planted it back on the table. "Okay Harold, I'll see you around," and I waved over my shoulder as I left the bar.

CHAPTER 15

Jane and I had virtually been living together for the past few weeks, as I said before, her health had been improving and she didn't appear to suffer from any ill effects from Tina's, as I now saw it, timely exit. She carried on becoming stronger and doing more and more for herself, she would look after the flat and when I came back in the evenings everything was always spick and span. I was insistent she still took time out during the day to rest and make sure she had some sleep during the afternoons. I really believed this noticeable improvement in her health was down to my influence and Jane's obvious recovery was brought on by my being around to help her, that good old-fashioned remedy TLC – tender loving care. These thoughts made me feel good and brought a new buzz back into my life.

Work was going well too, I was enjoying the office environment, and watching the buildings change and develop, there was something productive about it. I felt I was contributing and after months of inactivity followed by a rude awakening into the world of physical work it was a very rewarding feeling, I was beginning to feel part of something. So I was experiencing a happy home life and satisfaction at work.

Although I wasn't spending much time in my own flat I always popped in during the evening to make sure Dean was okay, some evenings he would come down to the basement flat and we would all have dinner together. He seemed to like Jane, they got on pretty well, but she is so gentle and understanding that I can't believe anyone wouldn't like her.

This particular evening, it was a Wednesday, the middle of the week, we were knocking together a Chinese-style stir-fry with chicken chunks and plenty of chopped veg, soy sauce, ginger, garlic et cetera and Dean was supposed to be joining us. I must admit I hadn't seen him for a couple of days, but that morning I had left a note in the flat telling him to come down this evening and naturally assumed he would show up soon after he returned from the market.

Once all the preparation of the food had been done I popped upstairs to see if he was ready, I opened the door to the flat and it was unusually quiet, generally the radio would be blasting out heavy modern twangs created by some modern day twangers, whom I must confess leave me a little cold. Dean was nowhere to be seen, I looked in the bedroom, he had taken to using my room recently as it seemed to make sense as I stayed downstairs to look after Jane. He had obviously been in and presumably changed and left without letting me know, which was strange as he should have known he was expected for dinner in the basement.

I checked the kitchen worktop where I had left the note, it had been read, screwed up and pushed to one side. I thought I would just try the bathroom on my way out.

I pulled on the door and it was locked, I put my ear to the door and listened, but there was no sound, no slush of water from the bath nothing just silence. I called, "Dean are you in there?" No answer.

I rattled the door handle it was definitely locked, so I called again, "Dean if you are in there open the door," I was beginning to panic something was wrong, I just knew it. "Dean" I shouted, and banged hard against the wood panel of the door, I then ran back into the flat and looked for a hammer or something hard to bash through the door, but there wasn't anything, I knew there wouldn't be, but you just have to make sure. I didn't really have any tools.

I ran down to the basement without any further delay and asked Jane if she had a hammer and screwdriver and we found a toolbox under the sink. Without waiting to explain I rushed back to the first floor bathroom and taking the screwdriver in my left hand wedged it between the panel moulding and the panel and tapped it with the hammer, loosening and levering it the bead came away with a splitting sound. I repeated this process to all four sides and then fixed the claw of the hammer under the exposed edge of the panel, pulling it free from the stiles of the door. I could then reach in and free the bolt securing the door.

I flung the door open and the bath was full of water and to my horror Dean was there totally submerged beneath the water level except for his knees. His eyes were wide open and staring up through the ripples, but deadly still, clogged up with water. I didn't know what to do, there was nothing I could do, he was clearly dead, I touched the surface of the water, it was lukewarm. His clothes were discarded about the floor, I rummaged through them throwing them onto the chair one by one, not knowing what I was looking for and then I noticed a scribbled note written on a torn open A4 envelope, it read:-

Sorry Vince!

It wasn't working. I couldn't go on like this anymore, you don't need me you've got Jane. I'm just in the way, like I always have been, like I was with my aunt. I should have stayed on the streets. Bye Vince, Oh and thanks. Oh and sorry again.

I sat down on the chair amongst his clothes and re-read the note, my hands were shaking, I couldn't keep them still and then my whole body vibrated with sobs, and I just cried with tears of salt and water running down my face. My eyes were streaming and then all I could see was a blurred figure standing in front of me.

"Vincent," it was Jane. "Oh my God," she exclaimed as she also realised what had happened. She disappeared immediately and I learned afterwards, she called for an ambulance and also phoned the police. When she returned she coaxed me back into my flat, made me lie down on the bed and then made me a cup of hot sweet tea which I cleared away the following day untouched.

I don't remember the police or the paramedics coming, but they clearly did as they removed the body taking it away I suppose to the mortuary. I stayed that night in my own bed and slept a little in between bursts of sobbing, my ribs and stomach aching with the effort. The pain in my heart was so bad and I just kept asking myself why? I was blaming myself, going over and in my mind, looking for any signs that Dean had been unhappy, but I couldn't find any, he always seemed so cheerful and he appeared to be enjoying his job in the market.

Had I been neglecting him? And spending too much time with Jane? Probably that must be the answer, it had made him feel unwanted and in the way. Therefore it was my fault, I had taken him off the streets with all the best intentions to give him a home, but then left him to fend for himself in an environment he just wasn't used to.

I took the rest of the week off work, my employers were remarkably understanding, especially given that Dean wasn't a direct relative. The police returned to take a statement from me, I could only tell them the truth as I have told you here, and of course, the note backed me up, in fact the note was the only evidence. They wanted to know if he had any other family and I could only tell them what Dean had told me, that his parents were killed in a motor accident, he had lived with his Aunt Ellen and her husband in Manchester, that they didn't really want him, and then about seven or eight months ago he ran away to London. But I had no address or contact details I could pass on. And it was then that I realised I didn't even know his surname.

And then there was obviously a post-mortem to be carried out and we had to go and identify the body. Well I went, Jane came with me, but I felt it was my responsibility and I didn't want to put her through any more than was absolutely necessary. It was a horrible experience being led into a white-tiled scrubbed room with a wall lined with large drawers storing bodies. The table in the middle of the room already had the body lying on it covered with a sheet. I was asked if I was ready and a man in a white coat pulled back the sheet and I looked, he looked clean and peaceful, his hair was combed smooth against his head in a tidy style.

I nodded. "That's Dean," but I couldn't say anything else because I didn't know anything else.

It was now left to the police to trace Dean's background and discover his real identity before the coroner could release the body for burial. I realised this had to be done but it was also a very difficult time for Jane and me just waiting to close the chapter. It was like being held in suspension and not being able to let go and move forward.

* * * *

It was about three weeks later just before six in the evening that there was a knock on the door of Jane's flat, I hadn't been home from work long. I answered to find a police constable on the doorstep, he introduced himself as PC Chesterman, he wasn't one I had seen before. He told me they had been trying to trace Dean's family and could he come in for a few minutes and have a chat with us.

"Mr Sleeve, we have been trying to track down Dean's family and I think we may have had some success. We think his full name was Dean Samuel Clitheroe."

"Well that's a Manchester name," I said.

Jane looked at me in a funny way.

"His father was Ronald Clitheroe and his mother Jean. His Aunt Ellen was married to a James Beech, we have found her and interviewed her and to be honest I can see perhaps why he chose to leg it and head for the bright lights. She admitted to bringing up the boy, but seemed little concerned as to his current whereabouts and hardly showed any emotions when we revealed his fate." He paused for affect, took a gulp of tea and continued, "We told her there would need to be a funeral and would she like it to take place in her area or in London, her response was you might as well do it down there. I asked if she would like to attend and she declined saying she wouldn't wish to travel that far and her Jimmy has a bad back."

"So what happens next?" I asked.

Following another mouthful of tea. "Well we have established the boy's identity and therefore we can instruct the release of the body for burial or cremation, which appears to be the favoured route these days, and as no one else appears particularly interested. If you wish to make arrangements and take charge Mr Sleeve I think it would be in Dean's best interests."

I nodded feeling very sad, but in another way proud that I had been granted the responsibility for this young man, whom I had grown to love, to help him on his final journey. I felt the tears prick my eyes again and Jane took my hand as PC Chesterman stood up to leave.

"Thank you Mr Sleeve, we will arrange the death certificate to be signed and the necessary paperwork to be put in place, here are a list of contacts, you may need to set the wheels in motion. You should be able to arrange the funeral for a week's time."

I thanked him and closed the door before turning to Jane who hugged me tightly, we stood still in each others arms for some minutes without talking.

* * * *

The following Tuesday was very autumnal, overcast and chilly we were only one week away from the clocks going back, just the sort of day for a funeral I thought. We were not having a church service, there seemed very little point as it was unlikely anyone would be there except for the two of us. There would just be a couple of hymns, a prayer and a few words said by a cleric at the chapel of rest attached to the cemetery. This seemed the best thing to do, I don't suppose Dean had any particular religious leanings so a quiet time of reflection was most likely to send him off with a sense of meaning.

Jane and I dressed appropriately and travelled in a car following the hearse, Jane had insisted on paying for this little luxury with respect for Dean. I was right, we were the only two people there which made supporting the organist an onerous task, but we manfully took up the challenge until I heard another voice in the background helping us along, and looking round I recognised PC Chesterman. He clearly realised it would not be a well-supported event and felt his presence would be appreciated.

The cold, clear atmosphere of the chapel was emphasised by its emptiness and though the service was poignant it was also clinical and in some ways unfeeling, the atmosphere was missing something, and obviously that was people. Two mourners and one policeman don't actually cut it and I realised that a young life had been taken away and for what? I truly didn't know and also how was I ever going to live with the guilt? Would I ever be able to forgive myself? Because the way I see it, it was all my fault, if I hadn't interfered and brought him to live with me he would still be alive.

The singing and service over the organist played a quiet dirge to accompany the rolling of the coffin as it slowly disappeared from view and the curtains closed leaving a feeling of finality.

214

The show over we walked home arm in arm without talking, just showing the respect that was reasonable for the occasion. We both knew that today would close this part of our lives and we could now look forward to a future together, and oh, how much I wanted that to work. The past year had seen so many changes.

I had been through the gates of affluence, tasted poverty, love, lust, infatuation, death and now I just wanted to experience stability and tranquility with the woman I loved. But...

CHAPTER 16

I decided to give up my flat, there was no point in keeping it going anymore, it cost money and I was never in it these days. Now Dean has gone, well we are not going to dwell on that anymore, Jane and I have got to move on. I had to give a month's notice, but that didn't make any difference, because I spent all my time with Jane anyway.

There was something I had been thinking about for some time ever since I saw Harold last, and we had that minor altercation. And now Dean was gone, I knew I had to do something to help and I said to Jane that now Dean is dead it just brings it all home. There is so much work that needs to be done out there on the streets.

"Jane," I said. "I really want to do something to help."

"Who?"

"The homeless, kids like Dean, adults as well, the last few months have opened my eyes and there must be something I can do! We can do."

She smiled and whenever Jane smiles my whole world surrenders, my heart beats just that little bit quicker and I succumb to her charms. "Oh you're so nice Vincent you're so thoughtful, what do you actually have in mind?"

I hesitated because I didn't really know, "I don't know but there must be something we can do."

Jane jumped out of her seat, came and sat on my knee and we kissed, long deep kisses and we held each other close, it felt so good I wanted it to go on forever. And then it stopped and Jane sat back next to me and said, "Okay what do we do? Set up soup kitchens? Start day centres? Perhaps educational seminars, no that is probably too much at the moment. A lot of the problems are most likely caused by drugs, perhaps we could try to help them with rehabilitation courses or something like that?"

I sat forward thinking, "It sounds a pretty tall order."

"Yes it does," she agreed. "But exciting."

"It is also going to take time and money and I haven't really got back on my feet yet, at least I've a proper job now and I suppose giving up my flat will save some money."

Jane said, "Vincent, I've often wondered if you have ever thought how I managed to afford to live in this flat without working and having a regular income?"

"I've never thought about it to be honest," I said.

"I haven't told you this before but I am by no means poor, I have a considerable amount of savings and all the time I have been living here I have more or less survived on the interest, thereby not eating into the capital."

I sat looking at her trying to take it all in and I came to the conclusion, she's not only beautiful, but rich as well. Hey that sounds a little mercenary, it wasn't meant to, but it has come as a bit of a shock.

"I think we would be able to manage fine, even if you gave up your job."

"Well I wasn't expecting you to support me as well."

"I thought we were a partnership now Vincent, all for one and one for all."

"Yes we are, of course we are," I replied smiling. I think I had just heard the most important words of my life, I couldn't have been happier. I stood up and moved in front of where Jane was sitting and dropped onto one knee, holding her hands in mine I said, "Jane... Will you marry me?"

She dropped her eyes to the floor before replying, "Vincent Sleeve, I would love to." And we fell into each others arms and once the tears of happiness had subsided we went to bed and didn't get up until the next morning.

In between making love, we made plans, the wedding, the future and our project to help the homeless.

* * * *

Until we were married we decided I would carry on with my job, I was quite enjoying it, but I realised it was never going to be a long-

217

term career position, it wasn't my field and from that point of view there weren't any ladders to climb. We planned a short courtship, in other words, as fast as we could make the arrangements, the licence and a few invitations, we weren't planning on a big event, but were going for a local registrar's office and then hiring the clubroom at the Assembly House in Kentish Town Road. A large old-fashioned style pub with very high ceilings and huge elaborate diamond-cut mirrors hung on the walls.

The guest list was a challenge, Jane had so many relations, many of which she hadn't seen for years, but her parents would expect them all to be included. And that was another thing, Jane was not even keen on asking her parents, but after she told them it was obvious they would be very hurt if they weren't there, and her father immediately took on the mantle of financial benefactor. I think that is something you should always let someone do if they make the offer.

We had some long talks about it and I was pleased that I managed to persuade her to invite her parents and two or three of her closer relatives.

On my side there was my mother, my father had passed away four years ago, that was a difficult period. But mum was keen and excited and I didn't want to spoil her pleasure, as she said she didn't like Rachel anyway (which is not what she said when we were married) and she wouldn't want to miss this for the world, I was pleased. Apart from mum I had no one else to ask, I thought of Harold, but why? I think our recent relationship was not an overwhelming success and anyway, I thought he was a bit of a shit, I still hadn't got over that article he wrote.

Jane was a tower of strength, she had made almost a complete recovery, it must have been a mental thing, (although I didn't want to belittle the condition of other sufferers) and now her life had changed and she had things to occupy her mind, the effects of the ME had slowly dispersed. Her muscle fatigue had diminished, she was a lot more active and her tiredness occurred far less often. I am not saying she was completely well, but a lot better and as long as she rested and didn't overdo it she could live life almost normally.

Also, since Tina had gone it appeared Jane was relieved of a considerable amount of strain and stress and I just wondered, was having to support Tina a bigger problem than I thought? Anyway these things didn't seem to matter now, we had each other and a long future ahead, it seemed as though all our problems were behind us.

* * * *

The wedding was a wonderful success, just the right degree of celebration and commitment or as one of the guests said afterwards, 'That was very tastefully done'. And it was, I was so proud, Jane looked absolutely fabulous, nothing like the girl I first met some four or five months ago when she could hardly move and appeared to be confined to a chair all day. She wore a cream suit incorporating a knee-length skirt, her hair had been dressed that morning and her make-up was laid on professionally.

It all goes to show she knows the contacts when it's necessary and wow was I happy with the final result?

It was agreed I would spend my last night of bachelorhood in my first floor flat, it was only three days before my month's notice would force me to give it up so it was like a farewell experience. I had still left some of my clothes there, so for this final act I moved my toothbrush back to the spot it had occupied in the half landing shared bathroom for a sullen nine months. It was sad, but I enjoyed the tranquility and the loneliness reminiscing over those times. Harold, Dean, Hilary, yes that was fun and even Simon Cheek, the bastard. Oh dear, that is a bitter response which doesn't suit my newfound image as a soon to be happily married man, having found the most wonderful woman in the world. I slept soundly, although I woke about four with an inexplicable desire to urinate and I once again had to trudge out to the half landing, but apart from that it was a restful and satisfying night leaving me rested and ready for the day ahead.

We had the ceremony, albeit in a registry office, with about twenty guests, all of which were on Jane's side except for mum who I was pleased to say really entered in to the occasion and made me feel good. She was certainly enamoured with Jane, which to be honest was a great relief, but she did remind me during the so-called reception, that she never really took to Rachel anyway. In a strange sort of way this hurt me, I found I naturally came to the defence of the one I chose, but that was in the past. Mother never gave any indication of those sort of feelings at the time, therefore, is that the prerogative of the parent? You may not like your children's choices and decisions, but because it is their choice you accept it with a graceful demeanour.

Of course I haven't delved into parenthood yet, still just treading the water, but having just caught a glimpse of Jane through the crack in the door leading to the bathroom and it is the first night of our honeymoon, I think I would be more than happy to embark on the erotic journey of copulation.

Of course I have been a bit cagey here, I haven't let on that we had been blessed with a particularly extravagant honeymoon and as I understand, it was being financed by most of Jane's affluent family. And though feeling a little guilty I was prepared to go along with it, especially as I have recently had a period of social under performance and my own life has been a bit mixed up. I know you are trying to guess where we have gone, well the sun is warm bearing in mind it is late November, UK time, and there is a great view of Table Mountain as a backdrop to rows and rows of vineyards.

We were staying in a five star hotel for ten days in South Africa just outside Cape Town, overlooking the bay on one side and Table Mountain on the other and it is fantastic. But perhaps more importantly I believe this break from our recent strains and stresses in the grime and smoke of London will go a long way to helping Jane's total recovery. She has been so happy since our wedding seven days ago, she has been constantly smiling and laughing and our love making has just got better and better.

We spent the days sightseeing and relaxing round the outside swimming pool and the evenings sitting on our balcony with a glass of champagne before going down to dinner in the plush and opulent dining room. And the nights were pure bliss as we held each other close and slept in unison. There is a pleasure that is indescribable and it is falling asleep with your arms wrapped around the one you love and waking some hours later to find you are still in the same position and the closeness of the bodies radiates such alacrity.

It was on our last night in Cape Town, we had had dinner, a mixture of local fish cooked in a paella style, a local dish with some fairly hot spices and washed down with South African sauvignon, cool and crisp. We were sitting on our balcony watching the sun drop into the ocean. It was still warm and we were content and satisfied, letting the atmosphere wash over us when Jane said, "Vincent, I have been thinking."

"Yep." I responded from my semi-conscious state.

"You know what you were saying before we were married and left England, how you wanted to help the homeless?"

"Yep." Again.

"Well I think I've had an idea." I suddenly realised this was the first time we had mentioned our lives at home, past or future, since we had been in the southern hemisphere, but of course now twenty-four hours to touch down we needed to prepare to bounce back to reality.

"Okay, what is it?" I was all ears now.

"We said no soup kitchens or things like that, well what about offering a service for some of the luxuries of life, like somewhere to have a haircut, perhaps dental checks, minor medical assistance, a full-on service."

I interrupted. "They are not luxuries, they're essentials."

"To you and me they're essentials, but to people who have spent months sleeping in a cardboard box in a shop doorway in The Strand or in tunnels linking underground stations they are a luxury. They can have toothache like anybody else, but they can't just go to a dentist and end up paying fifty pounds for a check-up and then be told they have to make another appointment to solve the problem. A haircut, a shave and a good wash could make so much difference to the way someone feels, to the way they feel about themselves as well. It could also be a place where people could come for company and to meet other people with similar problems, perhaps pre-arranged even."

"What a dating agency?" I asked.

"No, don't be silly."

"Well I did wonder."

"Now listen we could have a little area filled with advice leaflets answering the questions people want to know about sleeping rough, hygiene, sexually transmitted diseases, point out the dangers and problems. We could have some free samples, I am sure the NHS would be more than happy to supply certain things, preventative medicine is a cost saving in itself. And why not have a small area where they could get tuition and help with reading and maths, just the essential subjects. And..."

"Hey just hold on," I could see how excited she was getting, her mind was running away with itself. "Let's slow down, I think you have some good ideas, but one, we have to consider the costs, two, I have a full-time job, I know it may not be the best, but I have managed to make a go of it and to some degree I quite enjoy it and three, you are still recovering from being very ill and four, I am no barber."

Jane laughed at this and then said, "There is no need to worry about money, I have money for us to make a start, we will then raise money, we will apply for charity status and we will encourage volunteers to give up some of their spare time, people with skills, to cut hair, shave people, give medical advice, dental advice, teach. How do you think Childline started? And it is still manned mainly by volunteers especially in the call centres."

"I am not sure Childline is relevant to working with the homeless, it is far more of an escape route for children who feel threatened and need someone to talk to, isn't it?"

"Well yes, but the ideas of helping others is the same, once we achieve charity status, we would be able to set up fundraising ideas which could involve box collections on street corners or on pub and shop counters. We may be able to approach large organisations for sponsorship, perhaps naming our sites after them."

Jane had certainly been giving this a lot of thought, she sat back and waited for me to digest.

I considered her ideas and smiled my approval, the thought of working with Jane and at the same time helping the homeless was hugely appealing and I thought yeah why not give it a go? There was an enormous amount of planning to do but, and I looked into my wife's eyes and said, "Yep we'll do it."

"Oh Vincent, it will be wonderful, we can actually do something to help, we can make a difference."

She looked so lovely, I just melted again, you must be getting bored with my melting and going all gooey. But while we are on the subject I just want to make a point, you know when you think she looks absolutely wonderful and when you meet her everything just feels right, you realise she turns out to be everything you ever hoped for.

And then I thought, yeah perhaps we could, a chance to make a name for ourselves.

* * * *

The following day we travelled eleven hours before landing at Heathrow, this is when I appreciated that Jane was not a down and out because we travelled British Airways Club Class, with big seats and constant service which afforded me an ongoing supply of champagne and to be honest although I didn't let on to Jane, I was feeling particularly tipsy by the time we hit the tarmac in west London. It was a real autumnal welcome back to England, you know those days which are cold, dank and dark and you think what is all this about, especially when you have just left a sunny warm oasis and an atmosphere of romance and holidays. There is something terribly depressing about England in November. Those dark short days in the run up to Christmas, not always a time of year for many people to celebrate, not least those living rough on the streets. Perhaps this year we may be able to make a difference.

We took a taxi from Heathrow to north London and back to Jane's flat, it was cold when we went in, the heating had been off for a while now and it was late afternoon. We quickly turned on the fires and heating and I flicked the immersion switch to warm up the water so we would be able to have a nice hot bath in about an hour.

There was a pile of unopened post on the mat which we left in the kitchen until later, in the bedroom Jane unpacked and I lay on the bed and watched her. Domesticity, this is what I had been missing and I was now so happy and content, and this time I wasn't going to mess it up.

This was my wife, albeit my second wife, but my wife all the same and I adored her and I was determined I was going to do everything I could to make her happy.

CHAPTER 17

Now we were back home the whole thing went into overdrive, Jane fell right into the organisational stakes, first, she made arrangements for meetings with Westminster Council, researched the possibilities of porta-cabins, prefabricated sheds and even talked with contractors who could construct bespoke buildings.

Her first meeting with a representative from Westminster Council was not altogether successful. You would expect them to welcome any help with their homeless community, but they appeared more concerned about buildings being situated on their pavements or squares and the effect they would have on the environment, in other words the tourist industry. But Jane didn't give up she prepared a dossier like a business plan and lobbied the MP for the area and even wrote letters to *The Times*, *The Telegraph* and *The Guardian* in an effort to make powerful people aware of the obstructions being put in our way by the authorities. By the time these had been published she had received a phone call inviting us to return to the offices in Queen Victoria Street for an audience with a number of Council members.

Up until now I had carried on working full-time, but I took the day off to give Jane my full support and so that is why we were now sitting in an ante-room on the sixteenth floor of Westminster City Hall. A room starkly furnished with gloss painted walls in two colours, a pencil round dado line dividing them and an old oak desk with five chairs surrounding it. We sat waiting, a tray of tea and biscuits in front of us, I suggest a gesture of unilateralism, perhaps they were coming round to our way of thinking.

We weren't kept waiting long when two men, one in a smart three-piece suit, the waistcoat, I thought far too tight-fitting, and the other with a tie strewn to one side and the top button undone, he wore an out-of-shape sports jacket which instantly reminded me of my history master at school. Unkempt was the obvious conclusion and I did think this fellow may be the one most likely to be on our side, the third representative was a very shapely young lady, I estimated early thirties, she was neatly dressed in a knee-length black skirt, white blouse and a lovely smile.

"Mr and Mrs Sleeve," this was the three-piece suit.

"Yes," I said. "Nice to meet you." And I stood up and shook his hand, Jane leant forward and did the same.

He was obviously in charge and was about to direct operations. "This is Mrs Fulton," he gesticulated to the lovely smile, "and Mr Potts," who had already sat down and was pretending to read the paperwork in front of him. I, of course, knew he had fully digested it prior to entering the room and this was just for effect. "My name is Peters, Roderick Peters, I will be chairing this meeting and I trust we will be able to come to a suitable conclusion designed to benefit everyone."

He sat down and also appeared to assess the papers in front of him, before looking up and saying, "Right, as I understand it you and your wife, Mr Sleeve, are requesting permission or a licence to erect a temporary structure within the confines of the City of Westminster in order to operate a sort of drop-in centre for the homeless in our area." He paused.

"That's about the long and short of it," I said.

"What do you propose to do to draw people in? Because if it is just serving teas and coffees et cetera, these are usually done from a mobile format, which would be our preference, thereby not littering our streets with unattractive structures."

I spoke up again. "We have quite a few innovative ideas, but I am going to let my wife explain them in more detail," I turned and said, "Jane."

"Thank you," she said smiling at our interview panel. "Yes we have a number of ideas and I will try to take you through them one by one. Firstly we would like to have a building, albeit prefabricated, that we could divide into at least four different rooms plus toilets, shower room, kitchen and a small reception area. The rooms would each have a designated use, one would be for medical attention where people who needed it could come for medical advice, eye checks, dental checks and any advice on many types of medical problems.

We wouldn't have the facilities to carry out dental work on the premises, but a qualified dentist would be able to carry out the checks and identify any problems and encourage the patient to have it seen to, they could also advise on the hygiene elements."

"Mrs Sleeve," interrupted Mr Potts. "Where would you find these specialists?"

"We would engage a network of volunteers and allocate specific days to each discipline, am and pm and experience would soon tell us which ones would be most popular. We would set a day aside for haircuts, a simple thing which could make people feel so much better about themselves and the shower room would be available at all times."

"I presume that takes up two of the rooms?" asked Mrs Fulton.

"Yes," I replied to give Jane a breather. "The other two we propose to use more for social things, one providing an advice service and helping people with reading and writing, perhaps simple maths and we would have a selection of books, magazines and newspapers available. This could expand to other subjects if the demand was there and depending upon the skills of our volunteers. And the last room would be more of a common room where people can meet others in a similar situation, share their problems, we would provide tea, coffee, soft drinks and they could stay as long as they like. We wouldn't charge for these, but would most likely have a tin on the counter for donations."

"How would you propose to finance such a project?" asked Peters.

Jane spoke up again. "I will be putting up the money to get everything started, I have quite a lot of savings and in the meantime I will be advertising and recruiting volunteers. We also intend to apply for charity status and this would allow us to raise money via collections and fundraising events and donations."

The panel appeared to be digesting what they had heard when Roderick Peters said, "Where would you expect to put such a building?"

My turn again. "We clearly need to be close to the major problem areas, where the majority of homeless people are currently living, we have looked at the area between The Strand and the river."

"Very near The Savoy," said Mrs Fulton, "I'm not sure we could sanction such a position, the objectors would be all over us."

I was trying to work out their real opinions to look behind their bureaucratic fronts, to try and see what they really thought, when Peters said, "What are your reasons for wanting to do this?"

I was really surprised at this question, I would have thought it was obvious, but before I could speak Jane had responded.

"I would have thought that was obvious," she said. We clearly were in tune with each other on this one."

"Well maybe to you Mrs Sleeve, but we would like to know," responded Mr Peters.

"We want to help, my husband has seen the problems first-hand, he has helped in the research for a newspaper article reflecting on the plight of these unfortunate people. I would have thought you, as representatives of the council, would be overjoyed that we are offering to help you with one of the problems on your streets. It is not right that human beings have to live like this, all we want to do is help make their lives just a little more comfortable, we are not trying for any personal gain, if that was what you were thinking?"

I could see Jane was getting agitated and I wanted to intervene.

"Mrs Sleeve, may I apologise that was not my intention, if you would excuse us for a few minutes I think we need to discuss this amongst ourselves. If you go down the corridor there is a tea point on your right-hand side."

"Of course," I said and led Jane from the room, where we walked along the corridor and gazed out of the window towards Westminster Abbey. We had had enough to drink and really didn't want any more, you know that caffeine feeling when you start to feel sick.

"What do you think?" asked Jane.

"Do you know, I am not sure."

"Neither am I."

"Although I think your final riposte may swing it. You were very convincing."

"But they can't really believe we have an ulterior motive, can they?"

"I shouldn't think so."

* * * *

It was only a matter of about ten minutes before we were called back in, we sat down before Mr Peters spoke. "Mr and Mrs Sleeve, we think you have a good idea and on behalf of Westminster Council we would like to offer you our support."

"That's wonderful," Jane had jumped from her chair and was hugging me, I think she would have hugged Roderick Peters if I hadn't been there. I must admit at this stage I thought about hugging Mrs Fulton.

"Ah hum," grunted Mr Peters and Jane released me. "However," he continued, "we will need to choose the venue and land does not come cheap in Westminster. We will be looking into suitable areas and will contact you in two or three weeks with our recommendation."

"But do we have any say in this position?" Asked Jane.

"Yes of course you do, but you have to remember our decisions are not just based on your requirements, but all our existing tenants have to be considered, such as shopkeepers, hoteliers and businesses, many of which, given half a chance, would wipe all the homeless people off our streets with the repeated stutter of a Kalashnikov. So you must appreciate there could be very little sympathy from your neighbours if you were to set up shop somewhere in the West End. Therefore we need to work together to find a suitable location where there will be a minimal amount of objection and inconvenience to other people. If we are going to work together you need to trust our judgement, we know what we are dealing with, we also understand our homeless problem and anything that may help to alleviate the demand on our social services would, from our point of view, be very welcome."

I smiled realising we had won, knowing we had to work with the authorities, but why the hell not? We couldn't really expect to do it completely on our own. I stood up. "Thank you Mr Peters, Mrs Fulton and Mr Potts." And I shook them all by the hand, but I must confess I lingered with Mrs Fulton's appendage just a little longer than I should have done. And in a funny sort of way I liked it, but the like was quickly taken over by the guilt, I am a very happily married man now and sure as hell, I don't want to spoil that.

So I shook their hands and nodded and said yes and no and was so pleased that we had achieved what we set out to do, my new wife and I, it made me feel a bit like Bob Geldof and Midge Ure put together giving up my professional time to help the less privileged.

But yeah it felt good and as we walked from the room and took the lift to the ground floor I looked at Jane and realised how lucky I was to have found such a wonderful companion and I was so proud of her too. She sat there and voiced her opinions, stood her ground for what she believed in and it was only a few months ago she was laid up, incapacitated and with little hope for the future.

You must be wondering how I have managed to travel from being a thoroughly drunken down and out via a sexual rejuvenation with Hilary to being a happily married member of the middle classes with a priority to help the homeless of our capital city. Well life is an unpredictable experience and tends to leave one wondering so let this be a lesson to you. Ah that is a little arrogant isn't it?

* * * *

Winter hit us hard this year, it was sudden, four days into the New Year and we had twelve inches of snow covering the south-east of England and I understand further north it was much worse. The transport system came to a halt, the underground only managed to run a service through the centre of the city, because any of the routes which travelled above ground were impeded by frozen lines and piles of snow. The roads were not passable and most bus routes were running greatly reduced numbers. The mainline services were almost non-existent as points froze and would not operate, many of the staff could not get into work, because the whole transport system was in meltdown.

Catch twenty-two springs to mind, but clearly this inconvenience to the average city broker, banker or insurance magnate was nothing to the effect it would have on someone with no money, no job and a cardboard box and a blanket for a home. Living on the streets in mid-winter is about as bad as it gets, you can't actually appreciate the extent of the cold, how it eats into your whole body and leaves your bones aching. You don't want to move as this only increases the effect of the cold, the air moves through your clothing like a cold draught from a freezer and you shiver with pain. The rain also dampens the atmosphere and never dries and your clothes and blankets are always damp and cold. There is no reprieve from the bitter cold and the external pain turns into an inner depression, something that other people tucked up in their suburban-style homes will never understand.

And it was with this information and awareness that Jane and I embarked on our mission to improve the conditions of the homeless of our capital city.

Over the past few weeks we had been working very hard, well what I really mean is Jane had been working very hard with Westminster Council to find the best venue and how big a prefab we could erect. I had carried on with my position on the building site, where I was still working in the office and in a funny sort of way was enjoying it, the challenge of keeping the office going, getting all the orders in on time, so the supplies didn't dry up. It's a statistics thing, you know numbers, production, keep the materials coming in and production keeps going.

After a few weeks of negotiation it was down to two areas, one just north of Charing Cross Station behind the old church of St Martins in the Fields, where there was a corner of a disused site. Although building was due to start on a shopping development, there was this small area unaccounted for.

The second was on the north-west corner of Leicester Square, but to be honest we favoured the first option, it was more in the centre of the problem or was it just some nostalgia on my part and in remembrance of Dean. So once the site was agreed, we had to get through the red tape of planning permission and licensing to plant a temporary structure on site. To be honest Roderick Peters and his team did everything they could to speed up these processes, because I think they knew how this could really help to relieve the burden on the council. Also perhaps it could be a feather in the cap for Westminster City Council, you know the sort of thing, working with the community, instead of just handing out parking tickets and being obstructive.

Once the paperwork was settled arrangements were made to crane in three large porta-cabins and with some minor alterations a linking corridor was incorporated to unite them as one complex. This provided us with a small reception area and three reasonable sized rooms and the third cabin was a toilet and shower block which was entered via a door off the reception and an external passageway. The cabins were second-hand and once the ground had been prepared the supply and installation costs were only just over thirty thousand pounds, Jane provided all of this from her savings. Now the structures were in position it was clear that there was a lot of internal work to do to provide suitable comfort and facilities and with my recently found work contacts I coerced a few tradesman to give up a few hours of their time to help us.

Jane also spent a great deal of time advertising and interviewing prospective volunteers, which seems a strange requirement to carry out an interview for somebody who is volunteering for a position to help people who really need it. Surely anyone with any degree of skill, in whatever field, could only be of help. Anyway people were coming forward, teachers, dentists and doctors all offering different skills and with different degrees of commitment, some just a couple of hours a week others two or three half days, varying times from week to week so we could start drawing up a rota which would maximise people's time.

* * * *

Jane and I were sitting at home, we had just finished our dinner, it was a cold evening, the snow had turned to slush but the temperatures were still not sufficient to clear it away. We were lying in each other's arms on the sofa, I felt tired and the warmth of the food made it hard to keep my eyes open.

"Vincent," I felt Jane nudge me awake.

"Yes," I said.

"Are you asleep?"

"Yes."

"Well why did you answer?"

"I was only dozing."

"We've almost won you know, the signs are going up tomorrow and within a week we will have our first customers."

"Customers," I queried. "I'm not sure that is quite the right description."

"Well perhaps not, but what do you suggest calling them?"

I was fully awake now, "I don't really know, clients, but that is similar. But perhaps that is the right sort of title, something that shows them some respect not just demeaning their position and situation."

Jane spoke again. "Once we are open for business, I am going to make an application to the charity commission in the hope we can gain registration and then we can start up a fundraising campaign. I expect there will be plenty of form filling and I will need to put up a pretty convincing presentation and attend interviews."

"I am sure you will be able to do it," I said.

"Well I am going to give it my best shot, now we have come this far we have to go the whole hog. I also think it may be the best time for you to hand in your notice, Vincent the workload is going to increase ten-fold."

I unwound from her grasp and sat up all ears.

"I know you are a bit reluctant and concerned about losing your income, but I assure you I can support us easily for quite a long time. Once we gain our charity status we can both be fully employed by 'My Friend's In Need', it may not be high earnings, but it will be a living wage and as I said I do have some pretty big savings."

I nodded, knowing this decision would have to be made before long, "You certainly don't let the grass grow under your feet do you?" I observed.

"Oh Vincent I am so excited, I really feel we are on the brink of actually being able to make a difference."

I leant forward and kissed her tenderly on the lips. "You are a truly wonderful person Jane Sleeve, I think I realised that the first time I saw you and borrowed the iron. You appear to have such inner strength to come back from your illness and then work with such energy, but I am going to say it again, you must be careful to not overdo it, you must make time to rest."

She nodded. "Yes I promise I will be careful, you know I couldn't have done any of this without you Vincent, in fact if it wasn't for you I may still be sitting in that chair over there nursing my sorrows."

"Come on," I said. "Let's go to bed, I feel like making love to you."

She smiled and I knew I was in for a wonderful night.

CHAPTER 18

It was a Tuesday morning the last day of February, the 29th, leap year, and the skies were clear blue, but it was still cold, bitterly cold. The ice and snow had cleared but there was a stiff frost on the pavements, the trees had a crisp white tinge to them and it was our first day at 'My Friend's In Need'. Our dream was coming true, it was conceived on the back of our relationship, my second chance and in memory of Dean, who dying so tragically helped me to understand the deficiencies in our society and that we all needed to put something back and not just take. But today was to embrace not to bemoan the past, today we move forward, today we start to help people and today we achieve our dream.

Jane was up bright and early, we ate breakfast hurriedly before rushing off to the West End arriving at 'My Friend's In Need' before eight and stood back admiring our sign boards stating who we are, but more importantly the smaller vertical boards either side of the entrance doors explaining what was on offer and hopefully suitably worded to make people feel welcome.

One of the boards was a chalkboard so we could change it from day to day explaining which facilities were available, whether it was medical, academic, dental or hairdressing and the times to attend. Which day there would be English lessons or help with reading and writing or perhaps just simple arithmetic. We were really hoping the information would make them start to think, well perhaps we should take a look and see what's on today and then pop in and give it a try, have a coffee and a chat with someone.

I hoped this wasn't too much wishful thinking and I wasn't being too naïve, but clearly these people needed help and that was exactly what we were trying to do.

We unlocked the doors and quickly ran around the rooms, making sure everything was in place and as we wanted it. I checked the heating was working, turned up the thermostats to fight the bitter weather outside and heard the surge of hot water rushing through the pipes. We bumped into each other in the corridor linking the porta-cabins, hugged nervously and then laughed with excitement and apprehension.

"Vincent, I'm so scared,"

And she was. I suddenly realised how vulnerable Jane was, she had been working so hard and now this was the culmination of our plans. It could all go wrong, we had no idea who may walk through the door and even more worryingly, maybe no one would walk through the door and all our planning and Jane's expense would come to nothing. We would have let other people down, apart from ourselves, even Westminster Council.

I cuddled her, and held her tight. "Don't worry," I said and I loved the closeness of her body and the warmth, it felt so reassuring and even a little arousing. But this was not the time or place, but man is what man does, I think that's the quotation or is it something I heard somewhere else. I am not sure, but I think there may be a link with *Black Adder*, but perhaps that is a little too flippant for such a serious topic.

"I'm alright, I love you Vincent."

"I love you too Jane, it will be alright this will work."

"Will it?" She looked worried.

"Of course it will, we have done so much research and preparation and you have ploughed loads of money into it. It has to work."

"Yes, I suppose so."

She looked so delicate and unprotected, my heart went out to her, my wife, the woman I loved more than life itself and then I realised it was all my responsibility, I had to protect her, I had to make this whole thing work for Jane, Dean, and I suppose myself and Harold, the bastard, but there is no point in being bitter. This is a step forward and it has to work, we have put so much energy into it.

Nine o'clock came and went and we sat there with Gordon a gynaecologist and Linda a trainee teacher, we drank a lot of coffee and sampled the toilet block.

Linda was in her early twenties and keen to help, but I felt sorry for her because her and our expectations were so much higher, we presumed we would be swamped from 9am onwards. On this our first day, Linda was going to help with reading and writing, quite what the requirement would be we weren't sure.

Gordon, although a specialist, also had an all-round medical knowledge so would be able to advise on simple medical conditions and would be able to recommend when and where people needed to seek additional help.

We sat and discussed what motivated us to get into this situation and then we talked about football and Arsenal, not that I knew much about football, but anything was better than silence. Every few minutes I looked at my watch, after a while I found I was trying to guess the minutes as they passed, by not checking until at least one minute had gone and the next time two, then three and so on. Have you ever done that? I used to do a similar thing when driving long distances, only look up at the tachometer once in each mile, therefore judging when the next mile has passed. It's quite a good way of passing the time when the most boring thing in the world is driving. No I see what you mean it's pathetic, well back to the story.

Jane stood up and went outside, clearly she was disappointed after all the hype, it was now looking pretty flat, we had spent hours handing out flyers, leaving them in stations, cafés, park benches and wherever we thought they would be seen. And posters, with the help of Westminster City Council were plastered appropriately around the West End, and advertising space was bought in the free issue papers. So I just kind of assumed on day one there would be queues at the doors with eager applicants raring to sample our new style of generosity. But this didn't seem to be happening and I could see Jane was upset after so much anticipation.

After a few minutes I followed her outside, she was standing a few yards to the right of our entrance door, her arms folded and staring into the distance. I could see she was cold and shivering and I went and put my arms round her and kissed her neck and whispered in her ear, "Don't worry it's early days, people have just got to realise we are here, Rome wasn't built in a day."

She turned to face me and there were tears in her eyes, I kissed them away and held her close and she clung to me with a strength which made me tingle. When we finally turned back to the centre there were two young men tattily dressed in ragged clothes gazing at our blackboards, they must have been in their early thirties.

One of them was clearly more alert than the other, he was reading out the information to the other, I went over to them and said, "Why don't you come in and see what's going on?"

The one that was listening, pulled an open can of lager from the inside pocket of his misshapen coat and took a large swig.

"We are offering some help with reading and writing this morning and perhaps any medical advice you may require." I continued. "There are two rooms, one for medical advice, and the other for helping with reading and writing." I hesitated, "Or perhaps you would like to make use of the toilets or have a shower?" This was clearly not an easy conversation and I was beginning to feel I was talking to myself.

They looked at each other and grunted before stepping through the doors inside to the reception, I eased past them and quickly sat behind our small reception desk. We had devised a simple signing in system requiring as little information as possible so as not to concern them too much, we were careful not to put them under too much pressure. People living on the streets are usually suspicious of authority and too many questions may easily make them nervous and drive them away. All we were going to do was ask for a name, any name they wished to give and we would note their gender and keep a record of the reason for their visit, whether it was for information, reading lessons or just use of the showers and toilet facilities.

"If I could just take your names," I suggested.

They hovered over the desk, confusion obviously a disability they had to live with. (Oh I'm sorry I sounded a bit too much like Harold then, must be the slow start after all our hard work, I was really hoping it would kick off with a huge rush of enthusiasts).

"There is nothing to be worried about, I'll just write your names down, any names it doesn't matter what they are, any name will do, just so we can have some sort of record, if you want to be called

Vivian, well, that is fine by us, but if you don't that is also fine by us." I looked up and they seemed to understand.

"Roy," said the one with the reading skills.

"Thanks," I said filling in the letters on the form and then I looked up at his companion expectantly.

"Shamus," he muttered suspiciously, looking me in the eye with an untrusting expression.

I scribbled again, "What would you like to do? The options are available as I said before." I handed them a typed list each, all in bold capitals, as we were keen to minimise any embarrassment that may be caused. It is a fine line between patronising someone and making the information clear enough for them to grasp. They both gazed intently at the typed script and I noticed Roy was pointing out the words to Shamus and I could see the cogs turning and then Shamus made his decision.

"I would like a shower."

"Me too," said Roy.

"Fine," I said jumping to my feet. "Follow me." And as I led the way through to the shower area I pointed out the other rooms hoping I could instill some interest in them. I showed them the showers and how they worked, gave them towels and told them where to change and said to come out when they were finished and have a cup of tea or coffee with us.

I went to find Jane and she was also signing someone in, a middle-aged woman who clearly was not very well. We showed her to the medical room and introduced her to Gordon and left him to do whatever he could.

And then back in reception there were a few more people showing an interest, I managed to persuade one of them to take some time with Linda and as I expected, it was reading that so many people needed a little help with so I made a mental note that we should try and point them in that direction.

Our first two visitors had finished their showers and to be honest they looked and smelled cleaner and we sat them down in the relaxation area and gave them tea and biscuits.

"Have you no beer?" asked Shamus.

"I'm afraid not Shamus, we don't have a licence for alcohol." I thought that was the best reason to give.

Roy said, "I would like a haircut." His shaggy locks, still wet from the shower, and I could see what he meant.

"We are having a barber here on Thursday morning," I said. "Come along then and tell anyone else you know, you can have a haircut, another shower if you like and there is always the chance to socialise over a cup of tea."

Gordon stepped out of the medical area and asked if one of us could collect something from the nearest pharmacy, an ointment to help with a skin infection.

I quickly volunteered and rushed out to the nearest pharmacist in The Strand, I think I was keen to get away for a while.

Once I returned and the potion was administered and a few instructions given for future treatment, the middle-aged lady left quite happy and we hoped she would pass our name on to others. Whenever anyone was going to leave we gave them a credit card sized laminated sheet with our details on, address, phone number et cetera in the hope they would tell others.

As the day went on we had a continuous stream of visitors, most just wanting to nose around and see what was going on and this resulted in Jane making and serving plenty of tea and coffee. I was aware we didn't want to turn this into a soup kitchen, but on this, our first day, we could make an exception.

* * * *

"Cheers," we touched glasses with a chink.

"Cheers," I said in response.

We were sitting opposite each other in the Taste of China in Camden High Street, munching on prawn crackers and eagerly awaiting our mixed seafood starters. It had been an exhausting day both mentally and physically and we were pleased to be able to relax and wind down.

"I think that was a great day Vincent, I am so happy, all our expectations have come true."

"It was a bit of a slow start though."

239

"I know, but once the first two came in it seemed to gather pace."

"How many passed through the door in total?" I asked.

"We signed in twenty-two, the majority just had a look round and a drink, but it all means they are showing an interest and they should spread word. I am sure the word on the street will spread very fast, you can see they have little else to do."

"What do you expect tomorrow?"

"More of the same I suppose, we have a recently retired doctor in the morning and Linda is doing tomorrow afternoon and on Thursday Justin is offering his hairdressing skills, he appears to be suitably matched for dealing with either gender."

I laughed, but I knew what she meant.

Our starters arrived and we tucked in with ravenous enthusiasm, I glanced across at Jane as gelatinous juice from the crispy wontons ran down her chin and I thought how lovely she looked and what a lucky man I was. She wiped her chin with her napkin and looking up caught my eye watching her.

"What are you looking at Vincent?"

"You my darling you look so beautiful."

"What, with juice running down my chin?"

"It wouldn't matter whatever was running down your chin, you would always look lovely to me."

She smiled an embarrassed look of appreciation.

* * * *

The next day we were back on parade at early dawn and Justin, our tamed hairdresser, was all set up by nine o'clock with potions, oils and sprays, I wondered if this was suitable for our clientele but in a funny sort of way it was all part of the fun. An ambition to help people and with a bit of good fortune bring some joy and satisfaction to their lives. I walked through the rooms checking everything was neat, tidy and as we wanted it, that the toilets and showers were clean, which they weren't. So I spent twenty minutes scrubbing and wiping with the aid of Mr Muscle and some strong detergent. I thought I would have a word with Jane about employing a part-time cleaner to pop in early mornings and perhaps spending a couple of hours going through the rooms and toilets, cleaning where necessary and spraying around some air fresheners.

We needed the place to be inviting each morning and not smelling stale from the day before, the toilets should be clean and disinfected not full of detritus and effluence. It is important to remember the client base we are dealing with, without patronising them, we should provide something on a par with a low price hotel.

I felt a little despondent as I went back to the front desk, Jane was setting up and replenishing the communal lounge area. I think I would like to have a specific name for the lounge where we can hopefully create a community type of atmosphere.

As I was cleaning the toilets it hit me like a baseball bat between the eyes 'Dean's Den'. Yeah why not? A communal area for homeless people right in the middle of my everyday life, where people can come and enjoy a cup of tea and meet other people, perhaps even people Dean had met before, people he knew and talked with, or even stole from, (I quickly put this thought to the back of my mind).

I was excited, I really wanted to do this whole thing for Dean and somehow a room named after him made it work, and then I realised I hadn't any photos of him to display, we hadn't known each other long enough. But a plaque would do, with the right wording not too pretentious, simple and clear, something like 'DEAN'S DEN – HE WAS A FRIEND OF MINE'.

This would link in quite well with our name, 'My Friend's In Need'. I will have to speak with Jane, see what she thinks, I am sure she will approve, but there is always this nagging doubt because she is the one that is ploughing all the finance into this project. But I feel I just have to remember him whether it's just in my own mind or in a materialistic way.

Jane swept into reception, I have always thought girls should wear blouses and skirts or dresses, but Jane is the only girl I have ever seen who looks really good in jeans. But I must succumb to the realisation that it is the most appropriate form of dress for the situation, I would be pretty pissed off if all our guests spent most of their time ogling their hostess because she was dressed in more revealing clothes.

"Are we ready Vincent?"

"Yep, I'll open the doors. Let the buggers in."

"Vincent. That is not the way to talk about our guests."

I doffed my cap in a pretend bow. "No ma'am," I mocked.

Jane laughed and ran to me, her hair floated in the air and tickled my face as she embraced me and I thought wow, some girl. We kissed.

I opened the doors and Jane filtered in behind the desk ready to sign in the influx of eager recipients of our generosity. But there was nothing, I looked and the view didn't improve, zero was still the main character, I looked at my time piece, it was 9.13am, The Strand was busy with workers making their way to their offices, jobs or Inns of Court.

I checked the external blackboard to make sure the day's instructions were clear and Justin's preferred description of his talents were evident. As it was a warm morning, although it was still winter, I wedged the doors open and went back inside to sit with Jane. Justin had come out to join us and Linda was there too.

"Well boys and girls," I said leaning against the side wall.

Justin asked, "Do you expect a lot of people today, Vince?" He kept flicking his long flowing hair with the back of his hand.

"Justin, we really don't know, it is only our second day, we have no idea, but I am sure if we can get the word around it could start to snowball, in which case we had better be ready for it." I bounced from one foot to the other, impatient for action, I realised I was surviving on a high of adrenalin and oxygen and it was a heady concoction.

There was a silence and then Roy appeared at the door, that is, Roy who could read the notice boards. Shamus was not with him, well not yet anyway.

"Hello Roy," I said.

Roy grunted. What I am not sure.

"Shamus, not with you?"

"No, too much vodka," he gesticulated with his hands that Shamus was out for the count with too much vodka. (I know what you are thinking, how do you gesticulate vodka? Well that was just authorial licence).

"Well come in, Roy, what would you like? Jane, sign him in please."

Roy looked warily around our little group and said, "Tea and a biscuit and that haircut I mentioned."

Jane jumped to her feet. "Of course Roy come through with me, but of course you know the way," she held the door open for him.

Within a few minutes we were completely inundated with visitors of both genders, once things kicked off and the small amount of paperwork was completed, Justin was working full-time and he still made sure everyone left with a suitable quiff or bouffant and also found the time to squirt or massage in the appropriate potion. I personally was never one for elaborate hairstyles, but I am sure Justin was providing society with a valuable talent. Most did not require the sort of treatment that is usually dished out in top class salons, but just a cut and a tidy up and providing they go away feeling better about themselves, we have achieved our aim.

Roy had had his haircut first, a severe trim in the hope this would help to control his rather unruly locks and was sitting in the lounge with his tea and biscuits.

When the shouting erupted I was in the reception area and then we heard the crash of breaking glass. I rushed through the door and into the community area to be confronted with a vision I will carry to my grave.

Roy, who had just had his haircut and received our hospitality was standing over a middle-aged man who was cowering on the floor, blood was seeping from a cut to his forehead. Roy, a broken bottle in his hand was waving the sharp edges within a few inches of the man's face and his posture was extremely threatening.

"Look you fucking shit." This was Roy.

The man continued cowering and to be honest so did I, because I really didn't know what the alternative was, this sort of aggression was a little out of my league. I hadn't come across it that often, but I suppose I should have been prepared, at least aware that the possibilities could be there just by the nature of the people we were dealing with.

Roy's next move was the crucial one and we were not to be disappointed as he wielded his trusty blade screaming, "Look you fucking shit."

A little repetitive I thought but was not of the mind to point this out. The man on the floor was certainly shaken as he tried to sit up and was thrown back by the toe of Roy's soleless boot.

"Hey," he said, "give it a bloody rest Roy, there's no need for this."

With this Roy pulled back his arm and crashed the broken edges of the bottle into the man's face, blood squirted from the wounds as flaps of skin swelled open. "There take that you fucker," he shouted.

The man slumped to the ground all resistance shattered and I could hear him mumbling. "Roy you shouldn't have done this to your father," and with this he lost consciousness.

I rushed forward in the hope of effecting some sort of first aid, but all I could see was an old mashed-up face steadily swelling as blood rushed to repair the damage.

Roy had staggered back and thrown the remainder of the bottle to one side and crashed through the door and away.

I knelt over the still body and shouted to anyone. "Call an ambulance and hurry up." I cradled the man's head in my arms for what seemed like an eternity, his blood congealing on my skin as it slowly trickled from the wounds, the flaps of skin drying and stiffening as they dried. His head flopped against my arm, he was still breathing but his eyes were half closed and drowsy, I wasn't sure how long he could survive, he was not a young man and probably weakened by his lifestyle.

"Hurry up," I shouted.

It seemed like an eternity, but in reality it was little more than ten minutes, and then the paramedics burst through the door carrying bags containing a mixture of implements and tools of destruction and landed at the man's feet.

"We'll take over from here." said a pretty young woman dressed in green fatigues as she efficiently took control. Her companion quickly joined her and within minutes they had cleaned, patted, bandaged and whisked the unfortunate man back to the ambulance. My relief was more than obvious.

Jane was now beside me as I carefully got to my feet, my ageing limbs rebelling against the sudden movements. She easily fell into my arms and I could feel her shaking with fear, I held her tighter aware that she could break, but I didn't let up, I needed comfort and reassurance and Jane was my only sense of stability. But I was also aware of her vulnerability as well and that I had to be strong for her. This had been a very difficult situation something that had happened so quickly with nothing we could possibly have done to prevent it. It just came out of the blue and this is one of the problems when dealing with such volatile characters.

"Perhaps it won't be as easy as we thought," she said.

I nodded into her hair not knowing what to say. And then I realised there were clients all around and I had to clean up this mess and also the situation. We had only been open for some thirty-six hours and had already experienced an attempted murder. Not the best credentials for Westminster Council to defend their decisions to support us and even provide us with some financial assistance.

I groaned as I broke away from Jane's clinch and set about the business of cleaning up firstly the blood and detritus that was staining the floor, before moving onto our clients.

Jane had moved them away into another room and was trying to persuade them to carry on with their activities, but she was clearly upset and I didn't want to leave her to cope on her own.

It wasn't long before the police appeared although we hadn't called them, no doubt the ambulance service would have done so. At this point we decided it would be prudent to close the services for the afternoon and we ushered our clients off the premises with the promise we would be open for business as usual the following morning. However, we were forced to keep three of them back as they had been witnesses to the earlier proceedings. This turned out to be difficult as two were young men and they clearly didn't want to cooperate with authority and it wasn't long before another van was called and they were bundled in and taken away for further questioning.

I sat down with Jane on one of the sofas and held her tight, we were both in shock and didn't talk for a while until I went and made her a cup of hot sweet tea.

"This could ruin everything you know Vincent," she said.

"I know," I replied. "Only our second day and there is a violent attack on our premises involving ambulances and police."

"This could give some of the negatives at Westminster Council the ammunition they need to say I told you so."

I nodded, fully aware that what she said was true. But I also felt determined to carry on, this was only a minor set-back and we would beat it.

I kissed her on the cheek and said, "It will be okay, we'll persevere."

CHAPTER 19

It was some two months later, spring had sprung and the days were steadily getting warmer, the daffodils were out, leaves were opening on the trees and our little venture was gathering momentum. There had certainly been some teething problems and we had had to rethink certain aspects of the way we handled some things. We hadn't really judged the volatility of some of our guests and it soon became obvious that certain types would not mix well with others and this would nearly always result in a confrontation. But so be it, so we had to introduce a form of segregation and we did this by monitoring the type of people who would turn up for certain activities and ensure these didn't clash with other classes which could provoke an altercation.

I had been standing outside appreciating the early morning sunshine, the warmth felt good and I was now sitting at the desk, I had signed in two people a young girl, late teens was seeking advice from our doctor and an elderly woman was taking a shower of which she was certainly in dire need. But if this is the service we are offering it is quite reassuring that our facilities are being taken advantage of.

I heard the door open, looked up and did a double take as a smart but casually dressed man stood before me.

"Hey Vince, you bloody wanker, so this is what you are doing."

"Harold!" I stood up.

"I heard this new place had opened up to try and sort out all these bloody peasants who persist in littering our streets." He was looking around the room fidgeting from one foot to the other. "Well aren't you going to show me round?"

"Yes, well okay, right," I said.

"Just as decisive as ever I see."

I walked round the desk. "Follow me," and I went through into the communal lounge area just as the teenager came out. "Everything all right?" I asked.

"Good. Yeah." And she was off.

"Not staying for coffee?"

"Not today," she called over her shoulder.

"You seem happy." I said.

"I am," she shouted back and was gone.

"One satisfied customer," I said to Harold pleased with the opportunity to show off the good we were doing.

He grunted.

"This is the communal lounge," I said, "and through there is the medical room where we have a succession of volunteers holding morning or afternoon surgeries to treat minor ailments and more importantly to give advice on problems. In many respects to encourage people that they need to go to hospital or seek further attention is most valuable. We also offer a hairdressing service, which has actually turned out to be the most popular."

"Vince are you trying to tell me there is a smarter looking tramp gracing our streets since you started this nonsense?"

"Not really, but I am just making the point that a lot of people have taken advantage of the service and hopefully it helps to make them feel better in themselves, give them more confidence to face up to the problems they find out on the street."

The door opened and the elderly woman staggered through with her wet hair matted together and her tatty clothes hanging limply. She had been one of our regulars coming at least twice a week for a shower, she went to the drinks dispenser and pressed a couple of buttons to activate it before dropping onto the sofa.

"Nice shower Amy?" I said.

"Yep," she replied.

I took this opportunity to usher Harold through the rear door into the link corridor so I could show him the showers and toilet area whilst they were not being used. "We have showers and toilets through here," I said.

He grunted again still looking behind him where Amy was sitting with her drink. "I suppose they certainly need them. Anyway

Vince where is this amazing woman I hear you have married? First it was that tubby little bird Hilary you were trying to get hold of and the next thing we hear you have married a bit of a stunner. You're certainly a bit of a dark horse Sleeve, I always thought of you as being a bit of a wanker, but maybe I am going to be proved wrong."

"Jane, er she's out at the moment buying some supplies. You know this lot can drink us out of house and home if we're not careful."

"What you supply them with booze as well? Christ Vince what sort of charity is this?"

"Now just hold on Harold, we don't have any alcohol on these premises, Jane has gone out to top up on coffee and tea and some biscuits, she should be back before much longer. The offer is always there for anyone who has enjoyed our facilities to mingle in the communal lounge for refreshments, but is restricted to tea, coffee and squashes. We are careful not to turn into a soup kitchen, it is not the idea just to provide sustenance."

He appeared to raise his eyes to the ceiling, before saying, "Let's go and get" (that word again, you thought I had forgotten about it didn't you?) "some beer Vince, I can't be doing with poncing about round here much longer."

I agreed with a sigh, but as we walked to the door it opened and in stepped Jane her arms weighed down with carrier bags laden with the necessary groceries to keep our clients content.

"Jane," I said, by way of an introduction.

I noticed Harold visibly check and inwardly stutter before saying, "You must be Jane?"

Clearly obvious I thought, as I had just mentioned her name.

He held out his hand to shake hers but this was impossible as she was still clutching the shopping bags. I relieved her of her burden, no I don't mean Harold, and took them through to the kitchen area. When I returned they appeared to be chatting quite happily and Harold almost seemed attentive to Jane's conversation, but I suspected he was probably only interested in her obvious femininity.

My first reaction was to try and split them up and I said, "What about that beer then Harold?"

"Just a minute Vince," he waved his arm at me without taking his eyes from my wife as they wandered up and down her body.

"Fine," I muttered. "Just ignore me."

And they did and the conversation went on about how I had helped Harold with his journalistic piece in the local paper, how we had lived rough amongst these poor bastards (not my words, Harold's) and of course, if it hadn't been for him the idea for this whole enterprise would never have been thought of. This was when my blood began to boil, I found it very difficult to contain myself when it came to Harold's imagination and his different slant on events which happened only a few months ago, and I exploded.

"Harold, if you don't mind I think it is about time you came back to reality and appreciated this is not some sort of egotistical trip. Jane and I really wanted to do this because we have a conscience and we want to help people less fortunate than ourselves, it gives us some sort of buzz and makes us feel better in ourselves and if in the meantime others can benefit, well I think that is pretty good news."

"Well okay Vince," he had turned to look at me now.

"I think we should go and have that drink now," I said eager to remove him from the premises as I walked towards the door. Although I don't actually dislike Harold I can't say he will ever be a close friend and in many ways he tends to be a bit of an embarrassment.

In the Crown and Two Chairmen he had a pint and I stuck to the dry house white. Although he said he had only popped in to see how we were doing as he had heard about this new idea. I knew it would be the last time I would see him, you see Harold is a user, if you haven't got anything he wants well you are no use to him.

So we drank up and said our goodbyes.

CHAPTER 20

It is our four year anniversary today, we opened 'My Friend's In Need' four years ago today, you could say it is our first birthday as it is the 29th of February. Things have moved on a long way, we are now a fully fledged charity with fundraising achieving in excess of half a million pounds a year and we have opened two further sites, one in the corner of a car park at the Elephant and Castle. The second is situated on an area of disused land opposite the Building Centre in Store Street not far from Centre Point to the south, and Ridgemount Street to the east, both of these are good positions in needy areas where there are plenty of prospective clients. After all these years we still don't know the best way to address people, whether to call them clients, visitors or guests. It's strange but none of these descriptions really give an accurate description and we have been so careful not to patronise anyone.

Jane had worked so hard in building up the organisation from the initial planning and ideas to the endless meetings, presentations and form filling to gain the charitable status that was so important to the success of the project. There was a distinct cut-off point of six months when, if we hadn't been able to raise and inject additional funds into the organisation, Jane would have had to say no more, because her personal savings would have dwindled to an unacceptable level.

But the good Lord smiled on us and clearly wanted us to succeed, we set up a small fundraising department run by Carol and Gemma and they operate from a tiny office at the back of the Store Street site. They spend their days organising events, collection days, approaching large companies for donations and any other ideas that may bring in more money. They are full-time employees now as are Jane and myself and we have three other full timers Tim, Nathan and

Sally whose positions are managers of the existing sites, although none of us receive remuneration in line with the private sector.

As the paid side of the operation we hold fortnightly meetings to ensure everyone is up to speed and so we can discuss any new ideas and hopefully put them into practice as soon as possible.

We have created a network of volunteers which has expanded over the years, some just give a few hours of their time each week others will do two or three half days offering their skills in order to help others. Many are retired and are looking to put something back into the society that has served them so well and of course, they still have so much to offer with years of experience just waiting to be tapped. Others are just starting out on their careers or are part-way through and believe they have a part to play in helping the homeless people of our great city. It is amazing in this rat race of a lifestyle that surrounds us how many people are prepared to give up their valuable time to help others, it makes you feel good and confirms one's belief that the human race is not all bad.

Jane and I have moved from her basement flat in Kentish Town and are now the proud owners of a semi-detached, three bedroom house in Golders Green just down the hill from Jack Straw's Castle. There is a large garden at the rear and a small one at the front, the rooms are substantial and it is nice to have space. The largest spare bedroom, we have turned into an office where we keep all the paperwork appertaining to 'My Friend's In Need'. If it keeps growing like this we may need to rent some proper office space, but for the moment we are in control and I would like to think it could stay that way.

We have decided not to have children, it was mutual, I am not sure why, perhaps being together and our work is enough, but it also seems finite, no little Sleeves to follow in our footsteps, to carry on the name. Having read and digested this saga, you may consider that to be a good thing, well perhaps you are right but I also find it a little disappointing knowing my seed may never be sown.

We are just as happy as ever, our love for each other is just as fulfilling and passionate as the first day we met, or at least mine is. And I will never forget the first time I set eyes on Jane huddled up in a blanket in that bleak basement room, but at the same time there was

252

that amazingly magical moment when I thought yes this is a truly lovely woman. She looked so helpless and useless, but so beautiful at the same time and even now as I look back, I like to think I knew from that first moment that she would be my wife.

I smiled at the thought, content, tranquil and happy that after all the upsets in my life I now have just what I want and it's not the large salary I was making in the city, nor the flash cars and big house in Surrey, nor the glamorous Rachel with the rich parents.

But it is a nice house, big enough to live in and a hard-working wife who I love and adore and I think and hope she feels the same about me, why I can't imagine, because I am still the same bald, short ugly spud I was ten years ago. But true love is judged by strange parameters and I still can't understand it, and I suspect I never will.

* * * *

Well my tale has almost come to a close and I have put my authorial skills to the test. But only you can judge upon their success, I for myself am content that I have told the story as it was, albeit embellishing certain characters and situations to improve the reader's enjoyment and hopefully providing a more fulfilling experience. I also hope that perhaps the gentle reader may, when passing down Piccadilly in the hope of a decent lunch in The Wolsey or perhaps Green's, may give a little thought to the pile of human beings, wrapped in cardboard and blankets crammed into alcoves merely asking for a few coppers. And in a compassionate moment may lob a few coins or maybe a fiver into their hat.

'A fiver', I hear you squeal, well yes anything is of some help and the more the better for all concerned.

Oh and yes, there is just one thing that is always worth remembering when either relating a tale or being the recipient of some dubious information: 'Yesterday is history, tomorrow a mystery and today a gift'.

Make sure you enjoy every day to the full and whenever possible think of others, you may also get a second chance and may God be with you.